WIZARD for Hire

WIZARD for Hire

MAGIC REQUIRED

{OBERT SKYE}

SHADOW
MOUNTAIN

TO BYRON AND KAREN

I couldn't have written better in-laws. Thanks for being so exceptional, and for having such a remarkable daughter.

© 2020 Obert Skye

Interior illustrations by Brandon Dorman

Visit us at shadowmountain.com

Library of Congress Cataloging-in-Publication Data
(CIP data on file)
ISBN 978-1-62972-733-2

Printed in the United States of America
Publishers Printing

10   9   8   7   6   5   4   3   2   1

---⊙---

THESE WORDS DO NOT EXIST TO SIMPLY FILL A
PAGE. THEY ARE CAREFULLY ARRANGED BITS OF
MAGIC AND CODE THAT HIDE AND EXPOSE A WORLD
MORE FULFILLING THAN THE ONE YOU ARE LIVING IN,
UNLESS YOU ARE ME, AND YOU ARE LIVING MY LIFE.
IN WHICH CASE—GOOD LUCK KEEPING UP, WORDS.

—RIN

---⊙---

THERE'S ONLY NEED

Darkness pushed down like a fat wad of clay under the pressure of a heavy thumb—shoving itself into any cracks, crevasses, or corners it could find. The old moss-covered station sat to the side of the train tracks, a stone castle too worn out to punch its own ticket and move on. The dark rock walls and glass windows were decorated with thick vines and unkempt trees well past needing a trim. Three lonely bulbs lit small pieces of the station— two on the landing, and one inside near the shuttered ticket office.

The place was four beings shy of being deserted.

The last train had just pulled out of the station and the impish woman running the ticket booth had left for home. The smell of cinder and ash mixed with the dark night to create a palpable feeling of heaviness. One of the four beings there was a night watchman who was currently watching the inside of his eyelids while he dozed on a bench. Two others were simply passengers who had arrived on the last train and were now walking away to different destinations. The fourth person didn't move away from the station—he moved closer.

The tall man climbed the six stairs leading up to the landing and approached the sleeping watchman like a shadow. The guard was averaged-sized, in his late sixties, with a misshapen nose and wild eyebrows. He was wearing a uniform that consisted of black pants and a gray shirt with the name *Hank* stitched over the breast pocket. Hank was asleep on a worn wooden bench that rested beneath one of the two lights on the platform.

As the shadowy form moved in under the light, he became illuminated. Not only was the man tall, he was also wearing a pointed hat and sporting a yellow robe that was too short. The robe gave the dark night a bit of color.

"Excuse me," he said to the sleeping guard. "My name is Rin. You may have heard of me."

Hank continued to doze.

"Well, maybe you haven't," Rin added. "That's not surprising. I am quite modest, and I don't do what I do for the glory."

Hank kept on sleeping.

"Still," Rin went on, "it's always nice to be recognized for your talents."

Hank snored.

"Quick question: do you mind if I borrow your keys?" Rin asked politely. "You see . . ." Rin looked around at the empty platform and shuttered train station. "You see, I need to retrieve something of importance from inside the station. And, well, since it's you and me here now, I was hoping you wouldn't mind letting me use your keys for just a moment."

Hank snored some more.

"Right, you're thinking, *Great wizard, why don't you just use magic to unlock the station?* Certainly, I am capable, but I find it causes less damage and concern to doors and drawbridges if I use keys when available."

The sleeping guard continued to sleep.

"If it's agreeable for me to borrow them, say nothing."

Hank kept silent.

"Perfect," Rin said happily. "I'll get them right back to you."

Rin reached down and carefully unclipped the keys attached to the guard's belt. With his bounty in hand, he walked across the platform and to the large door attached to the entrance of the station. Sticking a key into the lock, he turned it and listened to the soft click.

"Is there anything more pleasing than the sound of a lock opening?" Rin asked himself. "Yes," he argued, "but it is definitely one of the top ten sounds."

Once inside, Rin closed the door behind him. Near the window for the ticket office was a single lightbulb hanging from a black wire. The light from the bulb was weak and humming—it struggled to dimly light the station's insides.

Rin passed beneath the light, crossed a wooden floor,

and avoided a row of benches while walking like a man who knew where he was going. Just past the benches was a short wall of copper-colored lockers. Looking up, he read the number he had written on the underside of his wide gray hat brim.

1983

Rin located locker #1983 and took a picture of it so he could post it on Instagram later. Then he fished around in the pockets of his robe for the small key he had been holding onto for days. The key was missing.

"Damp," he cursed. "Oh well."

Rin chanted a few words that drifted hypnotically around the empty station, then hit the locker with his right fist. The door popped open and he smiled. Rin removed the hat from his head and held it in his hands as an act of respect. Staring into the open locker, he spoke.

"I knew you'd still be here."

After taking a moment to put his hat back on and adjust it properly, Rin reached in and pulled out a metal toolbox. He cradled the item in his right arm and shut the locker.

"This feels right," he said happily.

Retracing his steps, Rin moved around the benches, across the floor, and back under the light. Once outside, he locked up the station and returned the keys to the still-sleeping guard.

"Thanks, Hank," Rin said as he hooked the keys back onto the watchman's belt. "You did me a favor. So, I'll leave you with something to think about: The person who sleeps through life masters many dreams."

The sleeping watchman snored lightly as a warm wind from the south drifted up onto the platform and filled Rin's nose with the smell of smoke and dirt.

"I'm sure if you were awake you would thank me for the wisdom. And since I am quite woke, I will humbly say you're welcome."

Clutching the toolbox tightly, Rin left Hank alone to master his dreams. He moved quickly down the platform, descended the six steps, and walked away from the station and into the dark.

Rin had gotten what he came for.

Once Rin was beyond the tracks, he looked up at the windy blackness as he clung to the box. He took out his phone and took a picture of the dark.

"It sounds cliché," he said to the air, "but a storm is coming." Hating the way his words sounded, he tried again. "A low front is sweeping in from the north and causing hot air to rise in a way that will bring rain." Rin paused. "That's much better."

A vertical slit appeared faintly in the dark night. Rin slipped through it like an actor moving behind the curtain. He had what he needed, and the final act was about to begin.

CHAPTER ONE

I FIND IT HARD TO TELL YOU

Sigi sat in a booth at Jeff's Diner, holding her cell phone to her ear. Her dark, curly hair was loose and full and complemented her brown skin nicely. She had on a yellow shirt and white shorts, and her nails were painted red. She smiled as she listened to her phone.

"Good night, Ozzy," she said, hanging up the phone and setting it on the table. She smiled again. "He says hi."

Patti, Sigi's mom, was sitting on the other side of the booth eating a hamburger and fries. The two of them had come to Eugene, Oregon, so Patti could do some work with a local company. They had invited Ozzy, but he decided to remain at their home in Otter Rock. There was little need to worry about him. Ever since the drama they had survived two weeks before, Sheriff Wills had made sure there was always an officer keeping an eye on all of them. Even as they ate, there was a cop car parked in front of the diner, and another parked in front of their house in Otter Rock.

"I say hi back," Patti said.

Patti was wearing a red shirt with white trim. Her dark skin and short brown hair made her look put together and stylish. She was described by many as being a lovely person. She was described by a few as being someone you shouldn't mess with. And she was described by a certain wizard as an ex-wife who refused to believe in magic.

Patti typed out a short text to Sheriff Wills on her phone.

"I'm wondering," she said as she typed, "is now a good time to talk about Ozzy?"

Sigi had just put a bite of pancake into her mouth, making it difficult for her to talk about anything.

"I know you two are close, and . . ." Patti paused to make sure Sigi caught her drift. When Sigi said nothing, she continued. "He's changed our lives dramatically. I just want to make sure you two are . . ." Patti paused again.

Sigi stopped chewing. "You're not finishing your sentences."

"I want to make sure this relationship you two have is healthy."

"Is this 'the talk'?" Sigi asked. "Because you probably should have tackled that years ago. But, for the record, Ozzy is extraordinary. He's extraordinarily unusual, extraordinarily complicated, and extraordinarily interesting. I don't know if the relationship is healthy. I mean, he's made things dangerous at times, but not the normal kind of dangerous. I like his grey eyes and how he acts like everything he doesn't understand is more interesting than scary. He also has a sentient metal bird, lives above our garage, and still can't match his own clothes. But I've never been happier to have someone in my life. So, if my happiness matters, then yes, it's a healthy relationship."

Sigi picked up her fork and took another bite of her pancakes.

"Okay," Patti said, holding up her hands. "I won't worry about that."

Sigi smiled and began to work on her scrambled eggs. They had come to the diner for dinner because Sigi was in the mood for breakfast food.

Patti watched Sigi eat a moment before saying, "I don't remember you liking breakfast so much. Especially for dinner."

"I guess I do."

"Your father likes breakfast," Patti said. "A lot."

Sigi finished chewing. "Right. Maybe it's genetic."

"Or," Patti said, "maybe everything you've been through has changed you."

"How could it not?"

Patti took a few bites of her hamburger before speaking again.

"Can I ask you something?"

Sigi nodded.

"I don't know why it makes me nervous to talk about this," Patti said. "But, well, your father . . . it's just that your father believes certain things."

8

"That's not a question," Sigi pointed out.

"Okay," Patti said, looking less confident than she usually did. "It's just, you know."

"I do?"

"I guess I'm worried about him and I'm even more worried about you. Sometimes his mind isn't quite right."

"Are you talking about him believing in magic?"

"Yes," Patti said with relief.

"Or the fact that he says he's a wizard?"

"That's part of it for sure."

"I've seen him do some remarkable things," Sigi said defensively. "I don't know how to explain them unless . . ."

"They're magic?" Patti guessed. "Sure, your father is . . . capable. He was a teacher once and he's done some good things, but I can't just pretend that his behavior is normal."

"Everything's normal somewhere."

"Right," Patti said, "but I worry about how his normal affects you." She took a deep breath. "I know this isn't easy to talk about, but I need to make sure you're okay."

"Should we call this the 'magic' talk?" Sigi asked, half-joking. "Are you telling me that when someone loves being a wizard very much, others should doubt them?"

"Then you *do* think he's a wizard?" Patti asked carefully.

"I'm glad he's back in my life," Sigi answered honestly. "Can't that be enough? For so many years he was never there. And when he was, he was an embarrassment.

Sometimes I felt more out of place with him as my father than I did being black in such a white town. And now that I'm beginning to feel connected to him, you're worried?"

"It's just that wizards aren't real," Patti said compassionately.

Sigi dropped her fork and locked eyes with her mother.

"If that hurts, I'm sorry," Patti added. "It's the reality of the situation."

"It doesn't hurt, it's just maddening," Sigi admitted. "And I'd like to stop talking about this."

"I'm just trying to help."

"I think you're just trying to tell me that my father's insane, when I have seen firsthand that he is much more than I ever thought possible. I can't justify everything he does, and heaven knows he drives me crazy sometimes, but he's *not* just a man dressing up as a wizard."

"That's exactly what he is," Patti said. "We all want someone in our lives to be magical, to take away the hurt or pain. But, when we're realistic, all—"

"When we're realistic, only the straight lines and that even numbers make sense. Dad has found something with more possibility than the stiff and angry reality we live in."

"You're scaring me, Sigi."

"Well, then, maybe I should leave." Sigi stood up. She was frustrated and her dark eyes were cloudy. "I'm going back to the hotel."

"Wait," Patti insisted, "I'll come with you."

"It's right across the street," Sigi reminded her. "It won't require any magic for me to make it there."

"Sigi," her mother said sternly.

"Mom," Sigi said, equally stern, "I'm capable of crossing the road. Besides, it's not like there isn't a cop watching us."

Patti sighed. "Don't be mad. You know I love you."

Sigi looked shocked. "Of course I know that. This isn't about you being a great mom. This is about the discovery that I just might have a decent dad as well."

"He's decent, but delusional."

"I hope you don't talk as kindly about me when I'm not around."

Stepping away from the booth, Sigi exited the diner and safely navigated her way across the street and back to the hotel. On the surface it seemed like she was right—it required no magic to get back. But had her father been there, he would have pointed out the traffic lights that changed on cue, or that the cars stopped when they should, or how the key card opened the hotel door, and how all those things were all operating under low levels of magic. Rin would have also pointed out that Sigi would be a fool to not acknowledge and be aware of all that.

Of course, what Rin would be unaware of himself is that as low levels of magic were happening, a low-level human was hiding in the shadows watching Sigi's every move. The low-level human watched her cross the street and enter the hotel. He also saw Patti come out of the diner and make her way to the Hampton Inn. He saw the cop car sitting near the entrance.

The man was standing beneath a tree outside the hotel. He took out a small notebook and scribbled down a few things. Then he moved over to his car, which was parked in a far corner of the lot and positioned in such a way that he could keep an eye on the front door of the hotel.

The man climbed into the vehicle and prepared to wait out the night.

CHAPTER TWO

CAN'T OPERATE ON THIS FAILURE

The low-level human was named Jon, and he was not complicated. His life in the past ten years had been all about his job, where rich people paid him to take care of unpleasant things for them. Jon would fix the problem, get paid, and move on to the next project without a thought. He wasn't complicated, he wasn't moral, and he also wasn't memorable, at least not in the classical sense. He was pale, bland, and balding—three things no respectable piece of fruit would like to be called, much less a human. His looks were, however, good for blending into the scenery, which worked well in his line of business. When he was thirteen, Jon had taken an aptitude test at school. The results had suggested that when he grew up, he should be a seat filler at large events that didn't want empty seats during a live broadcast.

Well, Jon was living up to the seat-filling part of that prophecy as he sat in his car staring out at the front of the Hampton Inn.

Jon was no stranger to tracking Sigi and Ozzy. He had been hired in New York by a man named Ray to find the boy. Once he found him, he had given Ozzy a package that had contained a plane ticket. Jon had followed the teenagers to the Portland airport, where Ozzy and Sigi had gotten onto a plane and flown to New York. When the two kids had returned to Oregon, Jon had tried in vain to take Ozzy as a captive. He had failed at every turn. The failure, he felt, was largely brought about by the strange man that the children were traveling with—a grown man pretending to be a wizard. At least Jon thought he was pretending. As events had unfolded, he had witnessed numerous things that had changed his mind. In the beginning he thought that Rin was nothing but an eccentric weirdo living his life in permanent cosplay. Then, as Rin performed wonder after wonder, Jon's distaste for the man turned into a need to find out where the wizard's power came from. Jon had been blown away when Rin had silenced his voice, and he had almost blown apart as Rin had destroyed the *Spell Boat*.

Jon had seen the light by escaping death.

Because of his change of heart, Jon no longer worked for Ray. He was working for himself, determined to find out what power Rin really possessed. He was a believer of sorts, and he wanted to be a part of the mystery that Rin had shown him.

Jon wasn't sure if Rin was magic, but he also wasn't sure that the wizard was not.

What Jon did know was that watching Rin's actions

had struck a chord within his soul. There was something about the wizard and the two kids and the impossible metal bird that made him feel things he had never felt before.

And Jon wanted more of that feeling.

After that fateful night on the ocean, he had come back a different person. He had rented a motel room in Corvallis, Oregon, and after recovering mentally from what he had been through, he had begun to track Ozzy and Sigi's movements again. This time, however, he was doing it for himself in hopes of finding Rin.

The two children weren't as easy to track. They had cops pinned to them and were never on their own. Even now Jon knew that there was a policeman parked in front of the hotel watching for trouble.

Ray, the man who had hired Jon, would have loved to have him finish the job and bring Ozzy to him in New York. But Ray didn't even know that Jon had survived the night in the ocean. So chances were good that Ray had hired someone else to find Ozzy. Which meant that as Jon spied on Sigi and her mom from beneath the trees at the hotel's parking lot, there could very well be another spy doing the same thing.

The forgettable man scanned the dark parking lot. He saw a cop car parked near the front, and a reasonable number of other cars. But he was in the farthest parking space with no one around.

Jon sighed.

The job had started off easy: deliver a package to one

kid. It had turned into something personal, complicated, and otherworldly. A simple job he could have done in his sleep had turned into an impossible quest, a mystery that could only be explained by the supernatural.

Jon shivered.

There was a knock at his car window. A security guard was standing next to his car. The tall, skinny man sporting a badge motioned for him to roll down his window.

Jon did so.

"Yes?" he asked.

"Are you a guest here?" the guard asked in a neutral tone. "Are you staying at the hotel?

"I'm thinking about it," Jon replied.

"Well, you'll need to think about it somewhere else," the guard insisted. "The hotel is full for the night, and you can't park here. It's private property."

"Right," Jon said, "let me just make a quick call."

"Make your calls somewhere else," the guard said in a less neutral tone.

Not wanting to cause any trouble, Jon nodded and rolled up his window, then drove across the street and parked at Jeff's Diner. He checked his watch, concluded that it wasn't likely that Patti and Sigi would leave the hotel, and then went in to get something to eat.

Jon was hungry for food, but he was equally hungry to find the answers he so desperately sought. And there was only one person who could stop that hunger and set him free.

Like so many in life, Jon needed a wizard.

CHAPTER THREE

WATCHED OVER

The morning sun was nowhere to be seen—it had slunk off behind the clouds to be someplace less depressing. The large home at 1221 Ocean View Drive looked faded and washed out beneath the dreary sky. The house was two stories with a detached four-car garage and a fountain that shot water into the air in various patterns sitting in front.

In the airy kitchen, a weak, moody light moped its way through the windows and flopped against the tables and floor. The dreary elements pouted and moaned, wanting the world to witness their misery.

"What a gloomy morning," Sigi said, giving the gray some of the attention it wanted.

"It feels like Oregon usually does." Ozzy shrugged as he stepped up to the table. It had been three weeks since the *Spell Boat* incident, and he was falling into a routine that included breakfast with the wizard's daughter every morning.

Sigi looked considerably more positive than the mood in the kitchen. Her long hair was pulled up on top of her head, forming a massive curly brown bouquet and giving her neck some room to breathe. Her dark skin created a silhouette in the dreary gray that had depth and interest. She was wearing a blue T-shirt Patti had bought her last week in Eugene with denim shorts. Her feet were bare, and her legs and arms were long and moved gracefully as she picked up a bag from the table and began to open it.

"Is your mom here?" Ozzy asked.

"She left early. Which means we're alone." Sigi's brown eyes smiled. "Should we skip school and do something exciting?"

"If you can get Sheriff Wills's permission."

Thanks to what they had recently lived through, there was always a police officer to escort them anywhere outside the house they wanted to go. The cops were there when they went to school, when they went to the beach, when they went to where the Cloaked House had once stood. They were even watched when they walked to the nearby convenience store. While they understood why they needed watching, to Sigi and Ozzy it was beginning to feel a lot like being held captive.

Sigi took the last bagel out of the bag and crumpled the empty container. "We're out of bagels. And I'd share, but I can't see a way to divide the two halves equally. You *could* always use your ability to make me give this up, couldn't you?"

Ozzy shook his head; his long dark hair brushed against his face and ears. He looked down at his left-hand pointer finger—the single digit was completely covered with a deep purple marking. Ozzy had thought it was a birthmark, but thanks to Rin, he had recently discovered that the purple finger came from his parents experimenting on him. The experiment had left him with a single marked finger—and the amazing ability to make some living things do what he instructed.

"You should try it on me," Sigi said excitedly. "We can find out if you're able to control the mind of someone who's clearly smarter than you."

Ozzy shook his head.

Sigi sat down to selfishly eat both halves of her bagel.

Ozzy poured himself a bowl of chocolate puffed cereal and milk and sat down across from her. After a few bites, Ozzy swallowed and asked Sigi the question he asked every morning. It was always asked half in jest and whole in desire.

"So—where's your dad?"

Sigi finished some chewing of her own food and shrugged. "I don't know. Where's your bird?"

The mere mention of Clark made them both half-happy and half-sad.

"I've waited my whole life for my dad to show up when he should have," Sigi continued. "He never did. Now I feel like we're in some dumb unending limbo, just waiting for them to return. What about Ray? Or Jon? Why is nothing happening? Are we just going to be babysat by Sheriff Wills and his officers until we die? Because waiting around for something horrible to go down feels like death. We don't even know if my dad's alive. He jumped into a dark ocean and disappeared."

"He's alive," Ozzy promised her. "Remember what he's capable of?"

"Sure," Sigi said, "but in my lifetime, he's also been less than capable—for example, he's not been around the last ten years. Also, he hasn't remembered most of my birthdays or been a part of anything normal."

"He wouldn't have left us on that boat if he didn't know what he was doing."

"I think that's one of the reasons he *would* leave us," Sigi argued. "People who know what they're doing don't abandon ships that could save them. And what about Clark? There's no way he would stay away if he was okay. That bird is connected to you. He's out there—and we can't go looking because we have no idea where they are. I mean, what if they're actually in Quarfelt?"

"I don't know. Is Quarfelt real?"

"Right," Sigi said, "because sometimes my dad's hard to believe."

"That's true. I mean, what about my parents? He said they're alive but I'm not sure I should believe him."

The wizard's daughter stood up from the table, leaving half her bagel uneaten. "Come on. We're going to be late."

Ozzy shoved the last half of the bagel in his mouth and then cleared the dishes.

After putting on their shoes and grabbing their backpacks, they met out on the driveway in front of Patti's house. Parked next to the fountain was the small white car that Ozzy and Sigi knew all too well, the same vehicle that had taken them on to a train, to Albuquerque and back, and into other insanely dangerous situations. It was small and had started its life as a hybrid, but Rin had changed out the motor a while back to give it something with a little more get up and go.

Before climbing into the car, Ozzy glanced around at the surrounding forest. There were trees on all sides of the driveway that hid any nearby roads and other houses. He watched three birds fly off to the west and felt a pang of sadness.

"I just don't think Clark would give up," Ozzy said. "Or Rin, or Jon—or Ray."

"Maybe it's best not to think."

Sigi drove the car while Ozzy sat in the passenger seat. At the bottom of the driveway, they passed a parked patrol car waiting to follow them and gave the cop a brief wave.

They were escorted the entire way to school.

When they reached Otter Rock High, the cop parked in front.

Sigi parked in the student section and climbed out of the car complaining.

"The whole school thinks you and I are nuts." Sigi shook her head in disgust. "Do you know of anyone else who has a personal policeman following them?"

"No, but I still don't really know many people here."

"Well, they know you, and they think you're nuts." Sigi threw her backpack over her shoulder and looked at Ozzy. "No offense."

"Some taken," Ozzy replied.

The two of them split up and entered Otter Rock High School with a river of fellow students who were unhappily doing the same thing. The air inside the school was filled with noise and cologne and fluorescent light. One student was yelling at another student about a recent TV show. Two girls were laughing about someone's hair. A teacher spilled her coffee and fought the urge to swear.

Despite the scene, or what Ozzy had been through recently, he liked school. He found it remarkable that everyone gathered together to teach and learn things. He liked the magical aspects, like hot lunches and access to a library. He felt powerful raising his hand in class and having the teacher focus on him. He had grown up alone and isolated. Now he was surrounded by others who were also trying to figure things out.

Ozzy made it to geometry class and into his seat just as the bell finished ringing. A large kid with dark circles under his eyes and chaotic blond hair sat down in the desk next to him.

Before Mr. Waite, the teacher, could address the class, a speaker in the room snapped to life and the sound of someone who didn't particularly enjoy their job spoke.

"Mr. Waite, please send Ozzy Toffy to the office."

Everyone glanced at Ozzy, all of them wondering what he had done to be summoned. The whole school was aware of just how unusual he was. He had been strange and singled out since the first day he had made his way to school. They were also aware of some of the unbelievable things that had happened to him in the last few months and had heard rumors about even more unbelievable things.

"What'd you do?" the big kid with dark circles asked.

"I have no idea."

Getting up from his seat, Ozzy nodded toward the teacher.

"Hurry back," Mr. Waite told him. "You can't learn if you're not here."

His point may have been true, but Ozzy knew there were plenty of things he could learn outside of a classroom. Gathering his backpack, he walked out of the room and down the hall toward the front office. His tennis shoes squeaked on the tile floor as he moved, the noise echoing off the lockers and walls.

In the office, two older women shuffled papers around and typed things into their computers. One had brown hair and was named Karen, and the other used to have brown hair but now it was gray. Her name was Glenda.

"Hello, Ozzy," Glenda the Gray said.

"Hello," he replied. "I was called down here. Is there a problem?"

"No," Glenda insisted, "at least I don't think so. A box arrived for you."

The gray-haired woman stood up and walked to a counter behind her desk. Sitting on top of the counter was a brown cardboard box. Glenda picked it up and brought it over to Ozzy.

"It's not very heavy," she reported. "You know, normally students don't receive packages here. But you've always been a little . . . more special than most."

"Thanks," Ozzy said sincerely, taking the box from her.

He studied the package with curiosity. It was a normal looking cardboard box, a cube with blank sides and bottom. Written across the top in large loopy letters were the words:

For Ozzy Toffy

Ozzy popped open the top folds of the box and dug through green and yellow packing peanuts. He saw something red and gray and . . .

Ozzy stopped tunneling and looked up at Glenda.

"Oh," he said excitedly, "it's just some clothes that my friend is returning."

Glenda stared at him.

"You see," Ozzy continued, "I lent these clothes to him . . . or her. Friends can be female. I mean, I have some female friends. Roughly half the population is female. Actually, I have one female friend. But I lent these to a male friend a couple of months ago and well, like I said, he's returning them. Sorry. I don't know why he shipped them here."

Both Glenda and Karen stared at the boy.

"They weren't mailed," Glenda said, still looking confused. "They were dropped off by a courier."

Ozzy's grey eyes went wide. "A courier?"

"A delivery person," Glenda said, thinking that Ozzy didn't know what the word *courier* meant.

"Right," Ozzy said excitedly, knowing perfectly well what a courier was. "What delivery person dropped them off?"

"I don't know." Glenda was acting like she was ready to be done with the conversation. "Just a man with a red cap and black shirt. He could have been friendlier."

"Was he tall?"

"No."

"Did he have a beard?"

"No. He was short and clean shaven."

"Thanks," Ozzy said, picking up the package. "I should get back to class."

"Do you want to leave your box here?" Glenda asked. "You can pick it up after school."

"No." Ozzy was insistent. "I mean . . . no, thank you."

Holding the box with both arms, Ozzy left the office and walked in the opposite direction of his class. His heart was beating at an alarming rate and his mind buzzed comfortably under the knowledge of what he had in his hands.

Sigi's classroom was on the other side of the school, and

when Ozzy got to her door, he stopped and looked through the small window above the doorknob. He saw that her teacher, Mr. Lastly, was talking about something while most of the students were resting their heads on their desks. Ozzy looked through the glass and spotted Sigi. He waved and she spotted him.

Sigi raised her hand and asked to use the bathroom.

As soon as she was out in the hall, Ozzy held up the box.

"Come on," he said. "I've got something to show you."

Sigi followed Ozzy down the hall and into the hidden space under the stairs that led up to the second floor.

"What's happening?" she asked.

"I got a box," Ozzy whispered.

"I see that. From where?"

"I don't know. Glenda said a red-capped delivery person dropped it off."

Ozzy set the box on the ground and pulled open the top flaps. He reached in and dug through the packing material. Grabbing the item at the bottom, he pulled it out dramatically.

Sigi gasped.

The two of them stared breathlessly at the object, both knowing that things were no longer in a holding pattern.

Stuff was about to go down.

CHAPTER FOUR

THE TABLE IS NOT BARE

Rin set the toolbox on the long wooden counter in the center of the odd-shaped room. Carefully, he opened the lid.

"A sight for sorcerer eyes." Rin looked around self-consciously. He was relieved that no one was there to hear the poor pun. Taking a second stab at it, he said, "A wonder to behold."

Rin pulled the small metal bird out of the toolbox and looked closely at it. He placed his hand over the silver strip on the back of the creature and took a moment to study what lay before him. Clark was a marvel, a miracle, a living bit of magic. His wings were an odd sort of pliable plastic stretched between thin wires. He had a tail of tin and a gold beak. Clark's feet were sculpted, each talon tipped with copper. Wire feathers stuck out of the top of his metal head just above his closed eyes. He was approximately five inches long with a tube-shaped metal body.

The wizard took his hand off the silver strip and placed the small artificial raven under a lamp on the table. Then he puttered around the workshop for a few minutes waiting for the bird to charge. Rin made sure to check on Clark every thirty seconds.

"Hello?" the wizard said.

The bird was lifeless each time.

Just as Rin was contemplating switching the lightbulb to a higher wattage, he heard, "If I open my eyes and that Jon person is here, I'm going to go birdy on him."

"He's not here," Rin said happily, looking at Clark lying on the table. "We're back in reality."

"Were we ever gone?"

"Yes," Rin said. "We were in Quarfelt for a spell."

"We were?" Clark said, his eyes still closed.

"Sometimes people's memories slip away during the trip to and from there," Rin explained.

"But I don't remember *any*thing," the bird admitted. "Last thing I remember, we were on that boat and Jon was pointing a gun at everyone."

"Well, a lot has happened between then and now. You must have forgotten."

Clark opened his eyes and cocked his head to the left.

"That sounds made-up," the bird said.

"It isn't," Rin insisted. "You were in Quarfelt and you did many amazing things to help defuse a number of dangerous situations."

"*That* doesn't sound made-up," Clark said, closing his eyes again as he continued to soak up the light.

"Only because it wasn't," Rin said excitedly. "Now we're back in reality and we have some things to do. I've got a whole list of stuff to check off."

The wizard pulled a piece of paper from one of the deep pockets on his robe. Written on it was a long to-get-done list.

"I've already accomplished the first item," Rin said proudly. "Collect the bird. Check."

"Where'd you collect me from?"

"Not important," the wizard said kindly. "Two—explain to Clark what has happened in the last three weeks. Check."

"I feel like you've fallen short on that one," the bird protested.

"I wouldn't have to explain anything if you remembered."

"What else is on that list?" Clark asked. "Is one of the items 'Take care of that Jon guy'? Because he was annoying."

"No, Jon's not around. It's just me."

"Oh," Clark said, his eyes still shut. "Well, to be honest, sometimes you're just as bad."

Rin gave an approving nod.

"My eyes are closed but I bet you took that as a compliment," Clark chirped.

Rin patted Clark gently on the head and the small

metallic bird opened his eyes again. He looked up at the wizard and tried to smile with his beak.

"Where are we?" Clark asked.

"In danger."

"Right," the bird said, still lying still and soaking up the light. "We always seem to be in danger with you. But *where* in danger?"

"We're in my house."

"Whoa," Clark tweeted. "This is where you live?"

The metal raven swiveled its small head, taking in the rustic room. He had a bird's-eye view of tools on a pegboard and loose lumber up in the open rafters. He could see a big fireplace at one end of the space and an old car at the other end. Using his talons and wings, he scooted like a metal worm across the table while trying to get a better look. When he came to the edge, he glanced down.

"Dirt floors," Clark said with wonder. "That's not surprising."

"This is my work shed," Rin said defensively. "There are wood floors in the house. Dutch pine."

Clark flapped his wings and flipped himself up on to his metal legs. He dug his copper-tipped talons into the table and then hopped back to the light. Standing under the glow, he stared at Rin and cocked his head.

"Where's Ozzy?"

"He's safe."

"Not very descriptive," the bird said. "For someone

who's always blathering on and on about things, you could do better."

"He's safe and sound."

"You're really painting a picture with your words. Is Sigi with him?"

"Yes."

"Okay, just let me charge a while longer and I'll set off to find them."

"Actually, you and I need to do something else first," Rin insisted. "Things are ratcheting up and there's great danger on the horizon."

"Don't mention ratchets," Clark said sadly. "Brings back bad memories. I had my heart broken by one once."

"Sorry," Rin apologized. "How about: things are getting heated and the fate of the world is in our hands?"

"That's better," Clark said.

Clark spotted an object sitting on the end of the worktable. He glanced at Rin and whispered, "Is that hammer taken?"

Rin looked over at the tool. It was made completely of metal and had been polished recently. Clark tended to fall in and out of love easily and often. He was attracted to things made of metal, but there were a few real birds that he had longed for in the past.

"I guess you're over the ratchet," the wizard said happily. "Tell you what—I'll introduce you to that hammer if you help me first."

"So it's not in a relationship?"

"No," Rin assured him, "it's quite available."

Clark took three hops closer to the hammer. Rin reached out and picked the tool up. He put it into the toolbox and shut the lid. Clark looked dejected for a moment and then perked up.

"What's the toolbox's story?"

Rin slapped his forehead.

"Okay," Clark said, "tell me what you need me to do."

"How about I show you?"

"I *am* a visual learner," Clark admitted.

"Well, I think you'll like the look of this."

Rin pulled a wooden box out from under the table. He placed it next to Clark and opened the lid. Clark jumped up onto the edge of the box and looked in.

The bird whistled. "Is that what I think it is?"

"Who knows?" Rin said solemnly. "You think a lot of unusual things."

Clark blushed, his cheeks turning a metallic rose color. "I guess it's my turn to be complimented."

"Now that we're both sufficiently full of ourselves, how about we shake things up?" Rin asked. "Ready to be improved?"

"As if that's possible," Clark tweeted.

"Ready to check off list item number three?"

Clark nodded.

Rin reached into the box and pulled out the molded black plastic pieces.

"You're like that one guy," Clark said reverently. "You know, the one with the tall monster."

"Frankenstein."

"No, I think his first name was Marvin," Clark said. "Marvinstein?"

"How about we stop talking and get working?"

Clark spread his wings and Rin pulled out more pieces.

"Nervous?" the wizard asked.

"I'm alone with a madman in his creepy woodshop," Clark chirped. "What's to be nervous about?"

Rin ignored the compliment and took a picture so that he could post a before-and-after later on Instagram. Then, without further ado, the wizard went to work.

CHAPTER FIVE

SPEECHLESS IN A MOST PECULIAR WAY

Ozzy and Sigi were in awe as they hid beneath the stairs, staring at the item Ozzy had pulled from the box. He held up the pants and unfolded them so that Sigi and he could get a better look. The pants were made from a red-and-gray tartan fabric. They had pockets and finely finished cuffs at the bottom of each tapered leg.

"He told me to watch the mail," Ozzy said, referencing some of the last words that Rin had spoken to him.

"So he's alive," Sigi whispered happily.

"Alive and purchasing pants."

"Good luck matching *those* with anything," Sigi said seriously. "You already struggle with getting dressed."

Ozzy looked worried. "You think I have to wear them?"

"I'm pretty sure that's what pants are for."

"Can't I just put them on a shelf like a trophy?"

The two of them carefully studied the pants. They were made from a heavy cottonlike material and stitched together

beautifully. There was no label indicating the size or brand—
just a small white tag on the inside of the waist that read:

> 90% magic
> 10% polyester
> Wash with like magical clothing.

"Who delivered them?" Sigi asked.

"Ms. Stalk said it was a short man with no beard."

"I guess this means you're officially a wizard," Sigi
said, her voice 90 percent excited and 10 percent jealous.
"You *did* pass the five challenges."

"Only because I didn't know what they were until they
were over."

"You need to put them on," Sigi whispered fiercely.

"That doesn't sound like something I *need* to do."

"Yes," she insisted. "He sent them to you for a reason.
You're no longer the apprentice. You've earned these pants."

"Do you hear yourself?" Ozzy asked. "These are *pants*—
and not particularly cool ones. I don't know fashion, but I
know these aren't it. Also, I've never been to Quarfelt—I'm
still not ready to say it even exists. But if it does, their system
of using pants to signify rank or importance is unsettling."

"Of course it is," Sigi said. "They're wizards. Now go
try 'em on before first period ends and the halls are filled
with confused teens like us."

Ozzy shook his head.

"You have to," Sigi insisted. "I've only gotten one piece
of clothing from my dad in my entire life. I was six and
he sent me an Andre the Giant T-shirt that would have fit

Andre the Giant. I wanna see if he's gotten better at guessing sizes."

Ozzy stared at Sigi. Her dark eyes were like spells he couldn't guard against and her voice was an incantation that made the air around him thin. He both feared and favored the effect she had on him.

"Please," she said.

Ozzy gave up. He sighed, turned, and walked toward the bathroom.

Sigi remained hidden beneath the stairs.

In less than two minutes Ozzy was back, wearing the pants, the red in his face an exact match of the red on his pants.

"Seriously," he said insecurely, "where do you think he got these?"

"They fit perfectly," she replied. "And they're way less obnoxious than that T-shirt he gave me. In fact, they look all right. How do they feel?"

"Amazing," Ozzy answered, embarrassed that he had used the word to describe pants. "I hate to say it, but they're *really* comfortable. Still, I should go change. I don't want . . ." Ozzy slipped his hands in the front pockets and stopped talking. With a look of excitement, he pulled something out of the right pocket. It was a small folded piece of white paper.

Ozzy opened it as Sigi leaned in to see.

There, in front of their eyes, was a message from a wizard. His handwriting was familiar, and the words were written in a dark brown ink.

Congratulations, Ozzy!

You have earned these trousers. Wear them with the kind of pride that only a wizard understands. There is magic everywhere, and these trousers make that more than obvious. Wear them well. You have passed the test and your life will never be the same because of it. Act accordingly. I will see you where the ashes settle and when the wind whispers that the time is right, or whatever.

Most magically, Rin.

They both stopped reading to look at each other in awe. "There's a PS," Sigi whispered.

PS—Make sure Sigi's recording Project Runway.

"He loves that show," she explained.

"Really?"

"As you can tell," Sigi said while looking at Ozzy's new pants, "he thinks fashion is magical."

"I think I'll get beat up if I keep these on."

"No one's going to beat you up," Sigi insisted. "No one's even going to talk bad about you. I mean, maybe they'll say some things behind your back."

"I have a feeling they already do."

"See," Sigi said, "you get it."

"There's still one thing I don't understand," Ozzy said. "Where's Clark? I mean if your dad's somewhere that he can send these to me, it seems like Clark would be able to dash in and let us know he's okay. I think—"

A door opened in the hallway and the sound of someone walking farther down the hall created soft echoes in the air. Ozzy leaned out from under the stairs to make sure the coast was still clear. As he did so, Sigi said, "Have you checked the back pockets?"

Ozzy put his hands in his back pockets—the left one was empty, but the right one had a small slip of paper in it. The paper was no bigger than a fortune from a fortune cookie. Written on it were the words:

Marsh and Meadow Motel
Room 213
Salem, Oregon

"Maybe that's where they are?" Sigi said with a large dose of excitement.

"Or that's where the pants were made."

"In a motel?" Sigi asked. "People don't make pants in a motel."

"Maybe that's where people make illegal magic pants. Seems like a motel would be a fitting place for that."

She ignored Ozzy. "No, it's got to be where they are."

"Why would they be—?"

The bell rang, interrupting them and indicating that first period was over. Doors opened down the hallway and students began to spill out.

"We've got to get out of here," Ozzy said.

"I agree," Sigi replied. "So, what's the plan? We can't just walk away—there's a cop at the front and locked gates everywhere else."

Ozzy thought hard as people continued to climb up and down the stairs. He glanced out at the kids making their way to second hour. Two students he didn't care for caught his eye.

"Do you remember last week when those guys called you that name?"

"You mean Adam and Jonas?" Sigi said. "The stupid, racist seniors who like to wind me up? Sure, I remember."

"Is that them?" Ozzy asked as he pointed.

Sigi looked and nodded. "But now's not the time for you to be chivalrous. I can fight my own battles. Look, I get that kind of crap all the time. They pick on everyone. They're just a couple of—"

Sigi stopped talking because Ozzy had stopped listening. He stepped out from under the stairs and motioned for her to follow.

The two meatheads in question were coming down the hall, surrounded by other students. Adam was tall with fat shoulders and a moon-shaped face. Jonas was taller than Adam and had more muscles than any three other students combined. The two were known for making school extra painful for those who were different.

Ozzy looked at them and plugged easily into their simple minds.

With a jarring halt, Adam and Jonas turned to look at each other. Some students bumped into them but quickly scattered away. The two seniors stood there like a lumpy roadblock. The expressions on their dim faces made it clear that they were as surprised by their own actions as everyone else.

"What are you doing?" Adam barked at Jonas.

"I'm not doing anything," Jonas growled. "Why are you staring at me?"

Instead of answering the question, Adam swung his left fist, connecting with Jonas's jaw. Jonas twisted and threw his right fist squarely against the side of Adam's face. Both boys screamed frantically as they unwillingly pummeled each other.

"What's happening?" Jonas yelled.

The students in the hall went wild, most of them enjoying the satisfying scene of two jerks dishing out their own comeuppance.

"I don't know . . ." Adam screamed before taking a punch to the gut.

"I can't . . ." Jonas yelled back as he received a swift kick to the right leg.

The chaos in the hall was deafening. Teachers burst out of their rooms and tried to break things up. But their actions were halted by Ozzy's thoughts. Instead of breaking things up, the teachers just stood there, unable to move. One of them managed to scream, "Get security!"

More and more students packed the hall, all of them

trying to catch a glimpse of those who had picked on them now picking on each other.

"I can't stop," Jonas cried.

"My face hurts," Adam cried back.

Someone had alerted the police officer out front and he had come running. The crowd of onlookers parted, and the officer dashed in. Just before he reached Adam and Jonas, they stopped punching each other and spun around to look at the cop.

Both boys were bruised, scratched, and sobbing.

"What's going on here?" the officer demanded. "You two better have a good explanation for what—"

Instead of giving the cop his attention, a sobbing Adam reached out to the nearby wall and pulled the fire alarm.

The entire gathering gasped.

The policeman grabbed Adam's arm and took hold of Jonas as the alarm created a new sense of panic throughout the school. Everyone began loudly running to the exits.

Sigi glanced at Ozzy with a look of amazement.

"You've gotten way better at that."

"It makes my brain hurt."

"I'd feel bad for you if the result wasn't worth it."

"Should we go?" Ozzy asked. "I want to break in my new pants."

Mixing with the crowd of students and teachers, Ozzy and Sigi worked their way out the front doors and easily slipped into the trees and away from the noise and confusion.

CHAPTER SIX

JUST HOPING YOU WILL PLAY

The hills near Corvallis, Oregon, were slathered in a fat blob of mist and fog—one big body of gray that dressed the landscape in a drab and dreary outfit. No birds were singing, no brooks babbled, but there was some movement. Near a tall hill with few trees, the fog, in a very unfoglike manner, began to pull itself apart, opening a rift that widened until a wizard stepped out.

Rin's presence divided the haze into two separate but unequal parts. A strong string of wind pushed through the divide and opened the view even further. The short yellow robe Rin wore was tied closed, making his torso look bulky. The gray felt hat on his head was wilted, the tall point hanging limply over the right side of his face. His appearance suggested that he had been through something rough, but he walked through the trees like a man with more confidence than his looks warranted.

Rin stopped and stood in the open space between the

two large sections of fog. He was on the side of a long slope. His brown eyes gazed down at the small bits of landscape he could make out. Below the fog he saw the edge of civilization—houses, roads, vehicles, and movement.

The wizard took a deep breath and took out his list. He studied what was written on it and then put it back into the pocket of his robe. He pulled open the front of his robe a bit and spoke down into his chest.

"You okay?"

"Yes," Clark said, "but I'd be better if you weren't so sweaty."

Rin walked down the hill, around a few trees, and past numerous stones that jutted up from grassy soil and wet ground.

"Reality feels funny under my feet. Much squishier than Quarfelt."

Before long, the wizard arrived at the edge of an asphalt-covered road. Rin turned north and hiked into town, directly to the address he had written on his forearm.

"Remember," Rin said, whispering into his robe, "don't come out."

"Seems like such a waste," Clark tweeted.

"This group wouldn't know how to handle it."

When he reached 811 Fieldstone Drive, Rin stood on the street and stared at the small, boxy church at that address.

A thin woman with bony shoulders and arms was in front of the church pulling weeds from the cracked sidewalk. She was perched on a small wagon that she shuffled back and forth with her feet to reach various spots of growth.

"Doesn't look very magical," Rin complained.

"Excuse me?" the woman asked.

"The building," he clarified. "It doesn't look very magical."

"You must be part of the group that's already arrived," the woman said with disdain. "I don't know what you all are, but I trust you'll not disturb anything."

"I try very hard not to be a disturbance," Rin said with a smile. "If things get out of line, I am always the first to scold myself."

The woman stared at Rin with a look of painful bewilderment. "I don't understand society," she confessed.

"And I'm bad at math," Rin said.

The wizard walked past the woman, entered the ugly building, and found the community room at the back end of the church. As he stepped into the space, he was happy to see that everyone had already arrived. There were four people—two women and two men—sitting on five folding chairs that were placed around an oval table. A large man with wild eyebrows (and a behind that required the use of two chairs) waved Rin in.

"Just like a wizard to be late," one of the women pointed out.

"I'd say sorry," Rin said with a smile, "but the trip I just took wasn't easy—and wizards don't need to apologize.

On occasion we have been known to explain, but we never apologize."

Rin took a seat on an empty folding chair.

"You looked chewed up," the large man who was taking up two chairs commented. "And a bit soft in the middle."

It was a pointless comment; Rin *was* chewed up and worn out. He also had a bird shoved down the front of his robe. Still, he sat like he had a fused spine—straight up, rigid, and focused. He let his brown eyes move around the oval table and get a good look at all of those gathered.

Rin smiled.

The weed-pulling woman out front had no idea what the community room in her church now held. Rin and the others were the Perennial Five, a powerful group of magical beings unnoticed by most of reality. Or if reality was aware, it didn't take them seriously. There were five members in all: two wizards, Rin and Bill; two witches, Flora the Older and Gemi the Younger; and one alchemist, Jayson. They were called the Perennial Five because they were eternal . . . and there were five of them.

They had joined together a year before because they wanted to be a part of something bigger than themselves— though to be honest, it would be hard for anyone to get much bigger than Bill. They had had no regular meetings or much communication, but now they were gathered around an oval table and Jayson was calling the meeting to order.

Rin nodded, cleared his throat, and smiled. He took off his gray hat and put it on top of the oval table. Without his hat it was easy to see Rin's full head of long, dark hair. His beard was equally long but growing in the opposite direction. Both his beard and hair were salted with bits of gray. He was wearing a black T-shirt beneath his robe, and he had on green crushed-velvet bellbottom trousers. The other members of the Perennial Five stared at him, waiting for him to say something.

"Thanks for coming," Rin finally said.

"How could we not come?" Flora, the older witch, said. "You made it sound urgent." Flora was wearing a black beret and black turtleneck, both covered in cat hair. She was older than Rin by ten years, but her thick dark hair didn't show a strand of gray. Her trousers were rust-colored corduroy and her black shoes were more rounded at the toes than most traditional witches would dare wear. Flora sat on her folding chair, her knees together and her palms on the table. "Your message said the fate of the world depended upon us gathering."

"It does," Rin replied, almost proudly.

"Well, then, get on with it," Flora said. "I've got things brewing that I need to check on."

"And why are we meeting *here*?" Gemi asked with concern. "In this place?" The younger of the two witches was thirty, but she didn't look an hour over twenty-one. She had red hair and blue eyes and skin the color of buttermilk. Her magical specialty was putting curses on things and people.

Gemi wore a one-piece jumpsuit that was purple on top and silver at the bottom. The outfit looked like something any mechanic with a sense of pride or fashion would refuse to wear. "I mean, why here? This building is so blah."

"It was cheap," Rin explained, "and available."

All five members of the Perennial Five had magical and interesting pasts. Each one of them had stories about impressive and imaginative places they had seen or been to. But they were in reality now and reduced to meeting in the community room of a boxy-looking church. Some churches are a joy to look at, but this one wasn't. It wasn't the kind of building that inspired others to be better, it was a church built in the 1970s with little budget for an architect with imagination—or for quality building materials. There were no stained-glass windows or spires. Just single-pane windows that let in a harsh, yellow light which exposed the fact that the janitor didn't like to dust. The church rented out the community room to anyone who was willing to pay and promised to not make a mess.

"Aye," Bill moaned, "this room lacks personality."

"And we've only paid for a half hour," Rin reminded them.

"Fer a half hour, you say?" Bill was an incredibly large man whom most people seemed to love. Not only was he a wizard, but his size and personality drew people to him. He was close to Rin's age—somewhere between forty-five and fifty—but he insisted he was well over three hundred years old in wizard time. He had a patchy gray beard and blotchy skin that looked rubbery and in need of smoothing out. The features on his face were almost lost in his putty-like cheeks and chin, but with a bit of staring, people could make out a kind smile, a wide nose, and a single right eye the color of lavender. Since few scales were large enough to weigh him, it was difficult to know just how much Bill weighed, but on a scale of small to large, he was enormous. His legs resembled water drums, his arms pickle barrels, and his stomach an over-inflated blimp. The T-shirt he was wearing was so tight that the printed image of a smiley emoji on the front of it was stretched beyond recognition. His trousers were tweed and fit perfectly. Despite his size, Bill was remarkably agile and quick. He wore an eye patch over his left eye even though both eyes worked perfectly, and he spoke like a pirate who was attempting to master an English accent for his role in a community theater's take on *My Fair Pirate*.

"Coursing, if we run out of time in this room," Bill added, "we can always gather in the back galley of Arby's. There's a right nice one just down the street."

Everyone but Bill shook their heads.

"What?" Bill asked with confusion.

They all knew there was an Arby's down the street. They also knew that Arby's offered no breakfast items, and magical beings were drawn to the food of the A.M.

"Ahhh," Bill groaned. "So, they don't have ye breakfast. Maybe we can get them to make a hash out of some curly fries."

Jayson the alchemist spoke up. "I can help with that. As you know I'm quite adept at changing something into something else. Melding a hash should be no problem."

It was no secret that the Perennial Five thought Jayson was the worst. They tolerated him, but he was annoying and intrusive—like a door-to-door salesman who had a habit of pushing open doors and demanding that others listen to what he had to offer. Plus, what Jayson had to offer was up for debate—his powers seemed weak at best. He was good at mixing food and drink, or melting wax to form small balls, but he had yet to impress any of them with anything epic. In appearance, Jayson was thin, like a straw, and none of his clothes fit him right—they were too big, or too long, or too loose. He had brown hair that he combed straight back, and ears large enough to catch the wind and spin him when he was standing still.

"Not all of us like breakfast," Bill protested. "I'm no less the wizard because of that."

"Sure," Rin said nicely, "just like not all wizards need to wear robes."

"Here we go," Bill argued. "I've told you—I don't like wearing a robe. I run hot!"

Flora banged the oval table with her right palm. "Please," she begged. "We all know that Bill would wear a robe if he could find one that fit."

"Thank you, Flora," Bill said.

"It wasn't a compliment," she informed him. "It's also not important. I want to know why Rin summoned us."

"You were summoned?" Bill asked her. "I just got a text."

"You can summon by text," Gemi argued.

"I don't—"

Rin held up his hands and silenced his four magical friends.

"I called this meeting as a precaution. There are things happening that I believe will require your assistance," Rin said. "I need to know that when and if the time comes, I can count on you."

"What kind of things are happening?" Flora asked.

"Dangerous things," Rin answered.

Jayson looked excited. "Like an ill wind?"

"Worse." Rin placed both of his hands on the table and tapped his long fingers. "You see, I am in the process of trying to solve something. I have discovered a secret that could change the course of all humanity. I hope to take care of this problem on my own. But as things have unfolded, I can see that I might need help. It will be dangerous, but it will be for the good of all humanity."

"I do like dangerous things," Flora said. "I don't get many chances to fight evil, and I'm not going to pass up a chance to do so. If I'm needed, I'll be there."

"Thank you," Rin said, trying to sound gracious.

"All right," Gemi sighed. "If I'm not busy when things go down, you can count me in too."

"I have no choice but to help," Jayson said proudly.

"My gift has been bestowed upon me and I will bear the responsibility of it."

The rest of the five groaned.

"What?" Jayson protested. "I am an alchemist!"

"Great," Bill said, ignoring Jayson. "When we formed this cluster a year afore, we all made a promise—a promise that we would all be there when needed. I don't feel any different now than I did then. If you need me, Rin, and if there be a comfortable seat—or several—that fit me, I will be there for ye."

"I knew I could count on you," Rin said with a smile. "When the need arises, you will all be summoned."

"Summoned by text?" Gemi asked. "Because I don't always keep my phone with me."

"You might want to start," Rin suggested.

"And you *promise* it's dangerous?" Flora asked again. "A few weeks ago, Jayson called me to help him balance the chemicals in his pool."

"I have a hard time figuring out parts per milliliter."

"Right." Flora grumbled. "But you said you were in trouble and needed the magic of a witch."

"I didn't say witch," Jayson complained.

"Don't worry, Flora," Rin said compassionately. "I'm not going to go into what specific trouble we're facing, but I promise you it's dark."

"Good," Flora said happily. "When it gets darker, let us know. I'd love to light something up."

"Why don't we just help you now?" Gemi asked.

"It's not necessary yet," Rin said humbly. "I'm still lacking a little information. But I'll get it. I have a secret weapon I haven't used yet."

"An unbreakable spell?" Bill asked excitedly.

Rin shook his head.

Jayson raised his hand.

"Yes?" Rin said impatiently.

"Does your secret weapon involve some precious metals that need mixing?"

"In a way."

"Is it a powerful new wand?" Flora asked.

"Something much better," Rin assured them.

"Better than a wand?" Gemi asked.

"Let's just say I have a dragon."

Nobody was impressed.

"Well, do you?" Flora asked.

"Just be ready in seven days," Rin insisted.

Gemi put the date into the calendar on her phone.

The five of them then sat quietly around the oval table looking amazed, worried, and excited about what might lie ahead. It was a full four minutes before Bill finally spoke.

"So . . . no takers on visitin' Arby's?"

All of them got up and left the boxy room. Four of them headed off to Arby's, but not Rin. He would have joined them, but he had things to do. The rest of the Perennial Five were on call, but Rin was already actively in the thick of it.

The wizard moved behind the church and back past

an Ace Hardware store. At the edge of the parking lot, he stopped.

"Did you hear all that?" Rin asked down the front of his bulky robe.

"They didn't sound impressive."

"Voices—and looks and behavior—can be deceiving."

The wizard took out his to-get-done list and checked something off.

"The next stop will be more difficult," he told the bird inside his robe.

"Bring it on."

The wizard took seven more steps and disappeared into a heavy patch of fog.

CHAPTER SEVEN

COMPLETELY IN COMMAND

Ozzy walked along the chipped and freckled Salem sidewalk with Sigi beside him. The day was gray, but long wands of sunlight were poking through some clouds and giving the blah a few bolts of glow. The two of them had taken an Uber from Otter Rock to Salem.

The driver dropped them off near a bus stop directly across the street from the Marsh and Meadow Motel.

Once the car had motored away, Sigi pointed.

"There it is."

The Marsh and Meadow Motel wasn't much to look at. It was an outdated two-story motel with forty-four rooms, all with brown doors. In the front of the motel was a small square building with a steeply pitched roof. The square building had a green door with the word *Office* painted on it. Above the green door, hanging from the edge of the pitched roof, was a white banner with blue letters that read:

Now under new management

"This looks like the kind of place where shady people would stay," Sigi observed. "Why would my dad stay here?"

"It's not that bad," Ozzy said, trying to sound positive. "It's not that great, either. What room?"

"Two-thirteen," Sigi answered.

"Let's hope they're here."

"Let's hope it's them," Sigi added, "and not some terrible misunderstanding. It's possible that my dad wasn't the one who put that address in your pocket."

"If it wasn't him, then who would it have been?"

"I don't know. Something about this feels wrong."

"That's only because we ran away from school. Sheriff Wills is probably combing Otter Rock looking for us."

"Right," Sigi admitted. "Either way, this day is going to end with us in trouble. I've never seen you do anything like what you did to Adam and Jonas. My dad would have been impressed."

"I don't know. He would have called it magic, but it's not. It's just the confusing result of something my parents tested on me."

"Wow," Sigi said. "It used to be me that dissed magic."

"I'm not dissing anything," Ozzy said, wondering if he was using *dissing* in the proper way. "I hope these pants mean something more than just your dad having bad taste in clothes. I wouldn't mind being a wizard, but my ability comes from something altogether different."

"It's hard to dismiss magic anymore," Sigi said seriously. "It took a lot to convince me, but I'm finally on board."

Both Ozzy and Sigi looked across the street at the motel. It wasn't pretty, but it was possible that behind door number 213 there was a wizard and a bird that they both needed tremendously. The last time they had seen Rin, he was in the middle of the ocean. Now they were hoping they would find him in the Marsh and Meadow Motel.

"Well . . ." Ozzy looked at Sigi and smiled. "Should we see if your magic dad is home?"

Ozzy held his left hand up. Pointing his finger like a wand, he felt his body buzz in a way that had become familiar. He looked out at the vehicles on the road and caught the thoughts of the people driving. Ozzy took over their will and most of the cars slowed and came to a stop. There were a few drivers Ozzy couldn't control, but they also had to brake to avoid hitting the cars in front of them.

Sigi's dark eyes widened as she gazed out over the street filled with unmoving traffic. Vehicles sat there running idle, the drivers dazed and bewildered. Those who weren't under Ozzy's control honked at the other cars in confusion.

"You realize we could have walked to the corner and waited for the light," Sigi pointed out.

"I need the practice," Ozzy said, trying hard to concentrate on keeping the cars stopped. "Come on."

They wove through the vehicles. Once they reached the other side, Ozzy relaxed. Cars began to move again as everyone tried to figure out what had happened.

"I worry about you," Sigi said as they walked up to the hotel. "What happens when all that power you have goes to your head?"

"These pants will keep me humble."

Ozzy and Sigi crossed the parking lot and walked past the motel's office, climbed the cement stairs to the second floor, then walked down the open walkway in front of the rooms. From where they were, it was easy to see and hear the noise from the street below.

Ten doors down, they reached room number two hundred and thirteen. It was the last room on the end.

The two of them stepped up to the door and stared at the faded number.

213

Sigi turned around and looked down at the traffic, running smoothly again. It was hard for her to keep her feet still—the possibility of seeing her dad made her jittery.

"This could be good or bad," Ozzy said quietly.

"My dad wouldn't lead us into a trap."

Before Ozzy could both disagree and give detailed examples, Sigi reached out and rapped on the door.

The noise from the street made it hard to hear if any sound was coming from the room. They leaned in closer and tried to listen.

Sigi knocked again.

The knob twisted slowly and then, with a swift tug, the door was pulled open.

Ozzy and Sigi gasped appropriately.

CHAPTER EIGHT

YOUR MIND IS WEAK

The thought had crossed Ozzy's and Sigi's minds that it might not be Rin who answered the door. But their desire to see Clark and the wizard had tricked them into forgetting that reality doesn't always give people what they want. And unfortunately, the person who answered the door was not what they wanted, not by any stretch of the imagination. It wasn't an illegal seamstress working on magic pants. It wasn't even a friendly stranger who they could apologize to for knocking on the wrong door.

True, it *was* the wrong door, but in a different way.

As the door swung open, the man on the other side of the door stared back at them, his light-brown eyes filled with a mix of bewilderment, fear, and surprise. The average-looking man was wearing a plain white polo and brown jeans, no shoes, no socks, and no welcoming expression. The man was no stranger; he was also someone they would have been perfectly happy never seeing again.

"Jon!" Ozzy said, jumping back.

Standing just a few feet in front of them was the very same Jon whom Ray had hired to track Ozzy down.

All three of them exchanged nervous and surprised looks.

Jon was awestruck. "I don't believe it."

Awe was not an easy expression for the man to make. Jon was a lot of things: ex-military, gun for hire, shady, and bland. He was an average height, had average brown hair, and unremarkable features. His teeth weren't too white or too yellow, and his ears were just standard-looking ears. His stance was unremarkable, his body was of an average build. He was a lot of things, but expressive wasn't usually one of them.

"You!" Sigi said.

The little bit of color in Jon's face disappeared and his knees wobbled. He was no longer intimidating. He was worn out and weak. All the fear of him that Ozzy and Sigi had once felt was gone. The average man's eyes went wide, and a panicked expression, like that of someone whose picture had just been unwillingly taken, flashed across his unremarkable face. He looked like he couldn't decide whether he should slam the door or take off running.

"You . . ." he managed to say.

"Us," Sigi said with a growl.

Ozzy wasted no time attempting to clip into Jon's brain. It was surprisingly easy. The man put both his hands back behind his head and stepped backwards into the room.

"What's happening?" Jon asked nervously. "What's going on?"

Jon continued to move farther into the room. Ozzy and Sigi stepped through the door, always staying ten feet away from the retreating man. Once they were all inside the room, Sigi closed the door behind them.

"I can't control my feet," Jon whimpered. "What's happening?"

Ozzy took a second to survey their surroundings. The room was a large suite with two beds and a separate sitting area to one side with a couch and a desk. On the other side was a kitchenette with a stove, refrigerator, and a small table with three wooden chairs tucked underneath it. An open door in the back led into the bathroom. Everything was old, and a few hairs and mystery stains shy of disgusting.

Ozzy had Jon stop near the small table. The confused man stood trembling as he fought his own body for control. It may have been gilding the lily, but Ozzy had Jon pull out two of the wooden chairs at the table and motion for his guests to sit down.

"Thanks," Ozzy said.

The two of them sat down.

Jon stood behind the third chair looking dumbstruck. He was at war with his own mind. He wanted to grab his gun from the holster on his ankle and run, but instead he moved his chair and sat down at a safe distance from the two teenagers.

Ozzy let go of Jon's mind.

"What's happening?" he said, relieved that he could speak freely. He tried to stand up, but Ozzy kept him in his chair.

"It's probably best to stay right where you are," Ozzy suggested.

"I don't understand," Jon argued. "Are you messing with my brain?"

"What brain?" Sigi said, still angry about what Jon had done to her in the past. "Just think of this as paying you back. I'm sure you remember locking me up in a shed."

"I remember you having no problem getting out."

"We weren't expecting you to be here," Ozzy said honestly.

"I wasn't expecting you to walk right up to my door. I was expecting the pizza delivery guy. Why are you here?"

Ozzy looked at Sigi and shrugged.

"I guess we need some answers about things," Ozzy said.

"What things?"

"For starters, how long have you been here?"

"After getting back from that night in the ocean I came here to this hotel."

"Motel," Ozzy corrected him.

"Right," Jon said. "Motel."

"Why?" asked Sigi.

"To keep an eye on you two."

"So Ray hasn't given up?"

"I have no idea what Ray is doing." Jon sniffed smugly. "I'm no longer working for him."

"Really?" Sigi asked suspiciously. "You quit?"

"I've had no communication with him since that day three weeks ago."

"Then why are you still hanging around?"

Jon sat there quietly.

"Why do you still care what we do?" Sigi demanded. "That's just creepy. Well, not *just* creepy, it's also pervy and wrong. Sheriff Wills won't put up with that."

"Sheriff Wills doesn't concern me," Jon said. "He's easy to avoid."

"We found you," Sigi argued. "You're not *that* good at what you do."

"Please," Ozzy said, sounding genuine and wanting to get the conversation back on track, "I don't understand. If there's no job, then why do you still care what we're doing?"

Jon locked eyes with Sigi. "I want to see the wizard."

Ozzy and Sigi glanced at each other with disbelief.

"Rin?" Ozzy asked. "You were there. You saw him disappear into the ocean."

"And he hasn't resurfaced?"

The two kids shook their heads.

"We thought he might be here," Ozzy admitted.

Jon scoffed. "No wonder you looked so disappointed when I opened the door."

"Actually," Sigi said, "the disappointment was all because it was you."

The average man stared at the above-average girl. "Your words don't hurt me. I don't blame you for hating me, but I am no longer your enemy. I am after Rin, and I will find him."

"So you don't know what Ray's going to do next?" Ozzy said.

"No. I'm done with him."

"I don't believe you," Sigi said.

"Well, I can't speak any plainer. It's the truth."

Ozzy closed his grey eyes and focused on Jon's mind and will. His power gave him the ability to control the actions of others, but it didn't bestow him with the power to make people give up their secrets—he could think for them in the moment, but he couldn't see thoughts they already had. Which meant that Ozzy had to be creative to motivate others to cough up what they knew.

Staring casually at Jon, Ozzy began to think. His thoughts caused the man to stand up.

"What's . . . happening?" Jon could hardly speak. "Come on."

Ozzy made the man dash across the room and slam up against the wall. Jon the Average bounced against the surface, fell onto one of the beds, and rolled off and onto the floor. He moaned for a moment before standing back up.

"What's Ray going to do next?" Ozzy asked.

"I told you—I no longer work for him."

"You've told us a lot of things," Sigi said. "Most of them were lies."

Ozzy pointed his finger at Jon. The helpless man walked to the kitchenette area of the suite. He opened one of the drawers near the fridge and pulled out a yellow ceramic plate.

"Don't . . ." Jon tried to say.

It was no use; Ozzy was making decisions for the man. Jon placed his left hand down on the counter. Then, with his right hand, he thwacked the plate against his fingers.

"That's for kidnapping Sigi."

Jon whimpered and smashed the plate down again. It broke into a dozen pieces and fell onto the floor.

"That's for trying to shoot us in the ocean."

Jon picked up another plate.

"I really don't . . ."

Whack!

"That's for owning too many guns," Sigi said.

Jon was beside himself but unable to do anything about it. Ozzy relaxed his thoughts.

"How are you doing this?" Jon asked, standing there frozen.

Ozzy didn't answer the question. Instead, he asked one. "What's Ray's next move?"

"How many times—"

Ozzy's finger buzzed as he took over Jon's will again.

The man stopped talking. He turned and opened the refrigerator. Inside was a gallon of milk, a few bottles of water, and some leftover spaghetti. Jon took out the milk, twisted off the cap, and poured the contents over his head. His face was milky and muddled as he tried to make sense of what he was doing to himself.

"Let go of my mind!" he demanded.

"Just tell us what Ray is going to do next."

Jon pulled out the spaghetti and smeared it all over his face. With milk in his hair and pasta pushed into his nose and ears, he finally looked more interesting than average.

"I don't know what Ray is doing. Don't—"

Jon spun on his heels, and under Ozzy's command walked into the bathroom. He closed the door behind him, screaming, "You have the wrong—!"

With the door shut, Ozzy and Sigi could hear Jon thrashing and struggling in the bathroom. The sound of water running, the toilet flushing, cabinets slamming, and walls being pounded filled their ears.

Sigi looked worried. "You're not killing him, are you?"

Ozzy shook his head. "Not unless the shampoo is poisonous."

The sound of the shower curtain being ripped down and Jon begging for help drifted angrily through the room.

"All you do is think it and he does it?" Sigi asked.

Ozzy nodded. "I see a switch in their minds and flick it on and off with a thought. When it's on I can place my own will into their head."

Jon screamed something about the taste of motel soap.

"Wow," Sigi said solemnly. "I hope the wrong person never gets ahold of your power."

"Me too."

The bathroom door swung open.

Jon was soaked. There was soggy toilet paper wrapped around his waist and legs and stuck to his shoes. His hair was painted with toothpaste and there was shampoo in his eyes. He spit out a tiny bar of soap. Unable to see well, he stumbled back and into his chair. His red, soapy eyes blinked erratically.

"Okay," he said, as a large soap bubble formed under his right nostril, "I'll tell you everything."

CHAPTER NINE

I CANNOT SEE THE REASON FOR THE PAIN

*J*on sat quietly on the wooden chair. He hung his head and tried to control his breathing. His eyes burned; his body was dripping with water and goop. He had no idea how he had gotten himself into the situation he now faced. He was an accomplished mercenary being bested by a couple of teenagers. He had taken down powerful people, manipulated governments, toppled regimes, and always gotten his mark. But somehow in the last little while, two kids, a toy bird, and a wizard had completely done him in.

Three weeks ago, Jon had followed all of them out into international waters. He had almost taken control, but then something had burst through the dark surface of the ocean and blown apart the wooden vessel he had been on. Ozzy and Sigi had departed the scene in the boat Jon had brought. He was left alone in the dark ocean with nothing but a small lifeboat and two oars.

He was also left with the nagging suspicion that magic might be real.

After the *Spell Boat* had been blown apart and Jon had been left for dead, he slowly rowed back to the Oregon shore. It had taken a day, but all the rowing gave him time to think. There were so many things he didn't understand and couldn't explain. He had seen Rin do some remarkable, magical-seeming things. At first Jon thought the wizard was a bother, but with everything Rin did, Jon became more of a believer. Now he not only believed, but wanted some of whatever it was that Rin had. Jon saw the wizard as a religion that he wanted to join.

He needed to find Rin and figure out where his power came from.

Jon's life had always been dark and selfish. Now he desired to believe in something bigger than what he had settled for his entire life.

When he finally reached the shore, he stole a car and drove to Salem. The town was big enough to hide him, and just far enough away from Otter Rock for him not to be spotted. Jon holed up in the Marsh and Meadow Motel, waiting impatiently for any sign of Rin's return. He had watched the news and done some spying, but so far, the wizard had not resurfaced.

Today, just before ordering a pizza, Jon had planned to take another trip into Otter Rock to see how close he could get to Patti's house without the cops noticing. He had felt certain that if Rin were back, Jon would be able to tell by the way Ozzy and Sigi were acting.

But Jon's plans had been upset when Ozzy and Sigi appeared at his door. Acting carelessly, he had opened the door without checking who it was. It was a mistake he'd never made before. But his guard had been down. No one knew he was alive, and he was hungry. He had thought he was opening the door for the pizza man.

The disappointment of not getting that pizza was second only to him now being pushed around by his own mind as it operated under Ozzy's direction.

The boy and girl wanted answers about Ray, but Jon didn't have any. He knew surprisingly little about the man he had worked for. Furthermore, he wanted nothing to do with him any longer. He hadn't enjoyed being sent to harm humans as young as Ozzy and Sigi. He also understood now how sick with power Ray was. He knew Ray wanted to control the will of everyone in the world—and he knew Ray was the kind of person who wouldn't stop until he did.

Jon would have been happy to never think about the man again. Ray was the past; the future was Rin.

Unfortunately, it didn't matter what Jon wanted. Ozzy had control of his brain and Ozzy wanted answers. The truth of the matter was that Jon also wanted answers, but the patterns of his past and Ozzy and Sigi's memory of how he had treated them gave them every reason to work him over. Jon was useless under Ozzy's control. All the boy had to do was look at him and he was suddenly knocking himself around or smearing himself with toothpaste. To make matters worse, the pizza had arrived and Ozzy and Sigi weren't sharing. Sigi had answered the door, paid the girl with some of Jon's money, and now she and Ozzy were eating the lunch of a man who once had filled them with fear.

Sitting on the chair, Jon watched them eat. He lifted his head, took a big breath, and spoke.

"Could I have some?"

"Could you tell us about Ray?" Sigi reasoned. "Also . . . who puts pineapple on a pizza?"

"You said you'd talk," Ozzy reminded him.

"There's nothing left to say. I've done work for him in the past," Jon admitted. "But I've never met him. He texts me on burner phones he sends me. He hired me to bring you to him and I failed. I don't think he'd want to hire me now. Failure is not something he tolerates."

"And why did he want Ozzy?" Sigi asked.

"You both know what he wants," Jon said. "Not many people have the ability to control other people. He knows your parents created the formula. He knows you have that formula coursing through your veins. He believes that the only way to recreate it is to extract it from you."

"That sounds painful," Ozzy said.

"I don't think Ray worries about the pain of others," Jon said sincerely. "He only worries about power. The job he wanted me to do changed as things progressed."

"How did it change?" Sigi asked.

"He wanted Ozzy to come to New York. Then he

wanted you held captive. He also wants that bird. He knows that Ozzy's father created him, and he can see some value in that flying piece of metal."

"That flying piece of metal's name is Clark," Sigi said sharply.

"Right. That's what *you* call him." Jon laughed. "Some of Ray's men call him the Angel of Death."

"Clark's going to like hearing that," Ozzy said, wishing the bird was there. "What other changes to the job did Ray want?"

"He wanted to silence the wizard."

"He wanted to kill my father?"

Jon wiped more shampoo out of his still-red eyes. "Yes, he thinks he's a nut who needs to be wiped out. His words, not mine."

"And we're supposed to believe that you no longer want to help him with all of this?" Ozzy asked. "You decided that it's too hard and you're out?"

"No," Jon said seriously. "I decided that maybe I'm following the wrong path."

"So you've had a change of heart?" Sigi asked doubtfully.

"Something like that," Jon answered. "I want what the wizard has."

"Really?" Sigi asked.

"Yes," Jon said. "I want to believe."

"In my dad?"

"In whatever's happening," he said quietly. "In the

past, I've been driven to take care of problems with violence and money. It seems like your father and you two take care of problems with mind control and . . . magic."

Ozzy smiled.

"I have one mission now," Jon confessed. "I need to know what Rin knows. I know Ozzy's ability comes from the serum, but not Rin's. What he does is bigger than controlling minds."

Sigi looked strangely proud of what Jon was saying about her dad.

"Rin's not easy to find," Jon admitted. "The only contact info I've found for him is an ad he posted in a magazine once."

"Not just once," Sigi said. "He posted that ad for years before Ozzy answered it."

"I found an old copy of the *Otter Rock Visitor's Guide* at the library. The sheriff's report said that Ozzy called him and started all of this. So I've called that number hundreds of times, but he never picks up."

"We're not sure he made it out of the ocean," Ozzy said, looking down at his pants. "Although we have our suspicions."

"Then I'll keep calling until I get him," Jon said soberly.

"Have you left him any messages?" asked Ozzy.

"Yes, dozens."

"I hope they were good," Sigi said. "He's big on messages."

"I just told him that I wanted to meet."

"That's not going to impress him," Sigi said sadly, picking pineapple off her pizza.

"It doesn't matter," Jon said strongly. "Because I won't stop looking until I have an audience with him."

"Oh, that's a good line," Ozzy said seriously. "If he ever comes back, make sure you say that to him. He likes audiences."

"So neither of you have seen him since that night?"

They both shook their heads.

"What about the bird?"

More shaking.

"They could be dead," Jon said without thinking.

"No," Ozzy insisted. "Not Rin—or Clark."

"How can you be sure?"

"You said you want to believe in something bigger," Ozzy reminded him. "Well, those two combined are too big to just disappear. We wi—"

A loud banging on the door stopped Ozzy mid-word.

All three turned to look at the door. Before they could even properly wonder who it might be, a voice shouted out.

"Open up! It's the police!"

"You told the cops I was here?" Jon asked in a panic, still not able to move on his own.

"No," Ozzy said.

"You've got to let me go," Jon begged. "I'll find the wizard. I won't hurt anyone in the process. I promise."

Neither Ozzy nor Sigi answered the man because they were both a little nervous about their own future.

"Can't you do something?" Sigi asked Ozzy as the cops pounded on the door again. "Make them turn around and leave."

"And then what?" Ozzy asked. "Spend the rest of my life controlling people to keep them from getting to us?"

"Can you summon the wizard?" Jon begged. "Send that bird in to take them out."

"We told you we—"

The police breached the door. What looked like a dozen cops poured into the room, yelling and knocking things over. They surrounded Ozzy, Sigi, and Jon, grabbing them and barking out orders.

"Don't move!"

"Stay where you are!"

"Keep still."

"Those are all the same thing," Ozzy pointed out kindly.

"Also be quiet!" The order was given by a police officer with tiny round ears that were too small for his big round head. By the way the other officers treated him it was clear that Round Ears was in charge. "Don't speak unless we tell you to."

Round Ears and his friends were less patient and gentle than Sheriff Wills and his crew usually were. But they were kind enough to not put handcuffs on the two teenagers. Sigi broke their rule, though, shouting out to inform them that

Jon was a bona fide bad guy and they might want to lock him up and throw away the key. Instead of doing exactly what she suggested, they handcuffed Jon and marched him out of the room and down the cement stairs.

Once they were all in the parking lot, Ozzy and Sigi were invited to sit in one car and Jon was thrown into another.

Round Ears climbed into the front seat of the car Ozzy and Sigi were in. He looked back at them through the wire divide and instructed the pair to sit calmly and not bother him.

"What did we do?" Sigi asked a little too loudly.

Round Ears shouted back, "I told you not to bother me!"

"Where are you taking us?" Ozzy asked, still debating if he should use his ability to escape.

"We're taking you back home," Round Ears said. "Sheriff Wills is looking for you. So just sit back and be quiet."

"I don't like people telling me what to do," Sigi said hotly.

"Then you're welcome to ignore me."

Round Ears spoke a few phrases of police code into his radio and then turned the car on. Jon was driven one direction, and Ozzy and Sigi were driven another.

It goes without saying—yet it's still being said—that the ride back to Otter Rock was less enjoyable than the ride there had been.

CHAPTER TEN

SAY WHAT YOU WANT

heriff Wills was tall—not as tall as Rin, who stood at six-three, but taller than Ozzy, who was almost six-one. Under normal circumstances, his height would never be associated with Rin and Ozzy, but since the last few months of his life had been nothing but a wild mess with those two in the middle, it made perfect sense to compare the point where he topped off to that of both the young and the old wizard.

Wills sported a thin mustache that he spent too much time delicately trimming in the mornings. It was the only delicate thing about him. He also possessed a full head of graham cracker–colored hair and eyes the color of watery mud. His uniform was faded green and tighter than it should have been. He wasn't fat—he just washed most of his clothes in hot water, and the results showed.

For most of his career, Otter Rock had been a quiet, peaceful town. There were tourists in the summer and the occasional drunken local year-round. But there had never been anything like the trouble that Ozzy, Sigi, and the man he had known as Brian had recently caused.

Back when Rin had first married Patti, his name was Brian and he was a middle-school teacher. He wore tweed sport jackets and didn't stand out much in normal society. But shortly after Sigi was born, Brian began to change. To the casual onlooker, the changes didn't look good. He and Patti began to have problems and Brian quit his job. Then one day Brian disappeared, leaving Patti to raise Sigi almost alone. Many years later he resurfaced, and was no longer Brian—he was a wizard named Rin. To make matters worse, he told anyone who would listen that he had spent the last ten years in and out of a place called Quarfelt.

Oddly, not everyone believed him.

Rin moved into a home he'd won in a bet, a place located in the trees a few miles out of town. To be more authentic, he began to wear a gray felt hat and a short bathrobe wherever he went. In the early days, the color of his robe had changed from brown to white to green to white again. For the last little while Rin had been consistently sporting a yellow robe, striped orange trousers, and red hightop sneakers.

The trouble Ozzy brought was different. The boy had come out of nowhere. He had lived alone until he was thirteen and then made the mistake of hiring Rin to help find his parents.

Sheriff Wills believed it was that move, that hire, that mistake, that was the catalyst for most of the problems that were happening. Ozzy and Sigi had nearly died or been seriously hurt repeatedly over the last little while, thanks to the trouble Rin had brought about. With Rin's help, the two teenagers had been chased by a powerful man in New York who threatened to do them further harm.

It was Sheriff Wills's duty to make sure the teenagers were protected. He had stationed officers outside of Patti's house and at their school. Wills would also coordinate with them and Patti to follow them if they needed to travel anywhere or get anything outside of Otter Rock. He believed more trouble was coming, and he felt the only way to be ready was to be on constant alert.

There had been no major problems over the last three weeks, but today had been different. Ozzy and Sigi had slipped away from school during a commotion two students started. But they'd been foolish and took an Uber. Wills had learned from before that Rin loved to use ride-share apps. So he'd set things up so that his dispatcher would receive a notification if Ozzy, Sigi, or Rin ever popped up as a rider. The Otter Rock police station had been contacted by Uber while Ozzy and Sigi were still on their way to Salem. With help from the Salem police force, the two kids had been picked up and were now being driven back to Otter Rock so that Sheriff Wills could have a little talk with them.

The sheriff had contacted Patti. She had been a couple

of hours away on business, but she was now on her way to the station as well.

Sheriff Wills stood by the front desk and listened to Wilma as she talked to someone on the radio. Wilma had been on the force for more than ten years. She had joined the force because she didn't like the way an officer had treated her years ago. Wilma was black and felt like the cops in Oregon could use a little more color and education. Wilma had worked with Sheriff Wills for the last four years. She had short hair and a look that made the people around her straighten up and get in line without her ever saying a word.

"They're just turning off Main Street," she told the sheriff. "Those kids really know how to get messy. I've never seen two people more attracted to trouble. Like we don't have enough things to take up our time."

Sheriff Wills looked at the mostly empty police station. Things were quiet—no one else was around.

"Okay," Wilma said, "maybe it's slow *now*."

"I don't know what it is about them," Sheriff Wills said. "Just when I think I have things figured out, they do something else stupid."

A cop car pulled up in front of the station. Round Ears got out and escorted the two kids into the building.

"Sheriff," Sergeant Ears said. "I brought you something."

Ozzy and Sigi looked properly beat.

"Hello, Sigi. Hello, Ozzy. I'm glad you're okay," the

sheriff said sternly. "Of course, that's about the only thing I'm glad about at the moment."

Round Ears sniff-laughed. "They were polite enough on the ride back."

"Thanks, Mark," Wills said. "Wilma needs you to sign the paperwork. I'm going to take these two and have a little talk."

"I don't feel like talking," Sigi said.

"Well, then we can just sit in silence until your mother arrives."

"You called my mom?" Sigi asked.

"Of course I called her. You were missing. You two are in potential danger and it's my duty to keep you safe. When you disappeared from school, Patti was the second person I called."

"Who was the first?" Ozzy asked curiously.

"My therapist," Wills said. "I wanted to see if she had an opening for tonight."

The two teenagers weren't sure if Sheriff Wills was joking, but they followed him as he opened the small gate in the counter and walked back to his office. They both took a seat on the chairs across from his desk and tried to look casual. They were a little too familiar with Sheriff Wills's office, and they knew him well enough to not fear him. They also understood that for the most part he was only trying to keep them safe.

The sheriff took a seat behind his desk and sighed.

"You two are something else." His tone wasn't mean,

but it wasn't complimentary either. "Who wants to tell me what happened at school?"

Ozzy looked at Sigi and she did the same right back. Neither one of them said anything.

"Right, you want to sit in silence."

"I'll tell you," Ozzy spoke up. "There was a fight at school and—"

"—And we were worried we might get hurt," Sigi interrupted. "That's why we left the campus. We were hoping to find someplace safe."

"Really? And Salem is the safe place you found?"

"It's the capital of Oregon," Ozzy said.

Sheriff Wills stared at the boy.

"Okay, let me ask you this: Why did you go to that hotel?"

"Motel," Sigi said.

"Is that important?" the sheriff asked.

"You motor up to a motel," Ozzy explained. "Hotels have indoor hallways."

More staring.

"Rin taught me that," Ozzy said.

"And was Rin at the motel?"

Ozzy and Sigi shook their heads.

"Jon was," Sigi said.

"The man who chased you out to sea?" Sheriff Wills was beside himself. "That's who they took to the Salem station?"

Ozzy and Sigi nodded.

A dark red patch spread up Sheriff Wills's neck from under his green collar. It made his face both festive and frightening.

"You two went looking for this man by yourself?" The sheriff snorted slowly. "What part of you thought that was a good idea?"

"Our brains," Ozzy said, thinking it was an honest question.

"You could have been hurt. Didn't he kidnap you once?"

"He did," Sigi said.

The sheriff put his hands in his head. When he looked up, he said, "I don't know what to do with you two. How did you know this Jon guy was there?"

"I got an anonymous note," Ozzy lied.

"From who?"

"I guess you don't know what anonymous means," Sigi said.

"Where's the note?" Any patience the sheriff once had seemed to be evaporating.

"I lost it," Ozzy lied again. "It was just an address and room number."

"And where did you get it from?"

Ozzy looked at Sigi.

"It was in Ozzy's locker," she said.

"So it didn't come in the box that was delivered to the school earlier today?" the sheriff asked, letting them know he had more information than they thought.

"No."

"What was in that box?"

"It's personal," Ozzy said.

Sheriff Wills may have been the sheriff of a small town, but he was no rube. Before transferring to Otter Rock, he had had years of success in Portland as a respected detective. He was using some of that deduction power now.

"Your pants are quite unusual."

"Thanks," Ozzy said.

"They look a little like the ones Brian was wearing the last time I saw him."

"His name is Rin," Ozzy said in a friendly tone. "It's short for Labyrinth."

"Sorry, like the ones Rin was wearing."

"I liked his so much I got my own," Ozzy said lamely.

"Where?"

"Yes, I wear them," Ozzy said, not understanding the question.

Sheriff Wills smiled. He knew Ozzy was different. The boy had grown up alone and was less jaded and sarcastic than so many other kids his age.

"That's not what I mean," the sheriff said. "*Where* did you get them?"

"I made them for him," Sigi cut in. "He liked the ones my dad had, so I stitched those together."

"Really? They're not the personal item you got from the box?"

"No," Ozzy said.

"Well, this is going nowhere," Wills said, throwing his

hands up. "You two know I'm only trying to help. Everything you keep from me makes my job harder. Can I tell you what *I* think happened today?"

"I bet we can't stop you," Sigi said.

Wills ignored Sigi's comment. "You got a box delivered to your school," he said. "In that box was a pair of pants and a note. That note was from Rin and it told you where to go. You helped cause a commotion in the hallway, slipped out, and traveled to Salem. Then you went to the motel room of someone dangerous. If we hadn't gotten the Salem police there quickly, you could have been in real trouble."

"We can hold our own," Sigi said defiantly.

"That's true," the sheriff admitted. "But there might come a time when you get into more trouble than you can handle. I don't know this man, Ray, in New York. But my contact there has made it clear that he is very, very dangerous."

Ozzy and Sigi made it a habit of not telling Sheriff Wills more than they had to. Clinging to that habit, they kept their mouths closed as Wills continued to talk.

"To be honest, Ray scares me as well. I'll sleep much better when all this is said and done. I'll also be happy when Rin returns."

"Me too." Ozzy couldn't stop himself from agreeing. There were few things in life that he wanted more than Rin and Clark's return.

"I still have so many questions about what happened to

you. I've been checking into every lead possible. Imagine how much easier my job would be if you just told me the truth."

"That's not really the kind of thing I like to imagine," Sigi said.

"For example—does Rin have a bird?"

Ozzy and Sigi couldn't help but smile. They both fought to keep their expressions blank, but Sheriff Wills noticed the small change.

"There was a bird that got into Bites a while back," Wills added. "The one that broke all the light bulbs."

"Animals are unpredictable," Sigi said.

"I just—"

The sheriff stopped talking because Ozzy's lawyer, Ryan Severe, had stuck his head into the office.

Wills swore.

"Let me guess," Ryan said. "You came back here where it was nice and quiet to tell these two that they don't have to answer your questions without having legal representation on hand?"

"Perfect," the sheriff complained.

"Thanks for the compliment," Ryan said. "But unless you're charging them with anything, these two need to get home and rest."

"I'm trying to help," the sheriff argued.

"Well, it would help if I take them home and talk to them first," the lawyer said. "Are they charged with anything?"

"No."

Ryan waved at Ozzy and Sigi. "Come on."

The two of them stood up to leave.

"We'll be watching you even closer," Sheriff Wills said. "I think you're in more danger than you know."

"Creepy, but thanks," Sigi said.

Ozzy and Sigi left with Ryan.

Sheriff Wills stood by Wilma at the front counter and watched them leave through the front doors of the station.

"Those two are going to be the death of me."

"I feel the same way about baked goods," Wilma said.

Wills went back to his office to make some calls. He was concerned about Ozzy and Sigi, but what he most wanted now was to have a conversation with a man named Jon.

CHAPTER ELEVEN

COULD YOU PLEASE EXPLAIN

Jon sat stone-faced in the interrogation room of the East Salem police station. It was a rectangular space with gray walls and a large stainless steel table in the middle. On the north wall was a wide mirror and a door. After being taken from the Marsh and Meadow Motel, Jon had been brought directly to this spot. The local police didn't know who they had, and when they questioned him, they got very few answers and little information. All they had figured out was that Jon had been registered at the motel under the name of Jon Smith, he was originally from someplace in the South, and he wanted to press charges against the two teenagers who had knocked on his door, harassed and abused him, and ruined his day.

When Sheriff Wills had shown up at the station, Round Ears was more than happy to let him have a go at the tight-lipped man. Jon had washed up as best he could, but there were still remnants of pasta sauce and toothpaste on his clothes and in his hair.

"Hello, Jon," Sheriff Wills said, entering the room and taking a seat across the table from him.

The sheriff and Jon were alone, but they both knew that other people were watching from behind the mirror.

Jon kept quiet.

"I've been looking for you," the sheriff said with a controlled voice. "I'm actually thrilled to see you even though you've caused some trouble in my neck of the woods."

Jon didn't speak.

"I know who you are," the sheriff said. "These officers here don't know your history, but I do. You work for Ray Dench and you've been hired to harm the Toffy boy."

Jon blinked slowly.

"I counted twenty-seven things I could charge you with right now," Wills said. "From kidnapping to gun charges. But here's the thing—I don't really want to take this out on you. I believe the real problem is your boss, Ray."

Jon couldn't let that go. "He's not my boss."

Sheriff Wills gave a small, calming nod. "Really?"

"I no longer have or want anything to do with him."

"That's a smart decision. Why?"

Jon didn't answer.

"This is a lot like talking to Ozzy and Sigi," Wills said. "They never give me any answers, either. I keep thinking how easy and clean this all might be if people would simply stop hiding what they know."

Jon looked at the sheriff and then stared at the mirror.

"Oh," the sheriff said in a friendly tone, "I see. Does it bother you that others are listening? Is that why you won't answer? Because, looking at you, it seems to me that you have something you'd like to say."

Jon glanced at the mirror again.

Sheriff Wills pushed his chair back from the table, got up, and left the room. A few moments later, a light went on behind the one-way mirror. The space in back was empty, letting Jon know that nobody was watching.

Sheriff Wills came back in and sat down.

"It's just you and me now, Jon. You can see there's no one watching, and they've turned off all the mics. I promise."

Jon closed his eyes and breathed slowly.

"How 'bout we just talk?" the sheriff suggested. "Some stuff has happened, and I'm thinking that we both have been through things that we would rather not have been through. Let me ask you this—are you loyal to Ray Dench?"

Jon's eyes flashed open. "No."

"That's good to hear."

"Ray doesn't even know I'm alive," Jon insisted. "And I want to keep it that way."

"Okay," Wills said. "Let's see how things play out. But if you do help me, I'll see what I can do to make sure Ray knows nothing about you."

Jon nodded in agreement.

"You were in pursuit of Mr. Ozzy Toffy and Ms. Sigi Owens at one point."

"It was just a job," Jon said. "I never wanted to hurt them."

"Looking at you now, I would say they've done more damage to you."

"It hasn't gone as planned."

"They frustrate me too," Wills admitted. "They disappear, they travel across the country doing who knows what. Strange things are always happening around them. They follow a lunatic around like he's a real wizard."

"He is," Jon insisted.

"Whoa," Wills said, leaning forward in his seat. "Are you saying you believe that Brian Mortley is a wizard?" The sheriff's voice had no animosity or judgment in it.

"I'm saying that for the moment I have no other way to explain what's happened."

Wills was intrigued. "Okay, then, tell me what's happened."

Those were the six words that cracked the dam. Jon wanted to get things off his chest, to have someone else know what he knew. And the floodgates were open. Jon told the sheriff everything he knew. He told him about a magical bird named Clark and a wizard that turned into a whale and blew apart boats. He told him about mystical staffs and grandfathers surrounded by tornadoes of books. He told him about Ray and his desire to control everyone's minds. He told him about Emmitt and Mia Toffy and what they had set out to do. He told him about expecting a pizza and receiving a self-inflicted beating from a boy that could control minds.

Sheriff Wills sat there looking composed and interested. He had known most of the reality-based details, but the introduction of so many magical pieces was astonishing and hard to believe. His mind staggered and spun as the new information filled in some of the pieces he'd been missing and gave him new clues. One thing was clear in all of this—what was happening to Ozzy was much, much bigger than Wills had ever imagined.

After an hour of talking, Jon stopped. The average man looked lighter, and even though he was sitting down, he appeared to be a few inches taller. A little color had returned to his pale face and he no longer resembled a glass of milk in brown pants and an off-white shirt.

After a full minute of silence, Sheriff Wills spoke.

"That's a lot to take in. I've been on the force a long time, and I've never heard anyone calmly tell me the kind of things you just did. So this bird, Clark. It's a living bird that *looks* like metal?"

"No," Jon insisted. "It's a metal bird that is somehow alive."

"Like a robot, or a drone?"

Jon shook his head. "It's alive. It thinks and acts and speaks for itself."

"That's not possible."

"I would have said the same thing a few weeks ago."

"So it's magic?"

"I don't know what it is. I know that Ozzy's father created it and Ray will stop at nothing to get it."

"Unbelievable." Wills shook his head in disbelief. "And Ozzy can control people's brains?"

"I think that's what happened to me," Jon said. "His parents used him as a test case for the serum."

"They were bad?"

"I don't know. I only know they were brilliant. And now their boy seems to have the ability to force his will on others."

"Could he make a police officer drive into the ocean? Or maybe cause a fight at school so he can slip away?"

"Yes, he could. He made me fight myself."

Sheriff Wills whistled, sounding more like a small-town cop than he wanted to. But the crazy answers and stories Jon had told were mind-blowing.

"And you're determined to find Rin and become like him?"

"I want what he has," Jon said.

"He's not well."

"According to who?"

"Almost everyone who knows him."

"Maybe they're just looking at him wrong."

"I don't know," Wills said. "I can *almost* believe in living metal birds and mind control more than I can believe in Brian being a real wizard."

"I suggest you believe in all those things."

Sheriff Wills drummed his fingers on the table as he thought. He closed his eyes and breathed slowly for a few moments. When his eyes finally popped open, he looked directly at Jon.

"Here's what we're going to do," the sheriff said. "I'm going to take you with me to Otter Rock. I want you locked up where I can keep an eye on you. I will do everything I can to keep Ray from knowing that you're alive. And if you continue to help, I will do my best to make sure that the courts know you cooperated."

Jon nodded.

"But," Wills added, "I have one more question for now. Do you remember Ozzy's grandfather's address?"

Jon nodded again.

"Excellent," the sheriff said. "I'm going to need that."

"If you're going to bribe him for answers, I suggest you bring him books."

"Duly noted."

Wills stood up and pushed his chair back. He left the room and explained things to Round Ears. After a small bit of paperwork, Jon was loaded into the backseat of Wills's patrol car.

It all seemed rather perfunctory and police-like, but inside, Sheriff Wills was having a hard time containing his excitement. He now had several solid leads. He also knew things that the wizard and his entourage had never told him. The possibility of solving the case for good filled him with a purpose and a drive so strong he could barely sit still.

For both Jon and the sheriff, it was a nervous, worrisome, fidgety ride back to Otter Rock.

CHAPTER TWELVE

SCARS STILL LINGER

Ray Dench was the worst kind of person a person could be. He wasn't an evil power-hungry tyrant who also had a soft spot for animals or volunteered at a soup kitchen once a month. No, he was an evil power-hungry tyrant who hated animals and purchased soup kitchens just to tear them down and laugh at the less-fortunates' lack of soup. He had no soft spot, no funny bone, and no milk of human kindness.

He did, however, have goals—a noble habit if your goals are to get good grades or to cure cancer, a disastrous idea if your goals are to be the wealthiest man alive by stealing everyone else's free will.

"No news of Jon?" Ray said unhappily to the large man standing in front of his desk. "He just disappeared?"

The large man was the new head of Ray's security team. He didn't particularly love his job, but the pay was just enough to keep him from standing up for his convictions and leaving to find something else. His name was Ty, and he was more than just large, he was wide, tall, massive, and hulking. He was dressed in the standard uniform of the men who protected and did Ray's bidding; a tailored blue suit with a white shirt unbuttoned at the collar.

"There's no news," Ty said. "Nothing has turned up as of yet."

"What about the boy?"

"Both he and the girl are being watched day and night by the police."

"And the bird?"

"No sign of any bird or the . . ." Ty felt stupid just saying it. ". . . or the wizard."

"Disgusting," Ray said hotly. "I'm trying to save the world and someone playing dress-up is ruining everything. When he does pop up, he needs to be taken care of."

"Understood."

Ray scratched the tip of his narrow pink nose as he took a few minutes to think. Ty would have loved to back out of the room and leave Ray alone, but he knew there were consequences to doing things like that. Ray liked to have people around to snap at or talk at. He also hated for people to leave before he'd given them his permission.

So Ty stood still.

Ray's office was adorned with a dozen stained-glass windows high up on the walls, currently creating colorful beams of light that fell across Ray's face. The man looked like a clown—or a puppet that had been created for no other reason than to terrorize people.

Time kept moving, but Ty stayed still.

Finally, Ray spoke. "I think I've waited long enough," he said. "It's been weeks since Jon disappeared, and we can't just have that boy wandering around freely. Those simple cops should be no problem for us. We need to plan a retrieval and bring Ozzy Toffy back to New York. Do you realize what that boy possesses?"

Knowing the question wasn't for him, Ty kept quiet.

"He possesses the secret to the most profitable and powerful possibility in the world," Ray answered. "If governments knew what he had they would tear Oregon apart to get it. We can't let that happen. What he has belongs to me and nobody else. I'd track him down myself, but . . ."

Ray stopped talking, bothered by his own words.

Ty knew the reason Ray couldn't track Ozzy down. The man was powerful, but he was also reluctant to leave New York. A crippling phobia prevented him from leaving the state. It had been years since he had done so, and he hoped that in his lifetime he'd never have to leave again.

"Do you think the wizard and Jon might have died in the ocean?" Ray asked.

Ty waited.

"Well?" Ray demanded.

Realizing the question was for him, Ty answered, "It's a possibility."

"If you had to wager on it?"

"I'd wager that both the wizard and Jon are alive," Ty said. "Jon is highly skilled, and the wizard has been known to disappear for years at a time."

"Fine," Ray snapped. "I have some calls to make."

"Then I'll leave you alone."

"No. You won't. Stay where you are until I say so."

Ty stood there trying to look placid and bored as Ray called in some favors from people who both feared and owed him.

CHAPTER THIRTEEN

NEED IS GREAT

Rin set the toolbox down on the bench behind the quaint bread shop. Maple trees growing around the bench kept it well hidden, helping to create a private spot in a busy city.

The wizard opened the toolbox and pulled out Clark.

The trees blocked most of the direct sunlight, so Rin retrieved a flashlight from the same box and turned it on. He held the light over the silver strip on Clark's back to speed up the charge.

Clark's eyes popped open almost immediately.

The bird stood up on the bench and looked around. Remembering that something was different, he took a moment to stretch his wings and look at himself.

"I feel powerful," the bird said.

The once-metal raven now appeared to be a small dragon. He had dark black spikes along his spine that stuck up five inches at his neck, decreasing in size until they met his tail feathers. His wings had been lengthened and transformed so that their now-longer span seemed to be less birdlike and more batlike. Two long horns spiraled out and up from above his eyes. The spikes and wings and horns were all adorned with a swirling textured pattern. The bird looked like a bulky but terrifying dragon—if that dragon lived on a world considerably smaller than Earth.

"I'm glad you like it," Rin replied kindly. "It's amazing what magic can do for one's self-esteem. Look at Ozzy, for example—he's much more confident than he used to be."

Clark looked around anxiously. "Is he here?"

"No," Rin said. "He's back in Oregon. I'm referring to how he acted on the boat."

"If he's back in Oregon, where are we?"

"In New York."

"How did we get here?"

"We took a shortcut through Quarfelt."

"Is that possible?"

"All things are possible for those who are willing to throw out the stuffy confines of reality. Did you know they now have bacon-scented soap?"

"I'm not interested unless it's metal." Clark stretched his wings again. "These things are heavy. And my beak feels funny."

"But you look amazing."

"I bet I do."

Clark jumped and shook proudly. He shot up into the

trees, wriggled around in the leaves, and then dropped back down onto the bench.

"I like the changes," he said, referring to himself. "Ozzy and Sigi need to see."

"They will," Rin said. "But right now we have a journey to complete."

"And it's in New York? Isn't this where that pinched looking man with the cinnamon-colored hair lives?"

"Yes. And yes."

A red sports car drove past, and the morning sun bounced off its windshield and flashed across Clark's eyes. The bird tittered, tweeted, and twirled.

"Are you okay?" Rin asked.

"I don't know," Clark answered. "I think I'm having a flashback of that felt place."

"Quarfelt?" Rin asked with concern.

"Did we fight something long and spongy?"

"Not that I remember."

"And was there a man there with a bad combover and three arms?"

"You could be talking about Ned," Rin said. "He wears glasses and has a really long nose."

Clark shook his head. "I wish I could remember being there."

"If wishes were fishes, we'd all have smelly hands."

"I don't have hands," Clark said. "I have talons. So I'd like to remember."

"Sometimes ignorance is necessary. Now focus."

"On what?"

"The task at hand."

"I'm not sure what that is," the bird answered honestly, still looking at his strange new wings.

"I was hired to find Ozzy's parents."

"Are they in New York?"

"No, but Ray is. And I'm hoping he might have a few answers."

"And my new additions are going to play a part in this?"

"Yes."

"Then let's move," Clark insisted. "I can't wait to put my new personality to the test."

"Okay," Rin said. "Here's what I want you to do."

Clark listened and, upon hearing the plan, smiled as much as his golden beak would allow him to.

CHAPTER FOURTEEN

IT'S A SAD AFFAIR

Patti was worried. Had she known all those years ago when she married Rin, who was then Brian, that things would turn out as they had, she might very well have said no to his proposal. Of course, then she would never have had Sigi, and Sigi meant the world to her. So much so that she was worried that her daughter was heading down an odd and unstable path.

Patti needed to spend more time with Sigi, but with Ozzy living at their house now, alone time wasn't as easy to come by. She had taken her daughter to Eugene for the day a week ago, but that had ended in a fight and more confusion.

To make matters worse, Sigi had skipped school yesterday and gone to Salem with Ozzy to track down a dangerous person. Patti felt lucky that the police had found them and locked up Jon so quickly. She had raced home from a meeting in Corvallis but by the time she had arrived,

Ozzy's lawyer had already picked both kids up from the station and had gotten them back home.

Patti was worried that her daughter was in a bad place.

Feeling desperate, Patti decided to take Sigi away for a few days. She wanted to go on a small vacation to California. However, she knew that Sigi would insist on Ozzy coming along. So Patti decided to be proactive and squash the problem before she sprang the news on her daughter.

Climbing the steps that led to the room above the garage, Patti went over what she wanted to say to Ozzy in her head. When she knocked on the door, he opened it almost instantly. The boy was wearing an orange T-shirt, purple shorts, and a somber expression.

"Hi," Ozzy said sheepishly.

"Hello."

"I'm still sorry about going with Sigi to Salem," he apologized for the tenth time.

"Me too," Patti said.

"We thought it would help."

"It was dangerous. We're lucky no one was hurt." Patti smiled to ease the mood. "Actually, I'm here for another reason. I have something to talk to you about. Can I come in?"

"Of course," Ozzy said sincerely. "After all, you do own this place."

Patti came into the room and closed the door. She took a seat on the desk chair and Ozzy sat on the edge of the bed. The two large windows lit the room completely and made the blue interior walls shine.

"Do you like living here?" Patti asked kindly.

"Yes," Ozzy answered. "I miss the Cloaked House, but this is a perfect second best."

"You've had an unusual life."

"It doesn't seem that way to me," Ozzy said. "It's all I know."

Sitting in the desk chair, it was easy for Ozzy to see how much Patti and Sigi looked alike. Patti's hair was short and neat while Sigi's was wild and full, but their dark eyes and strong cheeks had been set using the same mold.

"You're remarkable, Ozzy," Patti said sincerely.

"Thanks," Ozzy was confused. "Is that what you came to tell me?"

Patti laughed. "No . . . I came to say I need your help."

"You name it."

"Things seem kind of heavy recently." Patti held her hands in front of her as if she were lifting something weighty. "It just feels like life is more stressful than it should be."

"Sorry."

"You don't need to apologize," Patti said. "But because things are nuts, I was thinking I'd take Sigi on a trip with me to California. No business, just to get away for a few days. We would leave tomorrow."

"That sounds good."

"I feel like I need some alone time with her. You know, just mother and daughter."

Ozzy nodded even though he had no idea what it was like to spend some alone time with a mother or father. But being of above-average intelligence, Ozzy didn't need anything spelled out.

"Do you want me to stay here and watch the house?"

"Yes," Patti said sounding relieved, "but there's more. You know Sigi will insist you come along. And normally that would be fine by me, but you'll probably need to persuade or convince her that you *want* to stay here and that she should go without you."

"Nobody persuades Sigi," Ozzy said in a complimentary tone. "She's really good at doing what she wants to do."

"Right," Patti said. "But maybe you could nudge her, ease her mind about you staying here. Of course, there will still be officers watching, so you won't be alone."

"I'll see if I can nudge her."

Ozzy smiled and Patti smiled back. Both smiles were sincere. Patti was pleased that her plan to have some quality time with Sigi might happen, and Ozzy was thrilled at the possibility of having a few days by himself. He had grown up alone and isolated, and he missed the long days he used to spend in his own head.

"Thank you," Patti said standing up.

"There is one condition," Ozzy said. "Sorry, but if Sigi asks me point blank if you told me not to come, then I'll have no choice but to tell her. She's the one person I've never kept any secrets from."

"Fair enough," Patti said.

Ozzy stared at her. "Do you say 'fair enough' to upset

your ex-husband?" he asked without sounding like the jerk most people would. "Because Rin always says, 'More than fair.'"

"I'm aware of what he says." Patti was suddenly acting like she had a splitting headache. "I say it that way because it's just fair enough."

"I was only wondering."

Patti sat back down on the chair. "Look, Ozzy, you're a wonderful kid, and I know I'm not your parent, but I care about you. And sometimes—actually, a lot of times—Rin says things that aren't right, or shouldn't be taken seriously. It's not healthy to live a delusional life. Do you know where my ex-husband went for all those years he was gone?"

"Quarfelt?"

Patti looked at Ozzy and took a moment to breathe. "No, Ozzy. He was getting help."

"Where?"

"It's not important now. Maybe you can ask him next time he returns," she said softly. "If he returns."

"I don't understand," Ozzy said honestly. "Do you know for a fact that he wasn't in Quarfelt?"

"I know you've been through enough already," she said. "And I just don't want you to spend your life walking the wrong way."

Ozzy looked out the window toward the sea.

"What kind of help was Rin getting?"

"Life can be hard, Ozzy," Patti said gently. "Sometimes people need others to help them through it."

"And Rin needed help?"

"You're smart," Patti said sadly. "You must know what is real and what is pretend."

"I don't," Ozzy said. "I grew up alone in a forest with a metal bird. I have been picked on and worked over by people my parents shouldn't ever have hung out with. I hired a wizard. The line between real and pretend is a blur to me."

"Sometimes knowing what's real requires closing your eyes and using only your mind," Patti suggested. "You'll figure this all out."

"I will?"

Patti smiled. "Now, I'm going to be telling Sigi about the trip at lunch. So it would be nice to have you there to encourage her to go. It'll be good for all of us."

Ozzy looked back toward the ocean, hoping the view would help steady the strange new thoughts that were swirling up inside of him.

Patti got up, patted him kindly on the right shoulder, and then left the boy alone.

Ozzy closed his eyes and let his mind try to figure things out.

CHAPTER FIFTEEN

LACK OF DETAILS

Ozzy sat at the table in the kitchen feeling like an invisible weight had been wrapped around his neck. What Patti had said about Rin sat in his gut like a wad of wet cheese. The way she had said with such conviction that Rin had not been in Quarfelt made him uneasy. The whole world had become a ship and the motion of events was making him seasick.

"Are you okay?" Sigi asked as she sat on a tall barstool at the bar. "You look un-Ozzyish."

"I'm fine."

Patti was at the stove cooking some rice in a pot.

"Good," Patti said. "Because I have some news."

Sigi stopped what she was doing and directed her gaze toward her mom.

"We're going on a trip."

"We just went on a trip," Sigi reminded her.

"That was a one-day work trip. This is a four-day fun

trip," Patti said, sounding like a mom who was trying to sell something lame to her child. "I've already alerted Sheriff Wills and we're leaving tomorrow."

"What about school?" Sigi asked. "More importantly, where are we going?"

"Well, since we're leaving on Saturday, you'll only miss Monday and Tuesday. And we're going to do a lot of shopping and brave the crowds at Disneyland."

Sigi acted mildly intrigued. "I haven't been to Disneyland since I was eight and I threw up on the elephant ride."

"Sounds magical," Ozzy said.

"All right," Sigi said happily. "I guess that would be fun. You'll love it, Ozzy."

"Actually, if it's okay, I think I'll stay here."

Sigi looked shocked, and Patti did her best to appear likewise.

"What?" Sigi asked. "Why would you stay here?"

Ozzy was torn. Patti hadn't told him that they were going to Disneyland. He had never been there, but he had heard people claiming that it was the happiest place on earth. It's one thing to skip out on a mother-daughter outing, but it's quite another to forgo a visit to the earth's happiest spot.

"I know it sounds weird," Ozzy said. "But I would love to have some time by myself."

"We bother you?" Sigi asked.

"No, but I could read a ton of books and not miss the

math test I have on Tuesday. I guess solitude sounds more interesting than crowds of people."

"Okay," Patti said, pretending to sound surprised by Ozzy's wishes. "If he's out, then you and I can go."

"We can't leave Ozzy," Sigi protested.

"I'll get Sheriff Wills to add extra protection."

"Don't worry about me," Ozzy insisted. "I'll be fine."

"We could do a ton of shopping," Patti said.

"I'm definitely out," Ozzy added.

Sigi looked at Ozzy and questioned him with her brown eyes. He answered her back with his deep grey ones.

Turning to her mom, she asked, "Could we go to Harry Potter World?"

Patti didn't look happy about the request. "I guess."

"There's a Harry Potter World?" Ozzy said, trying not to sound excited.

"Yeah," Sigi said. "Now do you want to come?"

It was one thing for Ozzy to bow out of going to Disneyland, but it was another thing altogether to bow out of visiting the world of Potter.

"No," Ozzy said firmly, wishing he was alone and in front of a computer so that he could see what Harry Potter World was and what he'd be missing. "I have the books."

"Wow, you really *do* want some time away from us."

"Can I sleep on the couch in the living room while you're gone?" Ozzy asked.

"Of course," Patti answered.

Sigi shook her head. "It sounds like you're going to have a wild time."

"We leave early tomorrow," Patti told her daughter. "Bring an extra suitcase for any new clothes or souvenirs you'll be bringing home."

"California has souvenirs?" Ozzy asked.

"Yes," Sigi said. "I'll bring you a wand from Harry Potter World."

"They have wands?"

Ozzy was feeling less and less happy about the agreement he had made to stay home.

Patti left the kitchen to go pack.

"You're sure about this?" Sigi asked. "It seems like you'd want to go."

"I'm super sure," Ozzy said. "I hate shopping."

"Well, I don't. You won't get in trouble, will you?"

Ozzy held up his purple finger. "No."

"Right. I don't know why I worry about you. Oh, that's right, because you're constantly in trouble." Sigi smiled, put her plate in the sink, and then slipped away to do some packing of her own.

Ozzy left the kitchen as well—he had a need to look up a few things online. First, he wanted to see what he would be missing at Harry Potter World. Second, he wanted to see if there was any mention from anyone, at any time, regarding a realm called Quarfelt.

CHAPTER SIXTEEN

JUST TALK TO HIM

Sheriff Wills was not thrilled with the idea of Patti taking Sigi to California and leaving Ozzy alone. But he reluctantly agreed to park an extra officer in front of the home and contact the police in California so that they would be aware and ready to help. It may have seemed like overkill, but Wills knew that Ray was the kind of person people shouldn't turn their backs on.

The sheriff hadn't talked to the two teenagers since he'd questioned Jon. He wanted to confront them with the new information he had, but he also wanted to do some of his own detective work before doing so. What Jon had told him had opened dozens of new leads. The one that intrigued him most was the one he was pursuing now. He looked at the GPS on the dashboard screen in his car. At the top in bold type was the address he was heading toward.

1189 Alvin's View Lane

Since the first moment that Jon had mentioned that Ozzy had a grandfather, Sheriff Wills thought about little else. Ozzy's parents were the cause of most of the mystery, and the fact that there was another living relative who might have answers filled him with hope.

Pulling up to the address made him feel a little less hopeful.

The old blue house's yard was overgrown, with five large boulders scattered randomly around it. There were no trees and the view wasn't anything to name a street after.

Sheriff Wills walked up a cracked and crumbling sidewalk to a porch where a single rocking chair sat, growing old and splintery from time and weather. The front door was orange, ugly, and unwelcoming.

Wills knocked.

There was no answer.

He knocked again and called out. "Anyone home? I'm Sheriff Wills from Otter Rock!"

Having received no answer again, he walked across the porch to the front window. The curtains were drawn, but there was a small gap in the middle. Through the small opening he could see piles of old books. The walls were lined with shelves sagging under the weight of what they were holding. In the center of the room, sitting in a ruined chair, was a very old man, his eyes closed. He looked to be dead. More to the point, he looked like an Egyptian corpse that had been mummified for months.

Sheriff Wills rapped loudly on the window.

"Hello! Hello! Are you okay?"

The mummy didn't move.

Wills's heart sank. His most hopeful lead looked like it might be an actual dead end. He walked back to the front door and tried the handle.

To his surprise it was unlocked.

Without hesitation, Wills pushed the door open and entered the house. He could hardly get into the room. There were books everywhere, and Ozzy's grandfather was sitting there, crouched forward with a book in his hands, looking just as dead as he had through the glass. With all the titles and volumes surrounding him, he appeared to be a mummy who had been entombed with his favorite things in hopes of taking them with him to the afterlife.

Sheriff Wills made his way to the old man and groaned.

"Of course, he'd be dead," he complained reverently.

He took his phone out and called the local police station.

"Hello, this is Sheriff Wills from Otter Rock. I'm here following a lead and it seems as if I've found a dead man in his house. The address is . . ."

Something caught the sheriff's eye and caused him to stop talking. It was slight, almost imperceptible, but it looked as if the long nose hairs coming from the old man's big nose were moving slightly.

"Hold on," the sheriff said into the phone.

He stepped closer and stared at the man's face. The long white hairs poking out from his nostrils fluttered. The man was so old, the white hair on top of his head looked like a thick layer of dust on a wrinkled and deflated volleyball. He had a big mushy nose and a neck covered with loose folds of skin. He was wearing a purple velvet house coat, blue pants, and slippers. Wills reached down to feel for a pulse on the man's wrist.

"Do you mind?" the old man croaked.

Sheriff Wills jumped back two steps.

"You're alive?"

Ozzy's grandfather opened his eyelids to reveal two faded brown eyes. He looked at Wills and grimaced.

"Is this what they pay the police for these days?" he groused. "To break into people's houses and see if they're still alive?"

Sheriff Wills put the phone back up to his ear. "Sorry," he said to the person on the other end. "False alarm." He ended the call and stared at the old man in disbelief.

"Were you pretending to be dead?"

"Yes," the old man said, grumbling. "Yes, yes. I was hoping you'd leave me alone."

"I'm a police officer," Wills said. "When I see someone in trouble, I attempt to assist them."

"By breaking down their door?"

"It was unlocked."

"Of *course* it was," Ozzy's grandfather said mockingly.

"It's a safe neighborhood. Aside from the police who break in."

"I'm very sorry," Wills said. "But I'm happy you're alive."

"Not me," the old man said. "I began wishing for death over ten years ago. Fat lot it's got me. Here I am, still alive, still being harassed by reality and the police."

"I'm not here to harass," Wills insisted. "I'm here for Ozzy."

"Who?"

"Ozzy, your grandson."

"The boy with the wizard and the bird and that girl?"

"That's the one."

Ozzy's grandfather set down the book he had been holding and reached under a stack of encyclopedias that were piled up to his right. He pulled out a handgun and lifted it up toward the sheriff. Caught off guard, Wills quickly pulled his own gun.

"Put that down!" the sheriff demanded.

"Ah," the man said, "stop being so reactionary. I'm not going to shoot you; I'm giving it to you. That boy you claim is my grandson left it here after they almost killed me."

Sheriff Wills reached out and took the gun, holstering his.

"Ozzy had this?"

"Indirectly. Some pale person brought it. But Ozzy gave it to me."

Sheriff Wills examined the gun, then removed the

magazine, racking the slide until he was convinced it was unloaded. He set both pieces of the gun on top of a nearby pile of books.

"I've never seen so many books in one place," the sheriff said, making a weak attempt to be cordial.

"From your vocabulary I gather you've never read many, either."

"You don't waste energy on kindness, do you?"

"I don't waste energy, period."

"Well, what I came for won't take much. I just have some questions."

"Do I have to answer them?"

"No."

"I don't like people, I don't like interruptions, and I don't like you."

"You don't have to like me," Wills assured him. "But your grandson is in trouble and I think you might be able to help."

"No, I won't be able to."

The old man was an ugly wrinkled pill of a person.

Sheriff Wills glanced around.

"Okay," he finally said. "You don't have to answer my questions. I'll just leave you and let you be. But, looking around, I see some things that the local police and health departments might need to know about."

Ozzy's grandfather bristled.

"I see a very old man who can't take care of himself and who needs the aid of dozens of agencies to come in and check up on him. They'll need to give you tests and clean your house and cart off some of these books."

"The devil they will."

"Oh, they will, and in the end, they might realize that you would be better off in a home where you can be watched over by nurses and doctors and forced to read whatever book an orderly picks out."

"Stop!" the old man shouted. "I abhor horror, and the scene you are describing is more gruesome than a dozen murders. What do you want from me?"

"A few answers."

"Be specific," Ozzy's grandfather insisted. "A few? Few is less than many or most, and it could be as little as a couple."

"How about this," Wills suggested. "I'm going to ask you as many questions as I need to."

"Police brutality!" the man complained. "What's an individual to do?"

Sheriff Wills ignored him. "First question, what's your name?"

After a moment of looking disgusted, he answered, "Dr. Omen Doppler."

"Really?"

"Do I strike you as the kind of person who would make jokes?"

"No, no, you do not. What kind of doctor are you?"

"I have a doctorate in neuroscience and molecular radiation."

"So, Ozzy's mother was your daughter?"

Sheriff Wills couldn't tell for sure, but it looked like Omen might have nodded.

"Is that a yes?" the sheriff asked.

"What good is a nod if I have to back it up with a verbal confirmation?"

"That means Mia Toffy was once Mia Doppler?"

There was another tiny nod.

"And were you aware that Ozzy grew up alone in the woods not very far from here?"

"I thought he was dead."

"Right, otherwise you would have found him and helped him?"

"I didn't say *that*."

"Do you know what your daughter and her husband created?"

"They created numerous things," he said with a sniff. "Be more specific."

"The serum, the mind control formula."

"Yes, I'm aware of what Mia once figured out. Her husband, Emmitt, took some of the credit, but it was her formula. Emmitt made toys like that bird."

"Clark?"

"Ahhh," the old man waved as if bothered. "I think that's what they call him."

"He's something like a remote-controlled metal bird," the sheriff said, still not buying the fact that Clark was more than a robot or drone.

Omen Doppler looked at Wills with his weak brown eyes. "Oh. I see you're refusing to believe in anything that doesn't make sense. Another sign of poor reading skills."

"You're telling me that the bird is actually alive?"

"I'm telling you to find out for yourself."

"I'm pretty sure it was the same bird that busted up a bunch of lights at a restaurant and then fell nicely into the hands of a lunatic."

"I didn't ask for *your* history."

"Right, what do you know about the serum?"

"I know that if I were you, I'd stop asking questions about it. I'd quit my job, cut all ties with everyone you know and love, buy a house in another part of the world that is cut off from society, and hope that Ray Dench never finds you."

"You know Ray?"

"No, I brought up that particular name just by chance."

Sheriff Wills took a breath. "You're a tough one."

"I'm nothing but an old man who has hidden himself away to avoid danger. Now as I sit on death's lap and feel my bones turning to dust, I realize that I have no reason to fear him any longer. There's a good chance that before he ever found me, I'd be dead from natural causes."

Wills couldn't argue that.

"How do I protect Ozzy from Ray?"

Omen growled. "You can only hope that as Ray closes

in, he dies from eating undercooked chicken, or trips in front of a train before getting the boy."

"I'm not without resources," the sheriff said seriously. "We're protecting Ozzy."

"I guess you do have the ability to pretend." The old man said sarcastically. He then coughed, and dust shook from his white hair. "You can't stop Ray."

"You're incredible," Sheriff Wills said with disgust. "I don't know what happened to you in your life to make you like this. I'm not sure who wronged you or if you were dropped on your head repeatedly as a child, but this is your grandson we're talking about. Ozzy's had his parents stolen from him, and his life left for ruin. He's been a test subject and worked over in a way that even the most creative books wouldn't write about. Did you know that there is a possibility that your daughter and her husband are still alive?"

Omen stopped looking smug to look surprised.

"You say?"

"I say that some information might have come to light suggesting that Mia is not dead."

"I don't care about fairy tales unless they're printed in books."

"It's not a fairy tale," the sheriff insisted. "Your grandson almost died in the middle of the ocean trying to find them."

Omen sat up.

"What was Ozzy doing in the middle of the ocean?"

Sheriff Wills was surprised by the sudden movement and interest.

"He and his friends were pursuing a lead."

"What kind of lead? And where in the ocean?"

"They found some coordinates out in international waters."

"The Bern," Omen said reverently.

"What's the Bern?"

"It's an important lab housed in a submarine. I've wondered if it still existed."

"You're kidding."

"You're not much of a detective."

"Could Mia and Emmitt be there?"

"How would I know? Did anyone see the submarine?"

"No, something surfaced and tore their boat apart. Ozzy and Sigi made it back to shore in a small boat that Jon had brought."

"And the wizard and bird?"

"Rin?"

Omen nodded in a more noticeable way.

"He and Clark haven't been seen since."

The old man waved nonchalantly. "What's the use in any of this?" he said. "If I were ten years younger, I might care."

"I don't understand." Wills was angry. "If you know something that might help, don't hold back. This is your daughter and grandson we're talking about."

"You act like any of this matters," Omen said.

"It does to me, and Ozzy, and Sigi, and maybe many more."

"You miss my point," Omen said coldly. "There's nothing any of us can do for Ozzy. I saw the mark on his hand that the serum had given him. It's a wonder he's lived so long. It was affecting him when he was here. I figure it's only a matter of time before that boy's body is no longer able to contain what it holds. That serum is ultimately poison."

"What are you saying?"

"I'm saying that in a very short time none of this will matter to Ozzy."

"He can't be saved?"

"What am I, a preacher?"

"That's not what I mean," Wills insisted. "Can he be cured?"

"Who knows what can and can't happen?"

"I'm guessing not you."

"You're catching on."

Sheriff Wills asked a dozen more questions before Omen insisted that he'd had enough.

"Now, if you'd be so kind as to take you and your sterile vocabulary and leave me alone."

"I might have more questions later."

"I'll tell you the same thing I told that wizard," Omen said. "Write it down in a book and maybe I'll read it. Otherwise, leave me be."

Sheriff Wills left him be, but made no promises about not coming back.

The visit had been dreadful and uncomfortable. Still, as Wills climbed into his car, he was feeling a strange excitement. There were new things to think about—submarines, serums, and books. The visit hadn't changed any of the trouble that Ozzy and Sigi were in, but it had put a new face on things. Well, an old face on things. A very old face on things. It had also added a new level of worry. If Omen was correct, Ozzy could be in trouble on the inside as well as the outside.

Sheriff Wills flipped on his lights and sped back to Otter Rock.

CHAPTER SEVENTEEN

FEELING AND NOT BELIEVING

The Cloaked House had once been a place of hidden beauty and charm. It was the home Ozzy had grown up in alone. It had become one with the forest, overgrown with trees that had literally pushed into parts of the home. The round windows and wooden body were like a knoll with eyes. The inside had been a maze of boxes and books, arranged in such a way as to give the interior a feeling of charm and interest. Ozzy's attic room at the top of the starry stairs had been a source of great comfort and security.

That is what the Cloaked House had once been.

Now, thanks to Rin, it was nothing but a thick blanket of black damp ash. The remains of Ozzy's home were just a charred rectangular outline marking the foundation, a black smear on the dirt on the ground. The space was surrounded by partially burnt trees and miles and miles of forest that had been lucky enough to not have been torched.

There were only a few pieces of the house still standing. Part of the back wall leaned in at a precarious angle. It was the color of coal, thick wads of melted glass hanging where a window had once been. In the middle of the ashes, six steps from the starry staircase survived, but they couldn't take anyone more than a few feet closer to heaven. Near the end of the burnt rectangle, the brick chimney was standing alone, a tombstone for what once was and what would never be again. Ozzy walked through the ashes, feeling like a dethroned king whose kingdom was nothing but scorched earth. He was alone and wishing that a girl with dark eyes, or a wizard with striped trousers, or a bird with a big beak was with him.

None of them were.

Sigi had left early that morning with her mother to go to California. Rin had jumped into the ocean and not been polite enough to leave a forwarding address. And Clark was last seen in a toolbox.

Ozzy missed all of them, but standing at the ruin of the Cloaked House, he missed Clark the most. The metal bird had been a part of his life for so long that he couldn't remember a time without him. It was a miracle that he had ever found Clark hidden in one of the starry stairs, a sentient metal bird that didn't know when to keep quiet, or who to fall in love with. Clark had been by Ozzy's side all those years, and now he was AWOL, missing in action— the bird had flown the coop.

"Where are you, Clark?" Ozzy yelled out.

The wizard-in-training was supposed to be back at Sigi's house. It was against the rules for him to wander away without telling the police. But Ozzy's head had felt like a problem that needed air. He was tired of confinement and missed the forest and the ocean. So in the morning after Sigi had left, he helped the officer parked in front of the house feel a little confused. Then, wearing black pants, a black T-shirt, and some black Dr. Martens, he slipped out the back door. He had moved carefully and quickly through miles and miles of trees and bushes, doing everything he could to remain undetected. Once he was far enough away, he stood up straight and ran through the forest to return to the large dark smudge that had once been the Cloaked House.

The risk was worth it.

The home and the forest had been Ozzy's refuge for many years. They meant as much to him as anything. He had once hated Rin for destroying his sanctuary, but he was well past any ill feelings and had begun to think about rebuilding the home sometime in the future.

Ozzy bent down and picked up a piece of melted plastic. It had most likely been a part of a cassette tape, or a cup. Now it was just a dark hard blob. There were burnt pieces of books and bindings scattered everywhere in the ash. He found a half-inch piece of a page that had survived. He could make out three words on it.

. . . time is long . . .

Ozzy moved out of the rectangular imprint of ash and sat down on a large stone near what had once been the front porch. With the house gone, he could see and hear the small stream burping and spitting in the distance. It was acting like it always had, unaware of any changes the landscape had gone through. The missing porch was the last place Ozzy had seen his missing parents.

"Where are you, Mom and Dad?"

The wet air remained mute.

It had rained recently and it would soon rain again. The clouds above displayed their poor understanding of personal space and bunched in closer to watch the boy with the grey eyes and dark hair as he struggled to understand his life.

The boy stood up and began to walk away.

His intention was to leave the site and hike to the ocean, but a familiar sensation caused him to stop. Once again, a feeling like blood coursing through a sleeping leg was stirring throughout his body and accumulating in his left arm. Then, with a rolling whump, all the energy poured into a single finger.

Ozzy shook like a sinner at the feet of an angry god.

He looked down at his trembling hand.

"What now?" he whispered.

His finger buzzed with even greater intensity. His insides began to do battle with each other—kidney against lungs, gallbladder against heart. The sensation was startling, and it sent strings of thick knotted energy up and down his left arm. His body twitched and turned as he stood trembling. His mind sizzled and popped like a wet egg on a hot surface. He was facing the rectangular ashes now and his finger was pointing toward the mess. He could feel his hand grow heavy and his mind heat up.

"What?" he yelled at himself. "What's this about?"

Ozzy walked back to the wet ashes. He looked at the ruins with renewed interest. His mind and body were suggesting loudly that there was something he'd missed— something he needed to notice.

Walking through the cinders and dirt, he listed the things he could make out, hoping to steady his brain and body with words.

"Bits of book. Bits of box. Bits of wood. Piece of glass. Tin can."

Ozzy stopped in his tracks. Energy circled him like the rings of Saturn, twisting him and keeping him upright but tilted. He struggled to speak.

"Tin can," he said, looking down at a burnt metal container that had once held some of the food Ozzy had lived on—food his parents had packed into the house before they died. Food that had filled the basement.

Ozzy's grey eyes went as wide as puddles. He stopped twisting and looked down at the ground directly beneath himself.

"The basement," he said excitedly.

Ozzy ran to where the six remaining starry stairs were. On the side of the burnt steps, where the door to the basement had once been, there was nothing but a thick layer of ash.

There was no sign of the basement stairs.

The fire had consumed the house and the attic and had collapsed down on the foundation, completely hiding the fact that there had once been a basement.

Ozzy walked through the ruins, mapping things out, and trying to get a sense of what part of the basement was below him. In all the sadness of the fire, Ozzy and Sigi hadn't given a single thought to what condition the basement might have been in. It was most likely filled with remnants of the fire, but Ozzy's buzzing finger and crackling mind made him wonder if there was anything salvageable or important down below.

Stepping over the rectangle of black, he poked his toe into the ashes, searching for any hole in the floor or weak spot that he could break through.

"There were stairs that led down," he whispered needlessly as he pointed to the space where the basement door had once been. He moved five steps to the right. "I must be over the room where the food was." He moved ten steps to the left. "I have to be above the storage room." He stepped ten more feet to the left and stopped just outside the edge of the ashes.

"I need some . . ."

Ozzy's needs were cut short as a loud crack filled the forest air. The ground underneath him opened up and sucked him in. He reached out to grab for something, but it was no use. There was no time to even scream.

The boy was swallowed instantly.

He dropped twelve feet down into a dark hole and out of sight. His body slammed against a hard floor and his head hit an equally solid wall. Both his mind and his sight went black.

Up above him, the remains of the Cloaked House sat there looking as burnt and lonely as before. Ozzy had disappeared, and the large green forest with the black scar went back to behaving as it always had.

The clouds grumbled, and then, slowly, to mark the mood, they began to drizzle.

CHAPTER EIGHTEEN

SO GOOD

Sigi stood outside the Los Angeles shoe store waiting for her mom to pull the rental car around. The sun was low in the sky and the street smelled of gasoline and citrus. In her hands were two bags holding two pairs of shoes.

"I think I love California," she murmured to herself.

Their plane had arrived at one o'clock and, after eating French dip sandwiches at a restaurant, they had decided to go shopping before checking into their hotel. The rest of the afternoon was spent perusing all the shops that Otter Rock didn't have. They bought clothes at Top Shop, purses at Gucci, and shoes at Posers LA. The day was so stuffed with new things and traffic and sunshine that Sigi completely forgot to check in with Ozzy.

Her mom pulled a rented Land Rover to a stop in front of the shoe store. Sigi stepped off the curb and opened the back door to put her bags in. She climbed into the front seat feeling happy and exhausted. She loved her new clothes, but she loved not thinking about Otter Rock, or Sheriff Wills, or Jon, or any of the trouble they had recently been through even more. For the first time in a while her mind was at ease.

"You look happy," Patti said as they drove away from the shop.

"It's been fun so far," Sigi said. "Thanks for the clothes."

"You're welcome. We should do things like this more often. Where now?"

"Let's go to the hotel. I'm ready to lay down and do nothing."

"I couldn't agree more. Have you talked to Ozzy?"

"No," Sigi said. "I should." She reached behind her seat and found her phone in her purse. Pulling it out, she dialed the number for the landline at their Ocean View home. After seven rings the machine picked up and she heard her mother's voice telling her to leave a message.

"Hello, Ozzy, it's me," Sigi said. "You should call me and let me know that you're okay."

Sigi ended the call and bit her lip as she knitted her eyebrows.

"Don't worry about him," Patti said, picking up on her daughter's concern. "He's probably in his room and can't hear the phone."

"Right," Sigi said. "But he was going to camp out on the couch. He also said he'd call me at four. It's six-thirty."

"He's never been very good with time."

"That's true."

"If it makes you feel better, I'll text Sheriff Wills when we get to the hotel," Patti suggested. "He'll make sure he's all right."

"Good."

"Now," Patti said. "Let's check in, get something to eat, and then watch movies in the room and eat tons of unhealthy snacks that we'll regret later."

"Perfect."

Patti pressed on the gas and traveled down the street as quickly as the thick traffic would allow.

CHAPTER NINETEEN

AN ONLY CHILD IN AN ONLY ROOM

The darkness that surrounded Ozzy rivaled the deepest void, the cold so invasive it clung to every limb and crevice, and the dampness would cause one to long for a death by desert. The smell of smoke and ash filled the space and made breathing a chore. Ozzy rolled from his right side over onto his back. He reached out into the dark to find and feel a large lump on the top of his head.

The boy moaned, making the dark feel even more unsettling.

There was an inch of water on the floor that chilled his body to the point of chattering teeth. His dark hair clung to his forehead and covered his eyes, which would normally have made it difficult to see, but it was so dark it didn't make a difference.

Ozzy stared up in the direction he had fallen.

It was faint, but he could make out the outline of the hole he had dropped through, about twelve feet above him.

The tiny bit of forest he could see through it was black. The fall had knocked him out and time had been rude enough to continue to run on. It was late at night and he was disoriented, confused, and shivering.

"Where am I?" he whispered.

Pushing himself up onto his elbows, he rolled to the left and attempted to stand.

"Ouch!"

His legs begged him to stay still as his mind pulsated with a sharp, stabbing pain. The fall through the burnt ground had bruised his feet and done a number on his brain. His mind felt like a wad of putty that someone was using as a stress toy. With some more screaming and more agony, he managed to stand up. Ozzy patted his arms and body to see if anything other than his brain was broken or bleeding.

"I guess I'm alive."

Ozzy reached out and touched the wall he couldn't see. He lifted his arms, but he was more than six feet from the hole.

Shuffling carefully, he moved around the room, feeling for anything to climb up on or help him get out. There was nothing. The room was just a small, empty space with stone walls, a stone floor, and a cold steel door on one side. The door had a tiny metal knob and was locked tight.

"What is this room?"

It was a foolish question to ask himself, since he didn't know the answer. Ozzy had lived in the house for seven years, and spent a lot of time in the basement, but the hole he had fallen through was outside the foundation lines. He had never known of an extra room attached to the cellar. Also, the basement was only eight feet deep and the spot he was standing in was much lower than that.

Feeling for the steel door, he found the knob and lifted his right foot to use it as a foothold. He pressed his sore foot onto the knob and pushed himself up quickly, trying to leverage himself to the edge of the hole.

Ozzy reached up and out, scrabbling for the edge of the hole, but he misjudged where it was. His hands grabbed at the wall a few feet below the edge, and gravity grabbed back. Ozzy fell back down onto the stone floor. His head hit the wet ground with a terrific splash and thwack. He saw stars as more pain set his brain on fire.

The wizard-in-training was stuck. As his mind shut down, the world became darker and colder than it already was.

CHAPTER TWENTY

I CAN'T UNDERSTAND YOU

The sky above was black—no stars, no moon, just a dense darkness with the deep vacuum of space to back it up. Beneath a canopy of nothing, streetlights and signs gave the void a fuzzy edge at the point where it rested its dark body against the ground. Mixed in with the fuzz were thousands of people walking to thousands of different places—some to shows, some to restaurants, and some to places other than those two options. It's not important where most of the people were walking. What mattered most was where the man in a yellow bathrobe and gray felt hat was heading. Rin picked up the pace.

"East," he exclaimed. "East."

The wizard walked faster in the direction of his exclamation, and even in a city as diverse and unique as New York, he stood out. Rin walked through the crowd with such purpose that those who saw him coming moved to let the wizard pass. His beard blew gently backwards as he moved.

A group of Japanese tourists parted, some taking pictures as Rin walked through them. The wizard stopped to take a selfie with them and post it online.

Rin then turned down Avenue Ingracias, and there before him was the destination he sought—the Resort in New York, sitting there looking pretentious and old, large glass doors and outdated gold columns covering its front.

"Well," Rin said loudly to himself, "here goes something!"

The wizard crossed the street and walked up to the hotel. Without pausing he entered the spinning glass doors and spun his way into the lobby. Just like the last time he had been there, everything looked tacky. There was a gold-plated fountain choking and gurgling in the middle of the lobby, its basin filled with copper and silver coins. All over, gold chairs and tables were arranged like stiff bulky treasure. To one side of the lobby, a golden piano was being played by an old man in gold slacks, a yellow dress shirt, and a yellow vest. The old man had no hair on his head, and a back bent from years of incorrect posture while tickling the ivories.

"There's no accounting for taste," the wizard complained. "Would it kill them to paint something green?"

Rin took a picture with his phone and then slowly and dramatically looked around the place. What he was after was not in the lobby.

He moved through the area, passing the check-in desk, the concierge's station, and a gold-framed painting of a man standing in a field near a barn. There was no time to appreciate—or un-appreciate—the art, so Rin kept focused and headed out a set of glass doors that led to the court-yard behind the hotel.

Once outside, the wizard took a deep breath, drawing in the air as if it were more valuable than the air he had just been breathing in front of the Resort in New York.

The courtyard was familiar, but the last time Rin had been here, it had been filled with blowing and blinding snow. Now it was warm, and old, wealthy patrons were milling about, walking along a dozen different stone paths all lined with twinkling white lights.

Rin had no desire to stop and look around or to do any milling. He had somewhere to be and a to-get-done list burning a hole in his pocket.

The wizard marched forcefully across the courtyard, back toward the office of the man known to him as Ray—the man who had caused so much of what Ozzy had suf-fered. The man whose raw desire for power and control was as ugly as any attribute a person could possibly possess.

Rin stopped at one of the two pools in the courtyard. Sure, he was on a mission, but the lighted water looked inviting. Two old women were swimming; their movement gave the water sound and shimmer. On the west side of the larger pool, a lion statue was spitting up water and letting it fall back down in clouds of mist.

"Stay on task," the wizard told himself as he took a picture.

Rin walked between the two pools like Moses at a spa—water on both sides and a light wind blowing an invisible mist around.

As he reached the building near the back of the courtyard, Rin glanced about to see if he was being watched. He knew that Ray was no slouch—the man was legitimately evil. Ray surrounded himself with ogre-like bodyguards who loved to harass people.

There didn't seem to be anyone watching.

The wizard looked up at the ivy-covered building. It was a masterful piece of architecture, a five-story building as wide as the back of the courtyard, made from rough stone with multiple stained-glass windows. Rin counted a dozen gargoyles staring down at him like hungry demons with bad attitudes—their teeth bared and claws reaching forward.

"A+ for architecture," Rin said, taking a picture. "D- for cliché."

The wizard yanked open the front door and entered the five-story building. Inside, the walls were painted olive green and the carpet on the floor was thick, plush, and mustard-colored.

"I think I'm going to be sick," Rin said to himself. "Of course, if I throw up nobody will be able to tell, seeing how the carpet is the color of vomit."

"Excuse me," a woman said indignantly.

Rin looked across the room at a big desk, where an old woman was sitting and staring at him. She had hair the color of lavender and a brand-new blue pantsuit that appeared to have just come out of the package. On her desk was a small nameplate that read

SUSAN WHELPS

"What did you say?" Susan asked, her face smooshed together as if she had just tasted something sour and rotten. "Did you say *vomit*?"

"I was talking to myself," Rin said proudly. "But since I have no secrets, I don't mind you listening in, and what I said is that this carpet is the color of vomit."

"Pardon me," she said with offense, "this carpet is very expensive."

"Maybe you just got a bad deal," Rin said, looking down at it. "Home Depot has a lot of carpet way more attractive than this and at very good prices."

The woman scoffed. "Mr. Dench does not buy his carpet at Home Depot."

"Lowes?"

"I don't know what that is," Susan said, sounding personally wounded. "This is one-of-a-kind carpeting. Specially ordered from Sweden—and, I dare say, it cost more than most people make in a lifetime."

"I can see why you don't dare say it," Rin said compassionately. "That's not something I'd admit either. Maybe you could sell it and put the money to *good* use."

The woman's brown eyes became slits and she stared at the wizard. "Who are you?" she asked coldly.

"My name's Rin. I'm here to see Ray."

"These are private offices," she said with authority.

"Good," Rin said. "Because I don't think Ray is going to want anyone else to see what's about to happen."

Rin walked past Susan's desk and headed straight toward a set of large office doors. Susan jumped up from her seat and began barking words in a most unflattering way.

"You can't go in there! You need to leave!"

Rin ignored her. He walked right up to the doors and pulled the left one open. There was another set of doors behind it.

"Stop this instant!" Susan insisted.

She reached to grab Rin's robe, but the wizard spun in such a way that she was left grabbing at nothing.

"Wizards are hard to pin down," he said kindly.

"Stop!" she shouted.

Rin looked at her as he held the doorknob on the second set of doors. "If you knew me, you would know that I've never been good at doing what I'm told."

The wizard pulled open the second door and walked through it. Susan followed directly behind him, still shouting in a manner that angry secretaries don't usually have to.

As Rin moved into the office, Susan managed to catch hold of the back of his robe. Four feet in, he stopped and took in the room.

"Wow," Rin said. "Someone's overcompensating."

Ray's office was large, lavish, and cold. It was a big, square room with expensive but ugly art hanging on the walls. Above the art were small stained-glass windows too high and too colorful to see out. The carpet in the office was a boring gray, but decidedly less offensive than the carpet near Susan's desk. There were a few stiff chairs covered in yellow leather and a short wall of bookshelves that ran along the north wall. The shelves were filled with large leatherbound books and various small statues and awards. At the far end of the room was a massive desk made from dark glossy wood. The desk looked like the base of a great tree that had been chopped down and was now stuck like a large stump in Ray's pompous office. Sitting on the desk was a large hourglass filled with white sand on a gold base.

Behind the desk was a short, fake-looking man with red hair graying around the edges and brown eyes as dark and hard as the desk he was sitting at. The large desk made Ray look like a diminutive elf hiding behind a stump in the forest.

Ray stood up calmly and glanced out across the room toward Rin.

Susan let go of the wizard's robe and said, "His name is Rin." She was angry and her red face proved it. "I'm sorry, but he just barged in."

Ray waved a hand at Susan.

"It's okay, Susan. You can leave us."

"Yes, Mr. Dench."

"Close the door behind you," Rin told her. "I don't want to see that carpet again."

Susan made the kind of noise a person makes when they're disgusted with someone but they're still required to act appropriately.

"Hummf."

Stepping out, she closed the door behind her, leaving Rin and Ray alone in the pretentious, stuffy, and void-of-joy office.

"Nice place," Rin said kindly. "It really looks like the kind of room a cruel, power-driven individual might have. I know a man in Quarfelt who would love this place. Not my esthetic, though—seems anti-magic—but it fits what I know of you."

"Where's the bird?" Ray asked impatiently.

"Excuse me?"

"Don't play dumb," Ray said with an edge. "You know exactly what I'm talking about. I don't want that bird surprising me by shooting out of your robe and tearing up my office or knocking me up side of my head."

"I don't think you need to worry about that," Rin said. "I have no bird here. Clark disappeared a while ago. I can't say for sure, but maybe he's in Quarfelt."

"Quarfelt?"

"Really?" Rin said. "You claim to be this know-it-all genius and you don't know what Quarfelt is?" The wizard sighed in a way that let Ray know he was disappointed. "For your information, it's a realm where magic rules.

There's a wizard near every pot. Quite a special place. One of the last times I saw Clark he was there trying to impress a sword he had fallen in love with."

"So . . . no bird?" Ray asked again.

"As I just said twice, no. But if it makes you feel better, you're welcome to search me," Rin offered. "Seems unnecessary, seeing how the one constant in this world and the next is that wizards don't lie."

Ray blinked slowly. Under the fake light in the cold room it was clear to see that behind his dark eyes he was thinking. After a moment he spoke.

"Let's get something straight," Ray said seriously. "You're not in Quarfed."

"Quarfelt," Rin corrected.

"You're not in Quarfelt," Ray said cruelly. "And you're not a wizard. I want to put an end to that madness immediately. I've had people looking into you."

"That's flattering."

"I'm convinced that you're nothing but an unstable being who needs serious help. An unstable being who has caused me great inconvenience and aggravation."

"What?" Rin asked, taking four steps forward. "It's hard to understand what you're saying. My ears are immune to certain words. But don't worry, I'm not bothered. I'm aware that not everyone knows how to talk to wizards. I know a man in Quarfelt who always gets my breakfast order wrong. I do not like poached . . ."

Ray's fake-looking face tightened. "Stop talking . . ." he

paused for dramatic affect. "I don't care about your breakfast order."

"You should," Rin said encouragingly. "You see, breakfast, or the foods of the breakfast, is very important to—"

Ray held up his hands to stop the wizard from speaking.

Rin took it upon himself to move closer. He stopped at the front of Ray's desk and casually looked down and into Ray's cold brown eyes.

"It's kind of you to stop me from talking," Rin said. "Good conversations need time to breathe. And we don't have time for chit-chat. We have some big things to talk about."

Ray's expression remained unmoving.

"I'll go first," Rin offered. "I know in the business world it's a sign of weakness to speak first, but I don't live in the business world. It's a terrible place. All that filing and newspeak. Not for me. In fact, I have a hard time living in reality. But in Quarfelt, speaking first shows a strong upbringing and a great sense of decorum." Rin stopped and waved his right hand. "Look at me going on and on about myself. Hashtag humblebrag."

A blotchy redness moved over Ray's face like angry clouds.

"Are you okay?" Rin asked. "You look uneven."

"You should never have come here," Ray said seriously.

Rin laughed. "You'd be surprised how often people tell me that."

"This time is different."

"Good," the wizard said kindly. "I enjoy change."

"Well, then, I think you are going to enjoy what happens next."

"Good." Rin clapped. "Next is so much better than never."

"Do you *always* speak in such an infuriating way?"

"I speak like a wizard," Rin said strongly. "If you find that infuriating, it's on you."

"You're a ridiculous man."

"Ridiculous *wizard*," Rin corrected.

Ray tapped his fingers on his desk as he stared up at Rin. He was trying his best to stay calm. He had dominated and controlled truly powerful people in his life. He would not let some whack job in a bathrobe get the best of him.

"Enough." Ray exhaled loudly. "You're unaware of the stakes at hand. You talk like you have a say in all of this— like you know a way to affect the outcome. But what would you say if I told you that not only will you fail, but you are in grave danger?"

"Um . . . I would say, not bad, but I don't find it believable. I've never liked the expression *grave danger*. Too on the nose. How about, 'Things are getting ticklish.' That implies that there could be some discomfort, but there could be some fun."

"How about we stop playing games?"

"Never," Rin insisted.

Ray closed his eyes and counted to ten.

CHAPTER TWENTY-ONE

THE FACE YOU WORE WAS COOL

*C*lark sat perched on top of the roof by one of the twelve gargoyles. The demon was crouched and staring down at the courtyard below. The gargoyle had stone wings and horns and was baring his teeth with an open, angry mouth. Chiseled at the base of the beast was the word *vigilance*.

Clark looked at the word.

"Your name is a bit aggressive. Can I call you Lance for short?"

Lance seemed fine with that.

Before landing near Lance, Clark had flown around the courtyard a few times, making sure to stay high enough as to not be seen. It wasn't easy for him to keep away from all the gold-painted objects he could see in the lobby. The last time the bird had been here, the lobby doors had been hidden by falling snow.

"It's incredible," Clark said to Lance. "I don't know

how you sit here all day when just across the courtyard there's all that gold."

Lance said nothing.

"I get it," the bird said. "I'm intimidating."

Clark spread his wings and turned.

"I didn't always look like this. I used to be a raven. But then I found out what a group of ravens are called. Do you know?"

Lance had no idea.

"An unkindness," Clark tweeted in disgust. "Going through life with a label like that hanging over you isn't easy. So, a wizard hooked me up with all this."

Lance continued to bare his teeth.

"It is *not* dragon appropriation," Clark insisted.

Lance was silent.

"That's better," the bird said.

In the courtyard, someone heavy jumped into one of the pools. Their splash made other people near the water holler.

"I used to go to the ocean with Ozzy," Clark said longingly. "The water there makes those pools look like a joke."

Lance had nothing to say.

"You'd like Ozzy," the bird added. "He's a little naïve, but . . . well, I'm not really sure what naïve means. Maybe it has something to do with how much he likes soda."

Lance let the bird have a moment of silence.

"We're here to help Ozzy," Clark filled the gargoyle in. "I'm actually waiting for a signal. I probably shouldn't tell you that, but I feel like since we have so much in common it's okay."

Lance looked angry.

"Thanks for agreeing. Hey, you wanna know something, Lance?"

Lance didn't say no.

"I hate waiting for signals," Clark admitted. "I'd rather just rush in headlong and see what happens."

Lance bared his teeth.

"You get it."

Clark reached his right wing out and tapped the end of Lance's left wing.

"Can I ask you something else?"

Lance seemed cool with the request.

"Do you know where the electric box is to this building?"

Lance wasn't talking.

Clark looked around as the two of them sat, perched on the roof, impatiently waiting for the signal.

CHAPTER TWENTY-TWO

HERE ANGER IS

Rin stood in front of the large wooden desk with the large gaudy hourglass, keeping his eyes locked on Ray. The red-headed, power-hungry jerk was standing behind the desk, trying to make his five-foot-six height look intimidating to a six-foot-three wizard who was wearing a pointed hat that gave him at least four more additional inches of height. If Ray had his way, he would have called his men in and taken the wizard by force. But he wanted more information, and he did not like the idea of someone so unhinged getting the best of him.

He looked at the wizard and saw a new challenge to dominate. Ray brushed the sleeves of his mauve dress shirt and regained his composure inside and out.

"Listen," he said calmly, attempting to bring some civility into their conversation, "I think we got off on the wrong foot."

"Maybe *you* did," Rin replied. "Not me—for wizards, both feet are right."

Ray shook his head. "You honestly expect people to believe you're a wizard?"

"I expect people to believe whatever they want," Rin said. "I know people who don't believe in gravity. That doesn't mean gravity isn't real."

"I don't know why I'm surprised by any of this," Ray said. "Jon told me that you could be difficult."

"Is Jon the friend you used to aggressively chase after and intimidate two teenagers?"

"I object to your characterization."

"I object to the lack of fans in here," Rin said casually. "It's stifling. I find a little moving air makes a place much more tolerable and pleasant."

"Could we talk about things that matter?" Ray snapped.

"I thought we were."

"Listen," Ray said, trying to sound like a human, "seeing you actually makes me happy. I've been wanting to talk with you."

"Let's say it was magic that's now brought us together."

"You're incredible."

"Thank you."

Ray growled. "That's *not* what I mean by incredible. You've been a thorn in my side for a while."

"I can be irritating," Rin said with a smile. "But you've been more painful to Ozzy than I've been to you."

"Ozzy has something that belongs to me."

The wizard shook his head. "I really thought you'd be easier to understand."

Ray bristled. "I speak perfectly."

Rin shrugged. "If you think so. I guess I just prefer my villains to sound clear and clever when they talk."

"I'm a villain?" Ray asked briskly.

"In every sense of the word."

Ray did not smile. "You're much more annoying than I was led to believe."

"I guess it's nice to hear that you believe in anything," the wizard said, congratulating Ray.

"What happened to Jon?"

"Who?"

"You know who," Ray said. "You just mentioned him. He was . . . assisting me in Oregon."

"Oh, him," the wizard said happily. "Last I saw of him he was standing on a boat just off the coast of Oregon. He seemed upset."

"He seems to have dropped off the map."

"Well, if I see him, I'll say hi."

"I don't care if you see him." Ray was slowly growing angry again. "I've got other things to think about besides you two meeting up. Let's stop talking nonsense and you can tell me why you're here. Why you think you can just walk into my office and take up my time?"

The wizard locked eyes with Ray as he stood behind his desk. After a few moments of silence, he spoke.

"It's nice outside," Rin said matter-of-factly. "But your office is not."

"Your comfort is not my concern."

"Mine either," Rin replied. "Of course, being a wizard, I'm usually comfortable. Once you understand magic, very little upsets you. I slept comfortably on a futon once."

"I don't care how you sleep, and I don't believe in magic," Ray insisted. "I'm a man of science and technology."

"And you don't see any magic in science?" Rin said with disgust. "Have you never used a microwave?"

"Please be quiet," Ray said with a sigh. "Please. Let's stop talking nonsense."

"I wasn't. I was just commenting on it being nice outside."

"Why are you here?" Ray asked abruptly. "You know I've been looking for you everywhere, and you just waltz in and start talking about the weather."

"It affects everything."

"Please," Ray insisted. "Act like a grown-up and answer me—why are you here?"

"Okay," Rin said seriously. "I'm here because I have a job to do."

"And what job is that?"

"I was hired to find Ozzy's parents."

Ray laughed.

"Good luck, they're long gone."

"I believe otherwise."

"Trust me," Ray said. "Even if they were alive, you wouldn't want to find them. Why do you care about Ozzy? This shouldn't be your concern."

"This is my *only* concern," Rin said. "I was hired to find his parents, and I'm not going to stop until I have done that."

"They're dead," Ray stated.

"Maybe."

"They disappeared a long time ago!" Ray was getting agitated. "They were sick."

"I'm aware of that," Rin said. "That's why I need to find them."

Ray sighed a deep sigh. "Let's sit down," he suggested.

Ray sat down, but Rin continued to stand.

"Okay, stand if you wish. But I was hoping we might start over a third time." Ray spread out his hands in a gesture of peace. "I don't mean to insult you or cause any unnecessary trouble, Rin. In fact, I think you and I are both after the same thing. I would love to find Emmett and Mia Toffy alive. I know they tried for years to re-create the Discipline Serum, but they couldn't reproduce it. And when they failed, well, I think it was too much for them. Now Ozzy is the only key to what they once created. What he has inside him could change the world. Think of all the problems that formula could solve."

"Right," Rin said. "Not to mention how wealthy it could make you."

"Sure," Ray agreed with a thick tone of false modesty,

"it will make some people very rich. In fact, I'm sure there's money enough for you in it. We can change the world in a way that will make a real difference."

The wizard stared down at Ray, his dark hair hanging over his left eye.

"You'll have all the money you've ever wanted," Ray said, smiling. "I just need to talk with Ozzy. You bring him to me, and you'll never have to worry about money again. It's simple. I'll have a little discussion with him and then he can go. In the end, Ozzy will be fine and we'll both be rich."

"You already are rich," Rin pointed out.

Ray's annoying face looked perplexed.

"It's not just about the money, Rin. Do you mind if I call you Rin?"

"Yes."

"Okay," Ray said, sounding bothered, "then why don't you just think of all the problems that serum will solve?"

"So," the wizard said casually, "you see a serum that takes away everyone's free will as a problem solver?"

"Don't be so small-minded. People will still be able to make some choices, just not ones that will harm them. How many times have you seen someone make a dumb mistake that you would have easily avoided? Choices that could potentially harm others will be made by those who know better."

Rin looked calm.

"I can see it in your eyes," Ray said, beginning to sound more like his truly slick and devious self. "You know this is a good thing. Those who struggle to make the right decision when life throws them a curveball will have someone to make those decisions for them. Everyone longs for a powerful person to lead the way or to make difficult choices for them. People are hungry to be controlled—all they require is a place to sleep, food to eat, and phones on which to post about those things. I mean, you're an example of this. Ozzy hired you to make choices for him, didn't he?"

Rin kept quiet.

"The formula inside the boy will change the world as we know it. No more giving into dangerous cravings or poor habits. No more relationships that can ruin the planet for the rest of us. Things will make sense from every angle."

Rin stood as tall as he could and smiled so slightly that only an old-timey detective with a strong magnifying glass and a keen eye would notice it.

"You get it, don't you?" Ray declared. "You can see the wisdom in what I'm saying. Fantastic! Bring Ozzy here, heck, bring that bird . . . and your daughter—the more the merrier. And together the five of us will shape the world for good."

The office was silent for a minute while Rin closed his eyes. When he finally flashed his blue eyes open, he appeared calm and solid, like a statue carved by someone hoping to capture the emotion of tranquility in stone.

"No, thank you," the wizard said. "I don't see you as someone who could ever change the world for good."

"Don't be a fool," Ray argued.

"I have no problem being a fool, if that's what this task requires."

"Bring me Ozzy," Ray demanded.

"I didn't come to bargain," Rin said. "And I don't need to worry about you. You're afraid to leave the state. Holed up in your office and wanting the world to come to you. Look what happened to Jon. Send anyone you want—they won't succeed in bringing Ozzy back. Not as long as I'm alive. And wizards live for a very long time. We are perennial."

"That's where you're wrong," Ray snapped. "I *will* get the boy, and I *will* dispose of you. You won't be leaving this place; we need to visit a little longer."

"No, thanks—your office is uncomfortable."

"Enough!" Ray snapped. "I've tried to be nice, but now I'll have to be more direct. You might not believe me, but you *are* going to help me get Ozzy here."

Rin shook his head sadly. "I was hoping you'd be less you-like. If you knew anything about me, you would know that I would never help you do anything."

"You're making a huge mistake."

"I make a lot of them," Rin said. "I find the strongest magic is often hidden behind my biggest mistakes. Now, I have things to do. So if you don't mind, I will be on my way."

"I *do* mind," Ray said. "You're not going anywhere."

Using the tip of his left shoe, Ray pushed a hidden button on the floor behind his desk. Instantly the doors behind

Rin opened and three men in blue suits stepped in. A door behind the desk also opened and three more ogres entered. The men were tall and wide, and their eyes were all focused on the wizard.

Rin looked disappointed as the six ogres made a ring around him.

"It doesn't have to be like this," Ray said. "Just come with me and we'll find a solution that all of us can live with."

"No, thanks."

"You're not magical. And my men can be very persuasive."

All six men pulled open their suit jackets to expose the guns they had in shoulder holsters, then pulled the guns out and pointed them at Rin.

The wizard shook his head sadly.

"As you can see, your choices are limited," Ray said triumphantly. "Now let's all move to a more private space."

"Let's not," Rin said calmly. "We actually need to be leaving."

"We?" Ray asked, looking suddenly agitated. "We who? You said you didn't bring your bird."

The ogres in blue backed up. They were all familiar with the mysterious bird that had caused so much trouble in the past.

"I didn't bring the bird," Rin informed them. "And wizards never lie."

"So it's just you," Ray asked.

"Well, I didn't say that either."

Rin whistled a loud piercing whistle.

Instantly the lights in the office flashed off. All the ogres kept their guns trained on Rin, none of them feeling as sure about things as they had just moments before.

The room was filled with shadows and weak colored light flickering from the windows. The atmosphere made every non-wizard in the room jumpy. Ray shouted toward the outer office, "Susan, what's happened to the lights?" His voice was unsteady.

"I don't know," came a muffled reply.

"I do," Rin said to Ray. "You see, I might not have brought a bird . . . but I did bring a dragon."

"You're touched," Ray snapped. "You're not right. It doesn't take magic to turn off the lights, and I'll make you—"

Ray's rant was cut short as one of the high windows exploded in a burst of colored glass shards and orange flames came shooting into the room. The men in blue shifted their guns and fired up at the window.

A piercing screech filled their ears and shook their hearts.

Rin grabbed Ray's hourglass. He slammed it against the edge of the desk, causing the top to burst off. Then Rin spun, sending sand throughout the office and into the eyes and faces of Ray and his men.

"SQUAAAAAAAAAAWWK!"

A large plume of flame filled the room again, sparking bits of sand and filling the stuffy office with more heat.

"Don't let him . . . it . . . *that* get away!" Ray sputtered as his men kept firing upward into thin air.

The window across the room burst as Clark shot out of the office, then wheeled around and dove back down through the newly broken window. He breathed more fire from the opposite side. The men in blue turned to shoot in the new direction, but it was no use. Chaos had broken out and a wizard and a tiny dragon were very much in control.

Clark roared as men screamed and dragon fire and gunfire flashed through the space like deadly strobe lights.

As Ray jumped under his desk, the wizard and his dragon slipped out the back door. Thanks to the gunfire and not a few items that were now aflame, their exit went unnoticed and unimpeded.

CHAPTER TWENTY-THREE

HE'S DEPENDENT ON YOU

Sigi lay sleeping in the large, soft bed at the Hilton Garden Inn and Suites. The hotel's vibe was considerably different than that of the Marsh and Meadow in Salem. There were two queen-size beds with pillows as soft as baby clouds, a separate sitting area with a petite couch and an oversized TV, a small kitchen jammed with modern appliances, and a big table made from polished metal and glossy wood.

Sigi had chosen to sleep in the bed closest to the window. Her mother was asleep in the one near the bathroom.

The day had been full of travel and shopping and eating and swimming and it had worn them both out. They had attempted to watch a movie in their room, but the seductive call of slumber had lulled them both to sleep before the cheesy movie was halfway over.

In all the bustle of the day, Patti had forgotten to text Sheriff Wills and ask him to check on Ozzy. She had meant to, of course, but each time she had reached for her phone, something more interesting had popped up. It wasn't as if she and Sigi had gone off and no longer cared about Ozzy. Not at all. It was as if they had gone off and no longer remembered to worry.

Sigi turned over in her bed and pulled the comforter even higher.

The house at 1221 Ocean View Drive was a very nice home, but the beds in their hotel had tricked Sigi and her mom into taking a load off and slipping away from consciousness. Sigi's mind was filled with dreams that were happy and full of possibility.

Patti's dreams were just the same.

Neither one had said it, but it seemed clear that the vacation together was exactly what they had needed. Of course, they would have both felt differently had they known what was happening in other parts of the world. But they didn't, so why bother?

Which meant that Patti could continue to snore lightly and Sigi could continue to . . .

Sigi's eyes flashed open. While dreaming, her subconscious had taken a poke at her mind.

"Ozzy," she whispered.

She sat up in her bed, feeling a sense of panic building inside of her. She grabbed her phone off the nightstand near the bed and checked the time. It was just after eleven. Without worrying about calling too late, she pressed the button and dialed home.

Nobody answered.

She hung up and tried again. This time when there was no response, she left a message.

"Ozzy, it's me. Are you there? Pick up, please."

Sigi's words woke Patti up. She rolled over and looked at her daughter as she sat on the edge of her bed in the dark room.

"What are you doing?"

"I forgot about Ozzy," Sigi said with urgency. "He never called. Did you text Sheriff Wills?"

"I forgot," Patti admitted, "but I'm sure he's fine."

"He's not answering the phone."

"Maybe he forgot to sleep on the couch."

"I'm calling Wills."

"It's—" Patti rolled over and looked at the phone. "It's too late. We should wait until morning."

"No way," Sigi said. "I won't be able to sleep. I'll call the police station."

Sigi dialed the Otter Rock police station and waited three rings before someone picked up. It wasn't Sheriff Wills, but she was happy to hear that Wills was still in his office. She was patched through.

"Sigi," the sheriff said, "it's late. Is everything okay?"

"I hope so," she said. "We're in California and Ozzy's not answering the phone."

"Could he be sleeping?" the sheriff asked.

"He could be a lot of things," Sigi said seriously. "That's why I'm worried."

"I've been working on your case as we speak," Wills said. "I'll drive over and make sure he's okay. If he doesn't answer the door, can I use the key code your mom gave me?"

"Yes."

"I'll call you in a few minutes and let you know what I find," the sheriff said, in a tone much kinder than you might expect from someone at eleven-fifteen at night.

"Thank you!"

The sheriff hung up.

Sigi looked at her mother in her dark bed. "He's going to go check."

"That's nice of him. Now can you sleep?"

"Nope," Sigi said. "I think I'll watch some more of that movie until he calls."

Sigi turned on the TV and Patti sat up in bed to watch some more of a poorly made movie and wait for news of Ozzy.

CHAPTER TWENTY-FOUR

WHEN IT'S ALL TOO LATE

Rin and Clark crept through the trees at the back of the house like a wizard and bird-burglar. They had arrived at the house minutes before and easily spotted the police car parked out front.

"How did we get here again?" Clark asked.

"We stepped through Quarfelt, remember?"

"No, I don't. Last thing I remember is lighting a few things on fire in Ray's office and then us getting on a bus. Oh—and that bus driver staring at me."

"You *are* interesting."

"I really am. And why are we sneaking? I can just work my way into the house and let Ozzy and Sigi know we're here."

"Good," Rin said. "See if Ozzy's in his room."

Clark flew off. Five minutes later he was back.

"He's not there," the bird reported. "I could see through his windows and the room's empty."

"Makes sense," Rin said. "Being a wizard-in-training, he'll go for the couch now."

Keeping low, Rin and Clark crossed the back lawn and stood beneath the wide overhang near the back door. The wizard typed a number into the electronic keypad and the door unlocked.

"If I was Patti, I'd change that number," Clark said.

"She has. But I know where she writes her passwords down."

"It's weird that you two couldn't make it work."

"I feel the same way."

Rin opened the back door and the two of them entered the kitchen. He closed the door behind them and tiptoed to the living room, where the best couch was.

Ozzy wasn't there.

"Have I taught him nothing?" Rin said sadly.

The two of them combed the house but there was no sign of anyone. The only sign of life was the police car they could see out the front window. It was parked by the fountain with its lights off.

"Why do you think the police are parked out there?" Clark asked.

"I bet Patti feels unsafe without a wizard around."

A second police car pulled up the driveway and parked next to the other one.

"That one must be because they don't have a bird around."

Through the front window, they saw Sheriff Wills get

out of the car and wave to the other officer. The cop in the first parked car got out and the two men walked together up the sidewalk toward the front door.

"What do we do?" Clark asked. "Should I work them over?"

There was a soft knocking on the door, followed by Sheriff Wills speaking loudly.

"Ozzy? Ozzy, are you home?"

More knocking.

"Ozzy? We're coming in."

Rin and Clark heard the sheriff talking to the other officer.

"They're worried because Ozzy's not answering the phone," Wills said. "I just want to make sure he's here."

There was beeping as Sheriff Wills entered the code into the electronic lock. It didn't open.

"Shoot," Wills said. "I must have it wrong."

He tried again.

"Is this a nine or a seven?" he asked the other officer.

Rin motioned for Clark to follow him. He ran to the couch and took off his red shoes. Tossing them into the kitchen, he grabbed a blanket from the nearby cabinet and laid down. He put cushions up around his head as Clark jumped under the couch.

Sheriff Wills punched in the right number and the front door opened, just as Rin tossed his hat across the room beneath a large stuffed chair.

The two officers entered the house and Rin began to

make soft snoring sounds. The noise caused the sheriff to stop in his tracks and keep the lights off. From where he and his officer stood, they could both see that someone was sleeping on the couch.

"He's asleep," the second officer whispered.

"It looks like it."

Sheriff Wills moved a couple of steps closer to get a better look.

Clark was keeping an eye on them from beneath the couch. Sensing the need to make the act a little more convincing, the bird did his best Ozzy sleeping impression and mumbled, "Sigi . . . Sprite."

Sheriff Wills stopped moving closer.

"Wizard . . . bird . . . magic," Clark muttered.

The sheriff turned around and whispered, "It's him."

"He's a heavy sleeper," the second officer whispered back.

"If you'd been through some of the things he had, you would be too."

The officers exited the house and closed the door.

Once Wills had driven off and the other cop was back in his parked car, Rin sat up on the couch and Clark hopped out from under.

"I tried to snore like a teenager," Rin said. "It's all in the nose. But I must say you do a spot-on Ozzy impression."

"I'm used to hearing him sleep-mumble," the bird

chirped back. "And what about you under that blanket? You looked just like the right-sized lump."

"Thank you."

"So now that he's gone, where do you think Ozzy is? Do you think that . . ." Clark was out. The dark night and lack of lightbulbs had left him drained and uncharged. He fell over onto the carpet, his wings tucked in and his talons sticking up.

"I could use a little of that myself."

Feeling done in as well, Rin laid back down to do some recharging of his own.

CHAPTER TWENTY-FIVE

HAS HE GONE AWAY?

Jon sat in the jail cell, his legs hanging off his cot and his mind whirling. He needed to get out and find the wizard. He couldn't let some small-town police force be the end of him. Of course, he hadn't planned for two teenagers to be the end of him either. He'd been caught, but his long conversation with Sheriff Wills had been like therapy. Hearing the words come out of his own mouth detailing what he had seen Rin do felt like a rebirth, and made him believe even more that the wizard was real.

Officer Greg came into the holding area and unlocked Jon's cell door.

"The sheriff wants to talk to you."

Jon shrugged and stood up. He shuffled through the open door and walked toward the interrogation room at the end of the hall.

The Otter Rock police force wasn't huge. There were less than a dozen cops on the payroll. The station was never bustling with officers bringing in perps or throwing chairs around in an attempt to intimidate witnesses. Nope—there was Wilma at the desk during the day, another officer at the desk during the night, and a lead officer on hand. The rest of the staff was out patrolling the town or giving speeding tickets to tourists who were rude enough to try to blow through Otter Rock without slowing down to look around. Recently, the staff had been spread even thinner, with an officer parked in front of Patti's home and another always following Ozzy around.

Jon knew all of this. He was keenly aware that at that very moment there was only Wilma, Officer Greg, and Wills in the building. Had he been a wizard, he would have zapped himself free, but he had no magical powers, and he couldn't wait any longer.

It was Officer Greg's fault. The prisoner had been behaving so well and cooperating so completely. Greg let his guard down. He foolishly didn't feel the need to worry about a man who was ex-military, known to be slippery, and had gotten out of far bigger scrapes than the one he was currently in.

The two of them shuffled into the interrogation room and Officer Greg began to unlock Jon's right handcuff so he could attach it to the end of the table.

"Sheriff Wills will be in momentarily," Greg said as he undid the right shackle. "He just—"

In less than a second, Jon moved his free hand up and grabbed the officer by the hair. He then pulled Greg's head down hard against the table. The unsuspecting and newly unconscious officer slid off the table to the ground. Jon grabbed the handcuff key and moved out of the room. Wilma was up at the counter and Wills was still in his office, both unaware of what was happening.

Jon headed down the hall to the emergency back door. Without pausing, he pushed the door open and ran outside.

An alarm instantly began to wail.

Jon sprinted across the back lot behind the station, taking off his orange shirt as he ran. The chain-link fence around the area had a small strand of barbed wire running across the top. Not breaking stride, Jon jumped up onto the fence and threw his shirt over the barbed wire, flipped over the top, and dropped down on the other side. He could hear the alarm still wailing, now accompanied by Sheriff Wills shouting.

"Stop!"

There were other more interesting words thrown out by the sheriff as well, but the overall message was for Jon to give up and cease running.

Jon didn't listen. He shot across a street and into the trees behind a strip mall.

Sheriff Wills stopped at the fence, not willing to climb over it. He said a few choice words and then ran back into the station to rally his troops and recapture Jon.

By the time Wills got into his vehicle, the average man was already a mile away and moving through trees so thick it would be hard for any car to follow.

CHAPTER TWENTY-SIX

HALF ALIVE

Ozzy wasn't sure if he was alive or dead. Daylight appeared through the hole above him, the light looking like an oncoming train that had paused and was waiting to run him down after he had suffered longer. He glanced around the small space and wished there was something he could control with his mind. Knowing that there wasn't, he then wished being a wizard-in-training came with some real-life skills.

In between falling into black holes and worrying about staying alive, the boy had thought a lot about Rin. He had also thought about what Patti had said. She didn't believe. When Ozzy had searched for any sign of Quarfelt online, he had found nothing. It seemed to him that a place as important as Quarfelt would have been mentioned by someone.

Ozzy closed his eyes and slowed his breathing.

"What are you doing down there?" a voice questioned from above.

The boy lifted his right arm and rubbed the corresponding eye. Looking up, he saw a long beard and bits of light falling through the hole.

"Rin?"

"You look uncomfortable," the wizard casually shouted. "I like rain as much as the next magical guy, but just soaking in the stuff on a cold floor seems less than enjoyable. Oh, well, to each his own."

Despite the doubts that Patti had created, the thrill of seeing Rin gave Ozzy the sudden strength to push himself up on to his elbows and sit halfway up.

"You're alive!" the boy shouted.

"Is someone telling people otherwise?" Rin complained, just his head visible. "Do not believe those online comments. I swear, you put up one website and everyone wants to be a critic. Let's see *them* design better shoes."

Ozzy smiled.

"You look happy," Rin shouted with joy. "You're soaking in water in a very under-decorated room and you're still happy. You're acting just like a junior wizard should."

"No, I'm not," Ozzy said weakly. "I'm happy because I can tell from the nonsense you're blurting out that it's really you."

"Of course it's me."

"I've never seen you from this angle."

"I've never seen you wear earmuffs, but I'd still be able to tell it was you," Rin said happily.

"Where's Clark?" Ozzy asked.

Rin's expression changed. "He's not here."

"Where is he?"

"I can tell you all of that when you get up here."

"Tell me now."

Rin chastised the boy. "You have the patience of a first-year wizard. Remember what I've always said, 'Knowledge is a package that time unwraps.' I will tell you all about Clark when the time is right."

"You've never said that," Ozzy insisted. "Is he okay?"

"Sure, he's cool," Rin said. "I mean, I enjoy having him around."

"Not okay, okay. Is he *safe*?"

"Oh, well, that depends on what your definition of *is* is."

Ozzy closed his eyes and lifted his left hand. He pointed his finger up toward Rin.

"Are you trying to control me with your finger?" the wizard asked. "Because many people have attempted to gain access to my brain and it's never worked."

"I just want to know if Clark's okay."

"I'll tell you everything once you're up here." Rin seemed excited. "I prefer to speak to people who are not lying in rainwater. Now, why are you down there?"

Ozzy sighed. "I fell."

"It's a bad look," Rin said. "Your poor command of gravity makes me worry about your skills as a wizard. If you can't master one of the most magical things in existence, then how are you going to save the world?"

"I wasn't planning to save the world."

"That's good, keep yourself in the dark. It'll make the ending more exciting."

"Can you get me out of here?" Ozzy asked.

"It might help if I had a little backstory," Rin suggested. "For starters, why you are down there?"

"I fell," Ozzy said, "through the opening you're looking through now."

"Are your legs broken?"

"I don't think so."

"Your arms?"

"No."

"Then let's have you stand up and I'll see if I can reach down."

"Can't you just levitate me up?" Ozzy asked.

"The difference between what I can and will do is staggering."

"Is that a no?"

"It's an invitation for you to use some magic of your own. How can I expect you to grow if I'm doing all the heaving and lifting?"

"Right," Ozzy said with frustration. "That's a no."

It took some struggling, but Ozzy finally managed to get up on his feet. He wobbled for a few moments and then leaned against the stone wall.

Rin reached down and Ozzy reached up. The gap between their hands was still at least a foot across.

"Where's your staff?" Rin asked.

"I left it at home. It's hard enough to sneak away

without Sheriff Wills catching me. I didn't think a six-foot stick with a glowing orb would help."

"It always helps," Rin said. "Look how beneficial it would be now. And where are your trousers?"

Ozzy glanced down to make sure he was wearing some.

"Oh, you mean the pants you sent? Again, I didn't think that red and gray plaid pants would be the best thing to wear while I'm sneaking around."

"I didn't send them," Rin insisted. "They came directly from the QWA."

They both were silent.

"Do I have to ask?" Ozzy gave in.

"The Quarfelt Wizards Association," Rin explained. "And your magical powers are strengthened when you wear them."

"So is my humiliation level."

"Humility can be a powerful tool. I've won awards for mine."

"Rin," Ozzy complained, "if you're not going to tell me about Clark, and if you're not going to float me out of here or make our arms longer, maybe you could find a tree limb or something I could use to climb."

It took Rin ten minutes to find a decent branch. The first one he found didn't feel right, the second one was too splintery, the third one had an obnoxious personality, and the fourth one demanded that Rin set it down. The fifth stick was amiable enough to let Rin pick it off the ground and then lower it into the hole.

It may have been agreeable, but as Ozzy stepped on the handle of the metal door and pushed upward while pulling on the stick, it broke.

The boy fell back down to the stone floor.

"Try another," Ozzy said as Rin looked down at him. "Grab the nearest one. I don't care if it doesn't want to help."

"That's incredibly selfish," Rin said, scolding the boy. The wizard noticed something as he was gazing down. "Wait, what was that you put your foot on? Is that a door?"

"Yes." Ozzy turned his head to look at the metal door. "But it's locked."

"Not anymore," Rin said happily.

Ozzy grabbed the handle he had just used for footing and it broke off in his hand. The metal door whined as it slowly opened. He turned his head and looked up.

"It's open!" he hollered.

There was no need to scream—Rin was standing directly behind him. The wizard stepped back three inches.

"Inside voices," the wizard chided.

Ozzy was baffled. "What are you doing?"

"I jumped down," Rin replied. "I wanted to see what was behind the door."

"But now we're both stuck."

"What a foolish thing to say."

"Do you have your phone?"

"It's being repaired."

Rin reached past Ozzy and pulled the metal door open. He took out a small candle from one of his robe pockets and lit it with a match.

"You carry around candles?"

"The lighting is much more mysterious than a flashlight."

The flame made it possible to see that behind the door there was another subterranean room and a set of stone stairs. Most of the room was filled with burnt pieces of the Cloaked House that had spilled in from a collapsed hole in the basement wall. There were also broken glass vials and a metal table chained to the wall.

"Did you know this space was here?"

"No," Ozzy said reverently. "This is a part of the basement I didn't know existed. I wonder if my parents knew it was here."

Rin directed the candlelight toward some stone stairs that led up.

"What's that?" Ozzy asked.

Sitting on the second step was a big square block. It looked solid and black. Ozzy stepped over to it and picked it up. It was heavy and burnt and smelled like rubber.

"It must have fallen in from the basement during the fire."

"I hate to say anything *must* have," Rin complained. "It leaves no room for mystery. I prefer *may* have."

"Either way, it's weird," Ozzy observed. "It has ridges."

Rin moved around Ozzy and crawled as far up the stairs as he could. There were pieces of burnt board and tree roots crossing every step. At the top of the stairs they were stopped by a square metal hatch that was horizontal and at ground level. It had a handle and sliding bolt on one side and two hinges on the other. Rin slid the bolt back and pushed up with all his might.

The hatch didn't budge.

"You shouldn't have jumped down here," Ozzy said again. "Since I've obviously never seen a metal hatch behind the house, it has to be buried by years of dirt. We can't just push it open."

"I wish I had a wimpt for every *can't* I've turned into *can*," Rin said, sounding disappointed in Ozzy.

"What's a wimpt?"

"About half the value of a soom. They were part of the old currency in Quarfelt," Rin explained, while using the light of his candle to carefully study the metal hatch. "They used them for money back before the Great Mud Scrimmage."

Ozzy gave Rin a solid stare.

"It was a really messy war," the wizard added. "But that's not the point. As you can see, the hinges on this hatch are brittle. This might be a good time for you to try casting a spell to break them."

"I don't know any spells," the boy pointed out. "If the hatch had a mind, I might be able to will it open."

"It doesn't," Rin said. "But there are endless spells

inside of you. You're no longer an apprentice, you're a wizard-in-training, for trolls' sake—a genuine trainee. If we were in Quarfelt, they'd give you a sticker to wear."

"I'm glad we're here."

"Now you're talking like a wizard," Rin cheered. "So—give it a go. It's time to let those spells out."

The darkness kept Ozzy's expression hidden and prevented Rin from seeing just how uneasy he was with what the wizard was saying.

"Don't think about it," Rin instructed. "Just say whatever comes to your mind."

"You've doomed us both by jumping down here."

Rin tested the hatch. "Nope, that's not it. Try something else."

"I really wanted to see you again, but now I'm not sure why."

Rin pulled on the handle. "Try again."

Ozzy was exasperated. "This is ridiculous!"

The wizard tugged hard on the handle and the brittle hinges cracked, allowing him to pull the hatch down toward them. As it opened, a thick layer of dirt and grass caved in with it. The soil covered their heads and bodies and filled the stairs with mud and daylight. Rin reached up and pushed through the debris as he climbed the rest of the stairs and crawled out of the cellar.

Ozzy followed behind him, dragging the black cube.

CHAPTER TWENTY-SEVEN

LONG EXAGGERATED DRINK

The hatch opened up near the stream behind the burnt house. Moving like a motivated turtle, Ozzy let go of the cube and shuffled to the water. He threw his face into the stream and took a deep drink. With his thirst slaked, he scooted over and sat next to Rin. They were both dirty and streaked with bits of dirt, ash, and grass. The two of them looked like survivors of the Great Mud Scrimmage.

"Impressive spell," Rin said in a congratulatory tone. "I've never tried that one before."

"It wasn't a spell," Ozzy insisted.

Rin shook his head. "It's always disheartening when people fail to realize how powerful the words they throw out of their mouths really are."

"Super disheartening," Ozzy said impatiently. "Now, where's Clark?"

Rin looked away from Ozzy and stared at the ground directly in front of him.

"What?" Ozzy's face was now covered with ash and worry. "What is it? Where is he?"

"I'm not sure how to say it," Rin said. "But Clark's not here."

Ozzy was dubious. "What do you mean not here?"

"No longer with us."

The new wizard was speechless; the old one wasn't.

"You see, I brought him with me to Quarfelt, remember?"

"Yes," Ozzy said anxiously. "You snatched him up and jumped off the boat."

"Right. You were there. Well, once we were in Quarfelt, some things happened."

"What things?"

"I could go on and on about things, but the importantest thing is that Clark didn't come back with me."

"Then we need to go get him," Ozzy demanded.

"I can't."

"I thought you turned can'ts to cans!"

Rin looked touched. "You *were* listening. But this situation is different. You see, when your dad invented Clark, well, there were some things that needed improvement. And, when I tried to improve them . . ." Rin let his voice just trail off.

"What?" Ozzy asked. "What happened?"

"It's probably best that I show you."

Rin stood up and Ozzy followed suit, holding the large black cube. The wizard adjusted his hat and dusted off some of the ashes from his robe. For the first time Ozzy noticed what Rin was wearing.

"Your pants are different."

"I didn't want to brag, but I've been promoted. And I'm happy to say I'm still a size thirty-two."

"You were promoted to a hippie wizard?" Ozzy asked with genuine confusion. "I've seen pictures in old books of people wearing pants like that. Are they bellbottoms?"

"No, these are the trousers of a high wizard."

"That's unfortunate," Ozzy said with compassion.

"I had the choice of these or shorts," Rin explained. "But I've never felt very confident about my knees."

Ozzy took a deep, long breath of air and looked around the forest. The sky was growing darker and the threat of rain was becoming a promise. He looked at the wizard he had called all those months ago. The wizard he had hoped would find his parents. The wizard that Patti had said wasn't real. The wizard who had gone above and beyond for him countless times.

"I'm really glad to see you," Ozzy admitted. "New pants and all. And Sigi is going to be elated, but I really need to see Clark."

"Okay," Rin said excitedly. "Then you should probably scream."

"What?"

"You need to scream. Make it sound like your life's in peril."

"With you around, it usually is."

"Good, good, use that. Now scream."

Ozzy looked around at the burnt house, the hole to the secret cellar, the black cube in his hands, the ash-covered wizard, and the endless forest. He had plenty to scream about, but he was too exhausted to play along and do so.

"This is ridiculous," Ozzy insisted.

"No using spells, just scream."

"I'm not going to . . ."

Rin lifted his right leg and stomped on Ozzy's left foot as hard as he could. The boy dropped the black cube as a sharp pain shot through his entire being and then escaped out of his mouth in the form of a loud piercing scream.

Ozzy looked at Rin with wet, angry eyes.

"What are you *doing*?"

Rin smiled. "You'll see."

Ozzy was considering using his mind control to make every animal in the forest descend upon Rin and scratch him up. But that thought drifted away as a new and un-settling sound filled the woods. It was a piercing, dreadful noise.

"Perfect," Rin said proudly, as the noise grew louder. "You screamed good."

Ozzy looked around with concern, half missing the quiet of the stone cellar he had been sitting in just moments before.

CHAPTER TWENTY-EIGHT

A ONE-BIRD UNKINDNESS

Spinning around, Ozzy took in the sky above. He saw the whisper-thin edges of clouds as they struggled to show some definition in the endless gray mass. He heard a scream similar to a cat being waxed and saw a somewhat unfamiliar black shape racing toward him from the west.

"What is that?" he asked Rin. "Is that . . . ?"

A plume of flame filled the air, causing the approaching black shape to be temporarily lost in the orange. A moment later the black shape shot out of the flame and was screeching ever closer.

Ozzy smiled like a kid who had just been given the keys to the candy shop, amusement park, and auto dealership all at once.

"Clark!"

Rin held out his arm and the small black dragon swooped in and landed on it.

Ozzy gasped.

It was Clark, in dragon form. He was also smoldering, thin wisps of smoke coming off various parts of his body.

Clark tilted his head back and blew fire out of his beak and up into the cloudy sky. Ozzy stepped back in awe.

"What *happened* to you?"

"I've had a few upgrades," the bird bragged. "Not that I wasn't fine before, but now look at me."

Ozzy reached out and patted the bird on the head.

"I don't care how you look, I'm just glad you're back."

Clark was disappointed.

"But you do look amazing," Ozzy added.

Clark jumped off Rin's arm and onto Ozzy's head.

"Do I feel heavier?"

"Do you want to?"

"Yes," the bird chirped.

"Then yes."

"He's a dragon," said Rin.

"It's what I was born to be," Clark added proudly as one of his horns fell off.

Rin picked up the horn, licked the end of it and stuck it back on Clark's head.

"Where'd the fire come from?"

Clark leaned down so that Ozzy could see the small black canister glued under his right wing. A thin tube ran from the canister and into his beak.

"He's the real deal," Rin said. "The only problem is that he keeps blowing fire when he's flying. Which means he has to fly through the flames and the heat melts the glue holding his pieces on."

"And causes me to smolder," Clark bragged.

"How'd you do it?" Ozzy asked as he carefully looked Clark over.

"Magic," Rin said, waving his hand. "And there's a 3-D printer in the commons area."

Now Ozzy looked disappointed.

"Right," Ozzy said. "The commons area of where?"

"In one of the Hovels in Quarfelt. The one behind the incomplete castle."

"That doesn't clarify anything for me."

"Of course," Rin apologized. "I always forget you've not been there. Let's see, how do I explain it? Well, hovels are like your hostels here in reality, except there's always the chance you might have to pick up and run due to being chased by something."

"Sounds unsettling."

"Only the one located in Near East Quarfelt. The foundation is shifting."

"So you saw Quarfelt?" Ozzy asked the bird.

"Maybe," Clark answered. "I can't remember, but Riny here says I did. Now where's Sigi? She needs to get a look at me."

"She's in California," Ozzy said.

"Why did—" While asking the question, Clark accidentally shot flames from his beak. They hit Rin in the face, singed his eyebrows, and caught the brim of his felt hat on fire.

The wizard threw the hat down and stomped out the flame.

"Sorry," Clark apologized. "I still haven't perfected being a dragon."

Half of the plastic cover on his left wing fell off and cracked when it hit the ground. Ozzy could see Clark's real wing underneath.

"You might be better off just being you."

"Where's the fun in that?" Clark asked.

Rin picked up the cracked piece of plastic and put his now-flameless hat back on.

"I should get back," Ozzy told them. "I've been in that hole a while. I need to let Sigi know I'm okay. She said she'd send the sheriff if I didn't keep in touch."

"She did," Rin said. "He came over last night. But don't worry, we did a good job of pretending to be you."

Ozzy rubbed his forehead, smearing dirt and ashes around. He glanced down and noticed for the first time that the black plastic cube had cracked in half.

It was now two pieces.

Ozzy crouched down and studied them. Between the two pieces there was a single black record covered in burnt paper. Ozzy picked it up.

"It looks like your mystery cube is a stack of records the fire fused together," Rin said.

Examining the two halves, it was clear that only one

single record in the middle had survived. The paper around it fell off like dry grass and the label in the center was blackened from heat. Holding it just right, Ozzy could make out the word *Hurting*. Remarkably, the grooves of the record still looked intact.

"What do you think it is?" Ozzy asked.

"Probably a recording of bird noises," Clark guessed.

"You're not a bird anymore," Ozzy said affectionately. "It says 'hurting.'"

"Maybe it's a collection of dragon songs."

Ozzy held the record carefully, hoping it was a recording of his parent's voices, or at the very least, more music.

"You know, it really is a nice-looking piece of plastic," Clark admitted.

"It's vinyl," Rin informed the bird.

"Nice to meet you, Vinyl." Clark tipped his head and his other horn fell off.

Rin picked it back up and stuck it back on.

"I wish I had brought back some glue from Quarfelt," the wizard complained. "It's much stronger. It's made from the eggs of a mature tapeworm and the sticky disposition of a feathered obstinate."

The dragon stared at the wizard. "I think I'm glad I can't remember being there."

They all picked up the pace as they traveled quickly through the forest. Rin filled in Ozzy about Ray and what had happened. He also informed him of the Perennial Five and told him that he could put his mind at ease because they were ready and willing to help.

"I think I'm still going to feel uneasy."

"Suit yourself."

Ozzy filled in the wizard and bird about what had happened to him and Sigi and Jon and how he had grown to like the pants even though he wasn't wearing them.

"I'm not surprised," Rin said happily. "You're going to save the world in style."

"That's the second time you said I'm going to save the world."

"Keep counting," the wizard said. "It'll make it more dramatic."

Rin took out his to-get-done list and checked off another box.

"What's that?"

"It a list of things I need to finish before this is all done."

"Really? Can I see it?"

"No," Rin said strongly. "It's a to-get-done list, not a to-get-a-look-at list."

Ozzy left it at that.

Two hiked on, one flew.

CHAPTER TWENTY-NINE

PLAYING PRETEND

California was behaving just like the postcards and commercials claimed it would. It was a perfect seventy-two degrees, the sky was a shade of blue nobody could feel down about, and happy people milled about; smiling with their teeth, eyes, and cheeks. To make a beautiful day even more fulfilling, Sigi and her mother were enjoying that temperature, sky, and scenery at Harry Potter World. They had gotten up early and been two of the first people in line at the gates.

In the hotel, Patti had argued the fact that it would be better to go to Disneyland first and Universal the next day, but Sigi had argued for just the reverse.

"It'll be like I'm there with both you and Dad."

So in the hotel, and in the end, Sigi had won out.

The Wizarding World of Harry Potter was no Quarfelt, but the amusement park made Sigi happy in a way she had not anticipated. It made her happy about the books she had once read, proud of the father she now had, and it made her miss the boy she cared for. Butterbeer reminded her of how Ozzy loved Sprite, purchasing a wand at the wand shop reminded her of the fact that her dad already had one, and seeing pictures of hippogriffs reminded her of a small metal bird that she missed terribly.

"He's not a dragon," Patti said. "He's a robot raven."

"He's better than most dragons," Sigi insisted.

Patti smiled the kind of smile that made it clear she was both happy and concerned, but that it wasn't a fifty-fifty split.

"Are you glad you came?" she asked her daughter as they walked through Hogsmeade.

"Yes," Sigi said. "I wish Ozzy was here. He should have come."

"We'll bring him next time."

"And Dad should be here. Although he'd probably have a lot to criticize."

"You're right about that," Patti agreed. "But it would be good for him to see all of this *pretend* stuff. Pretend . . . stuff," she repeated.

"I get it, Mom, you're a non-believer."

Patti glanced at what her daughter had on her head.

"I can't believe how much you look like your dad in that hat."

Sigi smiled happily.

As soon as the gates had opened, the two of them had taken the Hogwarts Express and then walked through the shops, where Sigi had bought a wizard's hat. She liked the hat, but she loved the fact that it caused her mom some grief. Now she was wearing it to keep the morning sun out of her eyes and to fit in with all the other characters strolling about the park.

"Maybe magic is genetic," Sigi said.

Patti rubbed her forehead.

"I'm going to pretend that you're only acting like magic exists to give your mother a hard time. I didn't raise a daughter who supports make-believe." Patti was trying to keep her voice light and easy, but she had a genuine concern about Sigi trusting in something delusional. "This is fun, Sigi, but it's just that."

Sigi stopped abruptly, causing the people walking behind them to go around.

"Mom, I don't know what you think I believe, but I'm not going to climb up to the top of some building and jump off, thinking I can fly. It's just that for the first time in my life, I'm going to believe that Dad can do something remarkable—unexplainable, but remarkable. I promise I'll never follow him off a cliff or get a bumper sticker that says 'I love magic.' But I'm not going to discount what I've been through in order to fit my experience into a mold that everyone accepts."

The two of them slowly moved from the middle of the walkway in Hogsmeade, to the edge where they were blocking less people.

"My job is to be your mom," Patti said. "You're in

school a couple more years and then you'll be on your own. Mental health is a real issue."

Sigi stared at her mom.

"So you think I'm going nuts?"

"I think your dad has struggles you aren't aware of."

"You'd rather believe he's crazy than magical?"

"I'd rather he keep away if it means *your* life and mind are in danger."

Sigi shook her head as a large man dressed as Hagrid stomped past them. The wizard's daughter was going to let her mother know exactly how she felt about what she was saying, but before she could find the words, both her phone and her mom's phone buzzed simultaneously. The two of them took them out of their pockets and looked at the screens. It was a group text from Sheriff Wills, letting them know that Jon had gotten away, and that he was on his way to inform Ozzy.

"Jon escaped," Sigi said nervously.

"I see that," Patti said staring at her phone. "And Wills is on the way to tell Ozzy."

"This isn't good."

Patti pressed the number on her phone to call the sheriff and Sigi pressed the number on her phone to call Ozzy.

Only one person got an answer.

CHAPTER THIRTY

STICKY

It could be argued that when Rin had first placed the dragon pieces on Clark and hooked up the fire tube that the small black bird had looked impressive. But that argument was getting harder and harder to make now that parts had begun to drop off as they had hiked through the forest. Clark could barely fly since one wing was now bigger than the other. He also had a problem with the spikes on his back sliding down and jamming his wings. The bird perched on Ozzy's right shoulder to ride out the last bit of the hike.

"What kind of glue did you use?" Ozzy asked the wizard.

"It was white," Rin said. "And sticky."

"You couldn't just use a binding spell?"

Rin's robe caught on a low tree branch and the snag sent him spinning into Ozzy. The wizard tried to play it off as if he had meant to do that.

"Do you think us wizards have a book that clearly lists every magic spell step by step?" Rin asked. "The answer is—not yet, but soon. There's a committee working on it as we hike. But they can't agree on anything, so it'll probably never actually happen."

Rin shifted his feet and continued walking in the right direction.

"Maybe eye of newt works best in some situations," he continued. "But there are hundreds of substitutions for every ingredient. Eye of newt might cure a headache, but so does Advil. You can deliver a curse with the assistance of a letter-carrying owl, or you can use email. In a very real way, magic is slowly taking over everything."

Ozzy gave the wizard a side glance. "So much of what you say sounds made up."

"Whoa," Clark whistled from the boy's shoulder. "Shots fired."

"Made up?" Rin asked as if he had never heard those words in that order before.

"I did believe," Ozzy said honestly. "Do you remember when you followed me back to the Cloaked House the first time we met?"

"Wizards, elephants, and search histories never forget."

"Right," Ozzy said. "Well, I thought you were a real wizard, like from the books."

"I'm taller than most mentioned, but go on."

Ozzy stepped over a fallen tree and onto a dirt road near the edge of Otter Rock.

"Things have changed," Ozzy said. "I had lived my life alone, so I didn't know what to trust or believe. Now I know books like The Lord of the Rings or Harry Potter aren't real. Now I know that no other boys have hired a wizard to help them find their parents."

"That's not true," Rin said nicely. "There's a kid named Tim in Brazil who is trying to get a friend of mine to do just that. Of course, Tim's thirty-two, and his parents didn't disappear—they moved to get away from him."

"See," Ozzy said. "Stuff like that. Is that true?"

"Sadly, yes," Rin said. "But if you met Tim, you wouldn't be surprised that his parents ditched him."

Clark lifted his head to yell at a noisy squirrel and shot a weak stream of flame from his beak. Both Rin and Ozzy looked embarrassed for him.

"I think I liked you better as a bird," Ozzy admitted.

"One of my horns fell into my wing and my fire tube's pinched."

"I'm going to fix you when we get home," Rin said.

"You're implying that I'm in need of fixing."

"Only in that area."

Ozzy reached up and carefully patted Clark on the head.

"I'm also not great at Candy Crush," the bird admitted. "Metal beaks and talons are murder on phone screens."

Ozzy stopped and closed his eyes. His head throbbed like a subwoofer playing club music.

"Are you okay?" Rin asked.

"Something's up with my head."

"Your hair is a little long," Clark admitted. "I was going to say something, but you know how I hate to judge."

"You love to judge," Ozzy reminded him.

"No, I hate to *not judge*. You need a haircut."

"Quiet," Rin said. "Tell me what hurts. Is it like the sickness you felt before going into the ocean a few weeks ago?"

"No," Ozzy said. "I'm just tired and hungry."

"Let's pick up the pace," the wizard said with urgency. "We don't have much time."

"Time for what?" Clark asked.

"The boy's hungry!" Rin answered.

Clark squawked and the center section of plastic on his left wing dropped off and fell to the ground.

CHAPTER THIRTY-ONE

A FINE MESS

When they arrived home, the wizard, the wizard-in-training, and the half-dragon/half-raven snuck behind the house beneath the cover of long grass and trees. Then, crawling on their stomachs, they worked their way to the back door.

Once inside the house, they crouched in a spot where they could see through the kitchen windows and out of the large window in the living room at the same time. There was still a cop car parked by the fountain, and just like the previous night, Sheriff Wills was currently pulling up to the house and getting out.

"Get on the couch," Rin told Ozzy. "Quick!"

"But . . ."

"Language," Clark squawked.

Ozzy laid down on the couch.

"Get under the blanket," Rin insisted. "Pretend you're sleeping."

Ozzy pulled up the blanket and placed his head on the couch pillows just as Sheriff Wills knocked on the front door. Rin and Clark slipped into the kitchen to hide.

The sheriff rang the doorbell.

"Do I answer it?" Ozzy whispered.

"Of course," Clark whispered back. "It would be rude not to."

Ozzy got up off the couch, wondering why he had needed to pretend to sleep when he was going to answer the door anyway. He pulled open the door and there was the sheriff. His mustache wasn't quite as neat as usual, and there were bags beneath his eyes. He looked at Ozzy in a strange and accusing way.

"What happened to you?" the sheriff asked.

"I was sleeping," Ozzy said, trying to sound as if he had just woken up.

"Where?"

"On the couch."

Ozzy had spent a day and night in a dark wet room in the forest. He had climbed and walked through dirt and rain. He had ripped his shirt and pants on a couple of branches, and he was still wearing his muddy shoes. The sheriff looked past him toward the couch. Thanks to the few seconds Ozzy had just spent laying on it, it too was covered in ash and mud.

"How did you get so dirty?" Wills asked.

The wizard-in-training looked down at himself.

"Oh, that," he said. "I was trying to— I was out back trying to— I fell in something."

"Really?" the sheriff said suspiciously. "Do you mind if I come in?"

"I actually need to take a shower."

"I can see that, but I think it can wait."

The sheriff worked his way in and took a seat on a white leather chair in front of the window and directly across the room from the dirty couch. Ozzy closed the front door and returned to the couch. He sat down, knowing that Patti was not going to be happy about where he had chosen to sleep and sit.

"Listen," Sheriff Wills said. "The last place I saw black ash like the stuff on your clothes was at your cabin in the woods. But I'm not here to scold you about where you may or may not have been."

"Thanks," Ozzy said.

"I'm here because I need to tell you that Jon got away."

Clark squawked in the kitchen.

"Sorry," Ozzy said, "that's just an alarm I had set."

Sheriff Wills looked at his watch. "You had an alarm set for 11:13?"

"Yeah, I was going to call Sigi at eleven-fifteen, and I wanted two minutes to work on what I was going to say."

Wills looked like he needed a long vacation or a different career.

"Did you hear what I said? Jon escaped."

"How?"

"He assaulted one of my officers at the station and then hopped over the back fence. But there's no need to worry; we'll get him back."

"So he can escape again?" Ozzy asked curiously.

"No," Wills insisted. "He won't get away twice."

"But only if you catch him again."

"We will." Wills was frustrated. "I've talked with Patti and she's aware of what happened. They'll be coming back today."

"I thought you said we had nothing to worry about."

"I had a long discussion with Jon," the sheriff said. "He told me a lot of things. And he insists he's not working for Ray. But we can't take chances. I need to make sure you stay right here until Patti and Sigi arrive. Then we can all have a long talk and get things in order."

"What kind of long talk?"

Sheriff Wills stood up and put his hands behind his back. He looked out the front window at the cop cars and fountain.

"I've gathered a lot of new information," he said with his back to Ozzy. "I've visited with your grandfather. I even know all about Clark."

There was another squawk.

The sheriff turned around. "That alarm would drive me mad."

"It's just annoying enough to get my attention," Ozzy said loudly.

"There are a lot of things you haven't told me, Ozzy,"

Wills went on. "I don't know how you think I can protect and help if I don't have the right information. Jon escaping is a problem, but he's not the one I worry about. Ray won't give up on this. He wants what you have."

The sheriff glanced at Ozzy.

"Can I look at your finger?"

Ozzy thought about saying no, but he saw no reason to hold back now. He held his hand forth and let Wills take a good long look at his pointer finger.

"It's from your parents," Wills said quietly.

"Yeah," Ozzy admitted.

"And you can make people do things because of it?"

"I . . . well, I don't know exactly."

"How do you feel now?"

"What?"

"How do you feel?" the sheriff asked again. "Are you in pain?"

Ozzy was shocked. "I'm not . . . don't think . . ."

Sheriff Wills held up his palms to calm the boy.

"Don't worry," he said. "In all my years as a policeman, I've never had a situation like this. I like facts. I like reality. I don't read fiction because it's silly—pointless. One wizard kills one dragon and some troll captures a goblin."

"I don't know that book."

"My point is that this situation is a doozy. I can see no clear answers or solutions. I've talked about this with some of my colleagues, but my explanations end up sounding as insane as Rin."

This time Rin squawked.

Sheriff Wills winced. "It sounds like the batteries on your alarm are dying."

"When will Sigi be home?" Ozzy asked.

"Late today. They're catching a flight back to Eugene and then driving home."

"So we'll all talk then?"

Sheriff Wills looked at Ozzy as he sat covered with mud and ash on the dirty white couch.

"You need to stay put. Don't leave this house."

"I won't," Ozzy promised. "I'll just go to my room above the garage and stay there until they arrive."

The sheriff turned to leave, but stopped when an idea popped into his head.

"If you wanted, could you control me?"

"What?"

"Could you use your brain and that finger to make me do something I don't want to do?"

Ozzy was scared to answer.

"Well?"

"I couldn't," Ozzy lied. "I'm not sure I can explain some of the things that have happened, but me controlling other people's minds is just a misunderstanding."

"You made an officer drive into the ocean."

"That was him."

Sheriff Wills shook his head.

"Stay put, Ozzy."

"I will."

Sheriff Wills left the house and drove off down the drive.

Rin and Clark came into the living room and joined Ozzy on the couch as he stared out the front window.

"He knows too much," Clark whispered fiercely. "Maybe we should rubbish him out."

The wizard and trainee stared at the bird.

"What?" tweeted Clark. "Isn't that a thing? Like you rubbish someone?"

"No," Rin said. "Unless you're talking about the rubbish cycle in Quarfelt. But that just gives the city of Abra a lot of pride, and it helps with their recycling program."

"We're not rubbing anyone out," Ozzy said. "And I have to say put."

"Well," the wizard said, "*that's* not going to happen. Now wash up so we can get going."

"I told him I won't leave."

"I once told Patti I was good at sudoku," Rin said. "The point is sometimes we stretch the truth. You aren't really going to leave; you're just getting some fresh air. And I'm not horrible at sudoku—I just don't understand any of the rules."

"Is that the game where you throw around horse apparel?" Clark asked.

"No," Rin said, "you're thinking pigskins and that's football. Now let's get cleaned up and maybe make something to eat before we leave."

"Where are we going to go?" Ozzy asked.

"We need to get away from all this . . . *activity*," the wizard explained. "Cop cars parked in front, sheriffs with the door codes. I thought we'd go to my place."

"*Your* place?" Ozzy asked with a sudden excitement. "We're going to where you live? Like your home?"

"Don't get too excited," Clark complained. "He has dirt floors."

"In the workshop," Rin said defensively.

"I've always wondered what your house looks like."

"Well, the way I see it," said Rin, "is that you're one shower, one change of clothes, and two egg sandwiches away from finding out."

Ozzy needed no further motivation. He made his way to his room to wash up and get ready to finally see the home of a wizard.

CHAPTER THIRTY-TWO

ENGULFED

After taking a shower, putting on his QWA-approved trousers, and rapidly eating three egg-and-bacon sandwiches, Ozzy helped himself to a bowl of cereal and six pancakes. Then he tried playing the record he'd found on the record player in the study.

Remarkably, it worked.

They let the music play while Rin quickly washed and dried his robe and trousers.

"My trousers are in the dryer," the wizard informed Ozzy as a song about a mad world played. "What a lucky machine that dryer is. It's going to be enchanted for months. I'll have to tell Patti that she doesn't need to worry about sorting."

"Do you know this music?" Ozzy asked.

"It's not birds singing," Clark complained.

"Right—what about you, Rin?"

"Tears for Fears."

"I like words that rhyme," Clark admitted.

The album played on and filled the house with music until the dryer buzzed, alerting everyone that Rin's trousers and robe were ready.

Ozzy took the record to his room, and then met Rin and the bird in the garage. It felt like a fitting place to make plans. Sheriff Wills obviously didn't trust Ozzy to stay put. There was now a second police vehicle parked down on the beach behind the house.

"I can try to mess with their minds," Ozzy said. "But Wills will know that I did."

"Or," Clark suggested, "we could take one of these cars and see if they'll chase after us."

There were three cars in the four-car garage, a Honda that Patti drove some days, a truck that she used to haul things when needed, and the white car that Ozzy and Clark were very familiar with. Patti had driven her Audi to the airport, so that space was open. There were also three motorcycles parked on the far side of the garage, including the one Ozzy used to ride to the Cloaked House before being banned from doing so.

"Both fine ideas," Rin told them. "But I'm in the mood for magic."

"Really?" Clark asked. "You're actually going to do something?"

"No, but Ozzy is."

Ozzy and Clark groaned.

"Like what?" the boy asked curiously.

"You didn't get those trousers by accident," Rin said solemnly.

"Rin," Ozzy pleaded, "we need to get to your house."

"Then make it happen," he said. "You passed the Cinco-Wiz-Com, you are no longer an apprentice—you just haven't kicked it into gear. I can help, but eventually it will be all up to you."

"Okay," Ozzy said, "how about you show me the magical way to slip out of here, and I'll learn from that?"

"That's not helping."

The small canister glued to Clark's side fell off and dropped onto the garage floor. It rolled under the truck.

"I don't think this dragon thing is working out," the bird admitted. "I can't fly, and now I can't rain down fire on my enemies."

Clark jumped off Ozzy's shoulder and ducked under the truck to get the canister.

"Don't let him distract you," Rin said kindly. "Think about what you need to do to move us from this spot to another spot on the globe. We are here now, but we could just as easily be somewhere else."

Clark hit his head under the truck and chirped out a few choice words.

"What I'm thinking is that my head hurts," Ozzy said. "And what you're saying makes it hurt worse."

The rushing sound of air raced out from beneath the truck.

"Uh oh," Clark tweeted.

Clark's tweet was immediately followed by flames shooting out from under the vehicle. The black bird shot out to beat the heat.

"I tried to reattach the canister," Clark scream-splained. "I was just testing to see if it still worked!"

The fire reached up around the truck and began to increase in bulk and noise.

"Grab the fire extinguisher!" Rin yelled.

Ozzy pulled a fire extinguisher from the wall near him and threw it to Rin. The wizard pulled out the pin and pressed the trigger. Nothing but a small trickle of foam dripped out.

"Is that how it's supposed to work?" Clark yelled.

"No!" Rin replied. "I just remembered that Patti might have asked me to get this charged."

Flames leapt from the truck to the Honda.

"What'll we do?" Ozzy asked.

"I'm not sure," Rin admitted. "When I accidentally burned down the Cloaked House, I ran."

There was yelling from outside the garage as one of the officers pounded on one of the large garage doors. He had noticed that smoke was spilling out of the garage vents and filling the air with a deeper gray than the surrounding clouds.

Ozzy picked Clark up and ran out the small door at the back of the garage. Rin followed closely behind.

"Run for the trees," Rin yelled. "I've got to grab something. I'll be right with you."

"What about the fire?"

"Just run."

Ozzy didn't want to run away from the scene. He didn't want to leave the garage while it was burning. There was space between the garage and the house, but he couldn't be sure that the fire wouldn't spread. Also, his room was above the cars and he had grown to like it.

"Run!" Rin yelled as the police vehicle on the beach raced in from the back of the house. "Go!"

Ozzy dashed to the trees and ran until he felt sufficiently hidden. He then stopped to wait for Rin. The fire wasn't visible, but up above the trees he could see the smoke.

Clark chirped sadly while sitting on Ozzy's shoulder.

"It'll be okay," Ozzy said, reaching up to pat the top of the bird's head.

"I didn't get the canister."

"*That's* what you're worried about?"

"It was round and metal."

They could hear running and watched the trees. Rin appeared carrying the staff.

"You went back for that?" Ozzy asked with exasperation and disbelief.

"It's irreplaceable."

"Aren't there photo albums in the house?"

"Who can say?"

Ozzy looked up at the smoke above the trees. "You burned down the Cloaked House and now Clark's burned down Patti's garage."

"It was an accident," Clark insisted. "I feel a great sense of loss." Clark looked at both Ozzy and Rin. "Is that what I'm supposed to say?"

"It's perfect," Rin said. "And it's only the garage. Who needs a four-car garage anyway? Now, we should run. My house is just a hop, skip, and a jump away."

Rin led the way as the sound of sirens racing to the fire filled the moist Oregon air.

CHAPTER THIRTY-THREE

NO ONE'S AROUND

Rin's house was much more than a hop, skip, and a jump away. It was more like a run, traverse, and leap away. It was past the far side of Otter Rock, well beyond the town limits. The journey was made even more taxing due to them having to stay hidden and out of sight. And their hiding was complicated by the fact that one of them was dressed like a wizard of sorts, and carrying a staff, and another was sporting red and gray plaid pants.

"You said it was close," Clark complained from on top of Ozzy's shoulder.

"You can try flying," Ozzy pointed out.

"I can't," Clark argued. "My wings are messed up."

"I *can* fix that, once we reach my home," Rin said.

The hike went on for miles, through tall pine trees and rolling hills covered in lime green bushes and white rocks. Eventually, they came to a thin paved road overgrown with weeds growing up through the asphalt. A wooden gate stretched across the road, locked with a chain and padlock to keep cars from having access.

A sign on the gate read:

VERY PRIVATE PROPERTY

"It's just down this road," Rin said, sliding through a two-foot opening on the side of the gate.

"This doesn't seem very welcoming," Clark chirped.

"No one uses this road?" Ozzy asked.

"Only me."

The three of them hiked up the road, and as they did, the asphalt became more cracked and the weeds taller.

"You don't ever drive on this?"

"No, I usually park by the gate. I find the walk helps me think. Did you know that the word *picnic* is French in origin?"

"I didn't," Ozzy admitted. "That's what you think about?"

"That and where I might have put the key to the gate lock," Rin said. "I like picnics. Think of the freedom. You can sit down and eat anywhere. Besides, most restaurants are getting a little out of hand."

"Do you feel that way because you were kicked out of that one in New York?" Clark asked.

"That hostess had it out for me," Rin insisted. "Putting me at a table near the bathroom. Wizards, as you know, have a keen sense of smell."

Ozzy took a second to sniff the air.

"Smells like trees and dirt."

"A much better smell than that table I was placed at. Any rational person would want to put a wizard in the center of the restaurant, to class the place up. And then they gave me attitude when I asked the waiter to wrap up the food someone else hadn't finished."

"That's true," Clark said. "I think they were mostly bothered because you took those leftovers and tried to slip them into the pocket of the people who had left them."

"No room for neighborly these days."

"You should talk," Ozzy said, glancing around at the isolated forest. "You have no neighbors. This place is almost as remote as the Cloaked House."

"I don't like people prying."

Up ahead, arching across the road, was a large rusted sign with painted letters on it. The letters were faded but readable.

WetLand

"What's that for?" Ozzy asked. "Are these wetlands?"

"I didn't put it there," Rin answered. "I sort of won this whole place in a bet."

"Sort of?" Clark asked.

"Well, I bet a friend named Woody that he wouldn't live past forty. When he died at age thirty-nine, he left this all to me."

"That's pretty generous," Ozzy said.

"He owed me. I did some magic work for him. You know, cured a few ailments."

"But he died," Ozzy said.

"Some cures are fickle," the wizard said. "I once helped a man regrow all his hair so he could impress his wife. But . . ." Rin didn't finish his sentence.

"But what?" Ozzy asked.

"Well, his wife wasn't able to see the new hair. She lacked the gift of second sight."

"Do *I* have second sight?" Ozzy asked.

"No, you're up to at least eighth sight."

"His wife left him?"

Rin nodded. "It turned out okay, though. He got this place in the divorce."

"Wait, the hairless man was Woody?"

"Yes, this place was a dream he and his wife had," Rin explained. "But after the divorce Woody got it all. It used to be a small amusement park. Well . . . it never was, but it used to be a place that was *going to be* a small amusement park. Now it's just my home."

They walked under the rusted arch and across a torn-up parking lot. On the far side of the parking lot there was a long wooden fence with a steel gate that said, 'Welcome to WetLand.' Crossing the parking lot, Rin stopped to push open the right half of the gate. It squealed loudly into the wet air.

"That's terrible," Clark howled. "Reminds me of a hinge I once knew."

Once they were all inside the gate, Rin took a moment to stop and motion with the staff.

"This is WetLand Amusement Park."

The wet part was fairly accurate—the ground was squishy from recent rain. And the land part was also accurate, since it was land. Even the amusement part was accurate, because Ozzy and Clark were somewhat amused. But the park part seemed to be stretching it. WetLand was an overgrown and long-forgotten mess. There was an old carousel with a crumbled top and a few small buildings with faded signs. One building said: "Sweet Treats." One said: "Squirt Gun Range." And one just said, "Ho s o Wa rs."

"I think that was House of Waters," Rin explained. "It was some sort of maze."

Past the buildings there was a small rusted roller coaster, most of its track barely standing up, its main loop leaning to the side at an uncomfortable angle.

"That was the Rain Coaster," Rin said as they walked. "It never worked. Woody wasn't an engineer."

"But he liked water?" Ozzy said. "WetLand, House of Waters, Rain Coaster?"

"Who knows?" Rin said happily. "You can't judge a person by one amusement park."

Near the Rain Coaster was a small outdoor amphitheater filled with weeds and decay with a large field in front of it.

"He was going to build a field for a game he invented

called Kick-Run," Rin told them. "It was a lot like soccer, but the goals moved around."

Ozzy was listening to Rin talk, but his mind was preoccupied with what was at the other side of the empty Kick-Run field.

Ozzy squinted to get a better look.

Sitting there like a complicated dream was a large three-story Victorian house, with a gigantic round tower on its east corner that shot ten feet above the third floor. The tower was topped with what looked like a blue shingled wizard's hat. The entire structure was covered with intricate carvings around the windows and the slanted roofs and eaves. A wide front veranda was accessed by a set of grand wooden stairs. The stunning structure was painted a faded green with weak yellow accents. It was worn and in need of care, but it was a sight to behold, standing like a castle surrounded by tall trees and endless rolling landscape.

"*That's* your house?" Ozzy asked in astonishment.

"It's nothing compared to the one in Quarfelt."

"At least this one's real," Clark whispered into Ozzy's ear.

They walked across the Kick-Run field and up the stairs. On the veranda, Rin took a key from the trim above the door and unlocked the ornately carved front door. He pushed it open and the hinges screamed, sounding again similar to the one Clark had known.

The inside of the house was surprisingly clean. Ozzy

would not have been surprised to find the place filled with old trash bags, stacks of phone books, and an unidentifiable smell. But the interior was interesting and his wizard-in-training nose couldn't smell anything rotting. The place was filled with antique furniture and dusty paintings. The ceilings were covered in murals of nature scenes and parts of the night sky. Mixed among the antiques and old furniture were some more modern pieces—a long blue leather couch was pushed up against one wall and there was a black-and-white-checkered La-Z-Boy near one of the windows. The flooring in the house was wood, covered with colorful, old expensive-looking rugs, and the walls were mainly wallpapered in a busy pattern or painted a soft yellow.

"This place is unbelievable," Ozzy said.

"My brother and his wife loved the Victorian style," Rin said. "It's a little stuffy for me."

"Wait," Ozzy said. "Woody was your brother?"

"Yes, my older brother." The wizard sounded wounded. "He always had to do everything first. Even die."

"I'm sorry he passed away," Ozzy said with sincerity.

"Not as sorry as he was," Rin said without it.

Clark was still sitting on Ozzy's shoulder looking around curiously. "Where are the dirt floors?" he asked, sounding disappointed. "And the hammer?"

"Out in the workshop."

"I can't believe how big this house is," Ozzy said. "And there's an amusement park out there."

"It's more like a bunch of overgrown pieces of metal and wood," Rin said. "It's no Harry Potter World."

"Has Sigi ever been here?" Ozzy asked as he looked around.

"No. Patti's afraid of tetanus. Now come on."

Ozzy followed Rin through another room that was bigger than the first and into the kitchen near the back of the house. The large kitchen had an old cast-iron stove, an outdated sink, and a brand-new refrigerator that seemed both out of place and out of time. On the front of the fridge were dozens of colorful magnets. The flooring in the kitchen was linoleum in a colorful red-triangles-and-blue-squares pattern that was also cracking at the edges.

Stepping out of the kitchen, they entered the dining room that housed a table long enough to fit twelve chairs around it. In the corner of the room was an old phonograph with a black vinyl record sitting on it. Clark hopped off Ozzy's shoulder to go take a closer look at it.

"You should sit down," Rin suggested.

Ozzy took a seat at the table. It was covered with a lacy tablecloth made from stiff string.

"I have something I need to take care of," Rin said. "Hold on."

The wizard left Ozzy and Clark alone.

"I'm really glad you're back," Ozzy said to his bird.

"Me too," Clark said affectionately as he perched atop the needle arm of the phonograph. "This thing is amazing." He leaned his head down to read the label on the record beneath him. "What are the Spice Girls? Some sort of food experts?"

"Probably," Ozzy answered. "You can't tell me anything about Quarfelt?"

"No," the bird said, still looking at the needle beneath him. "I can only tell you that I don't think I was there. I don't want to be *that* bird, but I'm still not sure Riny's a wizard. I was built by a scientific thinker and I'm not easily swayed. Whoa, look at that knob."

Clark hopped off the needle arm and over to the round knob that turned the machine on.

"If you weren't in Quarfelt, then where do you think you were?"

"Remember when you found me?" Clark asked.

"Of course," Ozzy said. "You were in that box under the stairs."

"And when I came to, it felt like I had just been sleeping since the day your father put me in there. That's how I felt when Rin pulled me out of that toolbox in his shed. I was just tucked away while he did whatever." Clark hopped back onto the needle arm. "Do you know how many times I've begged Mister Wiz to shapeshift into a bird, or a raven, or a bird?"

"Those are all the same thing."

"Well, he never did."

"He changed into something in the ocean," Ozzy explained. "I wish you had been there, but it jumped out of the water and destroyed the *Spell Boat*."

"I'd be more impressed if that boat wasn't such a piece of—"

"My ears are burning," Rin interrupted as he came back into the dining room.

"Soak them in ice," Clark suggested.

"It's an expression," Rin said. "Like 'two knees don't make an elbow.'"

Ozzy stared at the wizard.

Rin sat down on a chair across from the boy and sighed the kind of sigh that wizards sigh when they want others to notice that they're sighing and hope someone will say something about it.

"Are you okay?" Ozzy asked, falling for Rin's ploy.

The wizard looked seriously at the boy. He cleared his throat in a way that he alone thought sounded authoritative.

"Seriously," Ozzy asked again, "are you okay?"

"Of course," Rin insisted. "Now, you know that I pride myself on always telling people what they need to hear."

"You've told me that a lot of times."

"Good, then you're up to speed about that. Now, we have some important things to discuss."

"Like the fire," Ozzy said.

"It's been contained," Rin reported. "It burned down half the garage, but it did not spread to the house."

"How do you know that?"

Rin shook his head sadly. "I'm a wizard."

"And according to you, I'm a wizard-in-training,"

Ozzy pointed out. "So, why don't you train me to know things like that?"

"Good idea," Rin said. "I'll put that on the agenda for later. But for now, I already know those things, so I'd have to pretend that I didn't just to teach you how to find them out. And that seems like a waste of our time. Like I said, we have important things to discuss."

"More important than a fire?"

"Yes," Rin said happily. "What would you say if I told you I found your parents?"

Clark accidentally scratched the needle across the record. It was a fitting follow-up to the news that had just been delivered.

CHAPTER THIRTY-FOUR

IDEAS AS OPIATES

Ozzy was beside himself. The news Rin had just delivered hit him like a truck filled with cement and possibilities.

"What?" he asked in awe. "You found my parents?"

"No," Rin said casually. "But I wanted to see what kind of reaction I have to look forward to."

Clark hopped from the record player to the table. He cocked his head at Ozzy.

"From the looks of it, I'd say his reaction will be bad."

"Please, I don't want to do this," Ozzy said. "I don't want to even talk about it. I know you're trying to help, but this isn't helping."

"This is what I was hired to do."

"But you can't possibly know if they're alive," Ozzy said boldly. "You found a note on the back of a picture—that's it."

Rin pushed up the right sleeve of his robe. There, written in pen, were the words he had shown Ozzy and Sigi on the *Spell Boat.*

No matter what you are told, we are not dead.

"Have you not taken a shower in three weeks?" Clark asked, disgusted. "Quarfelt? More like Quar*smelt*."

"I prefer baths," Rin said defensively. "And I've had plenty, but I've retraced this on my arm every day so that I don't forget what my purpose is."

Ozzy softened at the reminder of Rin's commitment.

"It's okay," Ozzy said. "You found out more about my parents than I thought. Those words on your arm are nice, but there's no way my mom and dad could have known they would be able to stay alive when they wrote them."

"That's true. Only a wizard can see far enough into the future to make promises now."

"My head hurts," Ozzy told them.

"It's an effect of the serum," Rin said. "We need to find your mother so we can find a solution to your condition."

"My mother? And my dad?"

Rin sat up straight in his chair. He reached across the table and patted Ozzy's hand.

"I have found your father," Rin said seriously. "I'm sorry, Ozzy, but he passed away three years ago."

Clark looked closely at Ozzy's expression.

"Right," Ozzy said. "You're testing me again."

"I'm so sorry."

"You're serious?" Ozzy asked. "He's dead?"

The wizard nodded solemnly. "I've seen his grave."

Clark patted Ozzy on the arm with a wing.

"I saw his grave too," the bird tweeted sadly. "He was like a father to both of us."

"I don't understand," Ozzy said. "How did you find out?"

"Magic," Rin said, sounding like magic was a next-door neighbor that he occasionally shared gossip with. "I've been busy these last few weeks."

"That can't be true," Ozzy said. "Maybe you found the wrong grave."

"Hold on," Rin insisted. "Don't drop the truth while reaching for a more convenient explanation."

Ozzy's grey eyes shook inside of their sockets.

"My dad's dead?"

"I'm sorry."

"My mom's alive?"

"I'm . . . yes."

"You paused," Ozzy said. "You know something else."

"I know a lot of something elses," Rin said soothingly. "You need to remember what I told you at the start. Sometimes the answers we so desperately seek come with sorrow that's heavier than we can imagine."

"Can you take me to my mom?"

"No."

"Use your magic," Ozzy argued. "Or show me how to use mine."

"It's not time."

"I think it is," the boy said boldly. "Or are you not a wizard?"

Rin appeared momentarily conflicted. He took a second to let the room grow quiet and then spoke. "Magic isn't a system of random ideas and rules, Ozzy. There's an order to what it can do. And the limit is not set by the minds of those who doubt—it's set by those who know no boundaries. Automatic garage doors and insulated thermoses are magical. But they are the kind of magic that hovers close to the ground. The kind of magic I need you to believe in can't be seen from where you are, because of how high it flies."

"Like a bird?" Clark asked wistfully.

Ozzy buried his head in his hands. "I don't know what to believe."

Rin took out his list and checked something off.

"Believe nothing," the wizard said, "no matter where you read it, or who has said it, not even if *I* said it, unless it agrees with your own reason and your own common sense."

Ozzy looked up. He could see that Rin's focus wasn't on him. The wizard appeared to be gazing at something just over his shoulder. Turning, Ozzy saw the refrigerator. The very words Rin had just uttered were a quote from the Buddha printed on a magnet.

"Great," the boy said dejectedly.

"Isn't it though?" Rin agreed, putting his list back into his pocket. "Now . . ."

Rin's words were cut short by the sound of metal clicking into place. The dining room had a fourth and unwanted guest.

CHAPTER THIRTY-FIVE

BREAKDOWN

The plane ride back to Oregon wasn't pleasant. Feeling concerned and helpless, Sigi could barely stay seated. It was bad enough that Jon had escaped, but moments before they got on the plane, her mother had been notified that the garage was on fire. Sheriff Wills had told Patti that nobody was hurt, but Ozzy was missing.

"We shouldn't have left him there," Sigi said to her mother.

"He's going to be fine."

"You can't possibly know that."

Patti was stung by the words and Sigi tried to back her comment up.

"Sorry, it's just that nobody knows that."

"Ozzy is the most resilient person I know," Patti said. "He's been through worse than a fire."

The flight attendant stopped the cart near their row

and asked if they'd like something to drink. They both got ginger ale, hoping it would help settle their stomachs.

While sipping their drinks, Patti said, "Ozzy is smart enough to avoid Jon."

"I know," Sigi said, "but I'm not too worried about Jon. I'm worried about the man he worked for."

"Ray?" Patti asked.

"Yes."

"Sheriff Wills said he's hodophobic."

"I'm sure he is," Sigi said with disgust.

"No, not that. He has a fear of traveling," Patti clarified. "He can't leave New York due to the condition."

"Well, that's why he has to get people to do his dirty work."

Sigi finished her drink and leaned over her mom to look out the window.

"Can't they make this thing go any faster?"

"We're already going hundreds of miles per hour."

"Reality is so slow."

Sigi leaned back and tried to control her breathing to keep calm.

CHAPTER THIRTY-SIX

SCRATCH THE EARTH

The sound of sliding metal had come from a gun being held by a hand attached to a man with more bulk than beauty. Ty stood in the doorway to the dining room, pointing a large handgun at the wizard. Clark tried to jump up and attack, but his wings were useless thanks to the few remaining pieces of dragon still stuck to them. Ozzy tried to clip into Ty's thoughts and get him to drop the gun and back away, but it had no effect on the man.

Rin stood up. "You need to leave. This is my house. Okay, maybe some of the paperwork still lists my brother as owner, but when I finally get things taken care of, this will be my house."

Rin lifted his staff to strike a blow, but before he could swing it, a second man hit him on the back of the head and sent the wizard and his hat sailing.

Rin fell to the floor, not moving.

Clark did his best to fly up into Ty's face, but one of his

spikes got caught on the long lacy tablecloth and he pulled the fabric up and over himself. Thrashing around, Clark chirped and tweeted wildly. One of the ogres kicked the thrashing tablecloth and sent Clark and the tablecloth flying against the wall with a crash. They fell to the ground in a heap of lace and material.

"Stop this!" Ozzy ordered.

"I'll give the commands," Ty said.

He grabbed Ozzy by the arm and dragged him from the kitchen and out a back door.

"Take the car!" Ty shouted to the second ogre. "We'll meet you later."

The second ogre ran off in the direction of the WetLand parking lot.

Ty pulled the boy down the stairs and into the grass behind the house. In the distance, Ozzy could see bits of the overgrown amusement park and wished his life was more fun than fear.

A powerful noise began to fill the air and as Ozzy looked up, he saw a helicopter descending from the sky, landing in the center of the Kick-Run field. The helicopter was painted green and had two open sides. A single pilot was flying it.

"Hurry," Ty yelled as he pushed the boy toward the helicopter. "Move!"

Wind and noise circled Ozzy as he was shoved into the machine.

"Take us out of here!" Ty yelled at the pilot. "Now!"

As the helicopter began to lift, Rin came charging out

of the back door of the house, his staff in one hand and the tablecloth in another. Clark was still trying to free his talons from the material as Rin ran. The wizard's robe caught on the bottom of the back stairs and caused him to fly forward onto the ground. As he was flung down, the staff flew from his hands and went shooting through the air, the tablecloth caught on the back of it. Clark ripped free and spiraled down to the ground with his one good wing.

The staff connected perfectly with the back rotor of the helicopter. With a tremendous crack, the stick splintered into a thousand pieces and the tablecloth tangled in the damaged rotor.

The helicopter listed to the right. It was only fifteen feet in the air and as it spun out of control, the skids caught the Rain Coaster's main loop. The machine was pulled back down to earth with an earsplitting screech. Ty flew out of the helicopter and landed on his side on the ground. The pilot slammed up against the windshield and cracked the glass with his helmet. Ozzy was thrown into a black netting at the back of the helicopter.

Rin got to his feet and took off running. He stopped just before reaching the downed helicopter to lean over and pick up a small piece of his staff.

"It was an original Gene Payton," the wizard lamented.

"Leave that!" Clark screamed. "Ozzy!"

Rin helped Ozzy climb out of the helicopter and steady himself. The machine's engine was still making an uncomfortable sound, and there was a large gash in the earth where the blades had come to a stop. Twenty feet to the right, Ty was lying peacefully in the long grass.

"Is he breathing?" Ozzy asked.

"Yes," Rin said. "What a shame. That roller coaster was Woody's life work."

"Your brother's dead," Clark reminded the wizard.

"Yeah," Ozzy echoed. "Just like we'll be if we don't get out of here."

"That's not happening," a voice behind them said.

Rin, Ozzy, and Clark turned to see Ogre Two. He had gone for the car, but now he was pointing a gun at them. His sweaty face made it clear that he was confused by the turn of events.

"I don't know how you did that," the ogre said, "but you're coming with me."

"Let the boy go," Rin said.

"It's the boy Ray wants," the man laughed. "Who wants a wizard?"

The ogre's laugh was cut short by a blow to the back of his head. The man dropped like a fat sack of wheat and there, directly behind the fallen ogre, was Jon.

"I want a wizard," Jon said, answering the now-unconscious ogre.

Ozzy was stupefied by the average man's sudden appearance and help.

"Thanks," Rin said, acting as if he had thought that

would happen. "Now, if you could tie these two up and make sure the pilot's okay, that would be much appreciated."

It was Jon's turn to look surprised.

"But I've been looking for you."

"Well, here I am," Rin replied. "But we have to run."

"I want to go too."

Rin looked at Jon. "You know the old saying . . ."

"What?" Jon looked thirsty for any knowledge the wizard might impart.

"I'm not sure," Rin said. "Just think up something comforting in your head. Come on, Ozzy."

"I'm not letting you go," Jon insisted.

Ozzy took over the man's brain and sent him walking to Ty.

"That's impressive," Clark said with a whistle.

"When it actually works," Ozzy replied.

The three of them ran through the park and out the front gate. There was a white unmarked van in the parking lot that Ogre Two was supposed to have gone back to.

"We don't have any keys," Ozzy said.

Rin chanted a few words and held out his hand. In his right palm was a set of keys.

"Stop saying *don't*," he lectured Ozzy. "It's a word that doesn't fit in the vocabulary of a wizard."

Clark looked longingly at the keys as he stood on Ozzy's shoulder.

"Get in," the wizard cheered.

Ozzy and Clark climbed into the passenger's seat as Rin took the wheel.

"Remember when we needed a car?" the wizard asked casually.

Ozzy nodded.

"Good times," Rin said happily.

The wizard turned the key, threw the van into reverse, and then tore out of the parking lot and down the thin, overgrown road.

CHAPTER THIRTY-SEVEN

GO SLOW

The ogres' van was large, with two tinted windows on the back doors. There was a driver's and a passenger seat, but in the back, there was just a long padded bench. The engine was powerful, which made it easy for Rin to drive along the highway at a speed much higher than the posted signs were suggesting.

"Is that the best you can do?" Clark asked as he sat perched on the dashboard.

"There's no limit to the best a wizard can do."

"There should be," Ozzy said, acting like the only adult in the car. "You should slow down. You'll get pulled over."

"Normally wizards like to obey the law, but we have someplace to be."

"Where?" Ozzy asked.

"Squeeze your brain," Rin challenged. "I bet you can figure it out."

"My brain's not functioning right," Ozzy said. "I couldn't control most of those men back there."

"It worked on Jon," Clark said, hopping down onto Ozzy's lap. The poor bird was a mess of gray plastic pieces falling off and tangling up his tail and talons. "Could you get this stuff off of me?"

"You don't like being a dragon?" Rin asked, disappointed.

"I miss being me. Besides, dragon appropriation is not very BC—bird-culture," he explained.

Ozzy began to pick at and pull off any bits of dragon he could get to. He pried a piece of plastic out of Clark's left wing and the bird made a noise of relief.

"Why do you think what I did worked on Jon but not on the other men?" Ozzy asked.

"Are you asking me?" Clark said. "Because I don't really know. Genetics?"

"No," Ozzy said, patting the bird's back affectionately.

"I have my suspicions," Rin said. "But it wouldn't be prudent to make guesses at this point."

"I don't mind guesses," Ozzy said.

"Spoken like a true trainee."

"Let me guess—you don't have any idea why I couldn't control them?"

"Duck!" Rin reached out with his right arm and motioned for Ozzy to get down.

The boy and bird both scrunched down in the front seat. Ozzy looked up and saw that Rin had taken off his hat.

"What's happening?" Ozzy asked.

"There's a police car on the highway up ahead," the wizard reported. "Everyone's looking for you. And since they're aware that we know each other, I thought it best to take my hat off. It's me being prudent again. Now, I'm going to pass them and see if it's Sheriff Wills driving."

"That doesn't seem very prudent," Ozzy hissed from his crouched position.

Rin pressed on the gas and sped up alongside the police car. The driver was a female officer by the name of Lena Smit.

"It's not him," Rin reported.

Officer Smit glanced over at the van and Rin smiled and waved at her.

"What are you doing?" Ozzy asked.

"It's important to be nice," Rin said defensively. "You never know who might be having a bad day."

Ozzy stared up at him.

"I saw that saying on Instagram," Rin informed them. He reached into his robe pocket and pulled out his phone.

"You can't text and drive!" Ozzy insisted. "I thought your phone was broken?"

"It is," Rin said. "This is a backup."

He tried to hand the phone to Ozzy. "Could you take a picture of me driving?"

"No, just slow down," Ozzy pleaded.

Rin let off the gas and dropped back behind the police car.

"Is she leaving?" Ozzy asked.

"No," Clark said. "She's slowing down."

The police car decreased its speed until it was going so slow that Rin felt compelled to go around it. He pressed on the gas again and, without using his blinker, switched lanes and passed the officer up.

The lights on the cop car flashed on.

"Looks like we have company," the wizard said, looking in the rearview mirror.

"Really?" Ozzy asked incredulously. "You pulled up beside her, showed your face, and now you're surprised that she wants you to pull over?"

"I've told you before, I'm never surprised."

Rin pressed on the gas and shot forward.

"This thing has some guts," he said happily.

Officer Smit was in full pursuit.

"You're going to try and outrun her?" Clark said excitedly. "Nice. Takes me back to the time we rode on that train. Hey," the bird said, as if having an epiphany, "do you think you can drive us onto another train, or maybe a boat? Wait," Clark said, jumping up onto the dashboard and looking out the window, "what about a blimp?"

"Don't make this worse," Ozzy begged.

Clark looked offended.

"We should just stop."

"I think we should go faster," Clark argued.

Ozzy stared out the tinted back windows at the police car racing up behind them. Seeing no other option, and despite his own wishes, he connected with Officer Smit's mind. She pressed on the brakes and brought her car to a quick stop on the side of the road as the white van continued farther.

Rin glanced casually into the rearview mirror and witnessed the parked cop car behind them growing smaller and smaller.

"It's amazing how magic works," he said. "So reliable."

"I did that," Ozzy told him.

"I know."

"It's not magic—it's my mind."

"As if the two aren't connected," Rin said wistfully.

"We're not out of trouble," Ozzy argued. "She'll shake that off in a few minutes and continue after us."

"Look at you predicting the future," Rin said proudly. "I think you're having a magical growth spurt. You're going to need new trousers soon."

Ozzy's head was spinning, but he couldn't deny that the journey was beginning to feel magical. Rin never seemed to worry about the things that he did. And magically, events seemed to play out just as he always said they would.

"Don't you ever worry about things not working?" Ozzy asked, putting Clark in his lap.

"Of course," Rin admitted, "but only until I remember how much I hate the feeling. Now, let's get to where we're going."

The wizard pressed on the gas and flew forward as Ozzy picked dragon bits off Clark.

CHAPTER THIRTY-EIGHT

YOU WON'T BE HOME SOON

Patti and Sigi were making good time. They had landed just over an hour before and were already past Corvallis and heading down toward the coast. They had been notified by Sheriff Wills that the fire had been put out and that there was no damage to the main house. They had also been told that Ozzy was still unaccounted for.

"This is too much." Patti was frazzled from the quick trip home and the circumstances that had brought it about. "What's happened to our quiet, simple life?"

"Sorry," Sigi said, as if it were her fault.

"It's your dad," Patti admitted. "His illness is going to be the death of me."

"He's not ill," Sigi said defensively.

"Yes, he is!" Patti shouted back, no longer trying to speak calmly. "He needs help. He's going to harm someone and then you'll see that the magic he's claiming to have isn't real."

"Can we please talk about this later?" Sigi begged.

"This is happening now," Patti said with force. "We can't find a solution to what is going on without talking."

"This isn't one of your lectures or a speech you give," Sigi said. "This can't be analyzed and charted. You don't know what to do, because this is not a spreadsheet. This is something you don't understand, so you refuse to believe."

"You're my daughter," Patti said. "I'm going to put a stop to all this."

"How? Are you going to keep me from seeing my dad, or kick Ozzy out?"

"If that's what it takes."

"You can't do that."

"I'll do whatever I need to if it means keeping you safe."

"You can't stop this!"

Patti slammed on the brakes. It would have been a fitting thing to do to prove her point, but she had stopped for a different reason, and that reason was because she hoped to avoid hitting the car in front of her. She had been so involved in arguing that she hadn't noticed the line of stopped cars. The Audi came to a halt just inches away from the back bumper of a blue truck. The jarring stop caused their seatbelts to lock up and stole their breath.

"Are you okay?" Patti asked.

"I'm fine," Sigi insisted. "I . . . don't believe it."

Sigi pointed out the front window at a figure running up the road. Patti followed the finger and saw the same figure.

Sigi smiled.

Patti did not.

Running up the highway was Rin. His hair, beard, robe, and flared trousers were blowing in the wind. He looked both majestic and maladjusted. The stopped cars in front of Patti and Sigi were honking and yelling things at the wizard as he passed.

Patti and Sigi got out of their vehicle.

Rin wove through the two cars in front of them and ran directly to Sigi's side.

"What are you doing here?" Patti shouted as she stood by her open door.

"Trying to find you."

"And you just happened to be stuck in the same traffic as we are?"

"No," Rin said with a wave. "I just happened to be the cause of this traffic. I'm parked across both lanes about a mile down the road."

"You did this?" Patti said with disgust. "Brian, this is unacceptable."

"It's Rin, and it had to be done," he said cheerfully. "We need Sigi."

"What?" Patti argued.

"I came to find her," the wizard said.

Sigi looked pleased.

"Come on," Rin instructed her. "We'll run to where I'm parked."

"Parked?" Patti hollered. "You mean where you're blocking traffic!"

"Some things can be two things at once," Rin said, sounding like a third-grade teacher explaining multiplication to his students.

"She's not going with you!"

"Yes, I am," Sigi said.

"Then I'm coming too."

Rin moved around the car so that he was closer to Patti.

"You can't come," he said. "I know you and I have our differences, but you have to trust me on this."

"*Differences*," Patti said. "Differences are things like one person liking cilantro when the other one doesn't. This isn't a difference; this is a crisis."

"Wait," Rin said. "Are you mad because I didn't like those enchiladas you made with all that cilantro?"

"That was over ten years ago, and no, that's *not* what this is about."

Traffic was backing up even further behind them. The impatient cars were all idling and wondering what the problem was keeping them standing still. Had the ones near Patti's car rolled down their windows they would have been able to hear the explanation.

"Sigi can't go with you," Patti insisted.

Rin smiled.

"We have joint custody," he reminded her.

"Really?" Patti put her hands on her hips, looking ready for a fight. "You've barely been around."

"Even more reason why I should make things right."

"Please, Mom," Sigi said as she stood on the other side of the car. "I won't do anything stupid."

"The very fact that you want to go makes me doubt your judgment."

"We're going to help Ozzy find what he needs," Rin said calmly. "I know I've provided you with more challenges than most ex-wives get, but this has to happen."

"Will it be dangerous?" she asked.

"Not at all."

"I should come."

"No," Rin said a bit too quickly, "you need to help Sheriff Wills understand that we're fine."

Rin and Sigi began to walk backwards and away from Patti.

"I have no choice?" Patti asked angrily.

"You always have a choice," the wizard said. "You're just having to choose the harder one."

"This is kidnapping," Patti shouted.

"I'm not a kid," Sigi yelled as she began to jog off. "Thanks, Mom!"

Patti growled and shouted. "Call me and let me know what's happening."

"Of course," Rin said, beginning to jog as well.

"Not you," Patti insisted.

The wizard and his daughter took off running down the car-covered road. Everyone had their motors running as they waited for whatever was up ahead to be straightened out so that they could move on.

When they reached the white van, Sigi saw that it was parked in the perfect spot, blocking both lanes and not leaving enough space on either side for cars to get through. People were standing outside of their vehicles talking loudly on their phones, calling anyone they could think of to come move the van.

Rin pressed the button on the key fob and unlocked the doors. As quickly as they could, Rin and Sigi climbed into the van and the wizard started the engine. Everyone in the vicinity began yelling unkind things at them. A man pounded angrily on the front window.

"Hurry," Sigi yelled.

Rin backed up two feet and then, like a professional driver, twisted the steering wheel and swung the vehicle to the right. With another twist, the van straightened out and shot down the road and toward the ocean.

"I didn't realize he was running off to get *you*," a voice said from the back of the van.

Sigi turned and saw Ozzy sitting on the padded bench. He had been hiding from the rows of traffic the poorly parked van had created.

"Ozzy!" she said happily.

"Hey, what am I? Scrap metal?"

Sigi spotted Clark on the floor and smiled even wider.

The bird shot up onto Sigi's lap and stood on her knees. She put her hand out and the metal bird pecked at her palm.

"I am so happy to see you," she said excitedly.

"I *am* fun to look at."

"You could have told me we were going to get Sigi," Ozzy complained.

"I told you to squeeze your brain," the wizard said. "I thought you'd be able to figure out that we can't move forward if we're not complete."

Sigi turned her head and looked at her dad like it was the first time she had ever really seen him. "Thanks, Dad."

"Yes, yes," Rin said brushing off the affection, "save that for later. We have more important things to talk about. For starters, how was Harry Potter World?"

Ozzy didn't let Sigi answer. Instead he filled her in on everything that had happened since she left three days ago. It felt like a world of information, but more than that, it felt otherworldly to have everyone back together.

"So where are we going now?" Sigi asked.

"California," Rin said.

"What?" Ozzy asked.

"I just came from there," Sigi reminded him. "We're not going there just so you can go to Harry Potter World, are we?"

Rin looked hurt. "Of course not. But remember, like things, journeys can have multiple purposes." Rin sighed.

"Not that it matters—we're not going to that part of California."

"What part?" Ozzy asked.

"It's just across the border. Should take us a little over four hours to get there."

"Sheriff Wills will be looking for us," Ozzy said.

"Not where we're going."

Ozzy glanced around the van. There was a wizard driving, the girl he liked most in the world in the passenger seat, and a metal bird that finally resembled the one he had grown up with sitting in her lap.

Clark looked at Ozzy.

"You okay?" the bird asked. "You look strange."

"I'm fine," he answered honestly. "I was just—"

"I think Ozzy needs to stop for one of those water seats," Clark chirped.

"You mean a toilet?" Rin asked.

"Humans really mislabel a lot of their stuff," the bird complained.

Rin pulled off at the next exit to get gas, visit the water seat, and stock up on snacks.

CHAPTER THIRTY-NINE

THE BURIAL GROUND

It was seven P.M. when they finally crossed over the border between Oregon and California. And it was seven-seventeen when Rin drove the white van thorough the Yeltin Cemetery gates.

"We're at a cemetery?" Sigi asked needlessly. "Again?"

Rin stopped the vehicle and they all got out.

"This way."

The boy, the girl, and the bird all followed the wizard.

It was a small cemetery with only a few hundred graves. There were trees surrounding the gates and trees shooting up between some headstones. There were also a few granite benches and a single mausoleum. A couple of the graves had dead flowers on them from loved ones who had been there recently, but not that recently. The grass between the graves was well trimmed and speckled with small yellow flowers. There were no other people around, and the sky was beginning to grow dark.

There were no people, but there were plenty of bugs.

Everyone swatted at their arms and faces as Rin led them to a grave located in the northeast corner of the cemetery, near one of the granite benches. The wizard stood in front of a plain gray headstone and watched Ozzy approach.

Ozzy knew what was happening—no words had been said, no explanation given, but as a wizard-in-training, or as a human with more than two brain cells, he had figured out where they were and what he was walking up to.

"My father's grave," he said to Rin before even looking at the headstone.

Rin slapped his neck and nodded.

Ozzy looked down and read the words chiseled into the granite headstone.

E. O. TOFFY

"No dates?" Sigi asked, swatting away a bug almost as big as Clark.

"That's not right," Ozzy said softly. "Doesn't that mean he's still alive?"

"No," Rin said kindly. "He is the opposite of alive." Not liking the way he'd phrased it the wizard tried again. "He is no longer undead? Wait, that's worse. How about, like old food, he is perished?"

"Wow," Clark said. "I always forget how bad you are at some things. Luckily, you constantly remind me of that fact."

Ignoring Clark and wanting to get it right, Rin took another solemn stab at it. "Ashes to ashes, butt to dust."

"Seriously, Dad," Sigi begged. "Stop talking."

Rin was sweating now, much to the delight of the mosquitos. "What I'm trying to say is that your father is resting in places—in place. He is resting in this place."

"Beautiful," Clark said sarcastically.

Rin nodded proudly.

Sigi apologized for both Ozzy's father's death, and her father's poor choice of words.

"I don't understand," Ozzy said as they looked at the headstone with so little information on it. "This could be for someone named Ed Otto Toffy. How do you know it's my dad?"

"I was here last week. I talked to the grave-digging man who buried him," Rin said as he put a hand on Ozzy's shoulder. "He had the paperwork with the details and dates. It was requested that nothing but his initials and last name be on the stone."

"Who requested that?"

"Your mother," Rin said, sounding like he was telling a joke.

"Burn," Clark chirped, not realizing he wasn't.

Sigi picked up Clark and carefully held his beak closed.

"I don't understand," Ozzy said angrily. "You said he died three years ago."

Rin swatted and nodded.

"That means three years ago, my mother was right

here. She was four hours away from me as I sat in the Cloaked House alone? Why didn't she go there? Why didn't she bury my dad at the place he was taken from?"

"Your mother informed Mr. Gravedigger that it had been your father's wish to be buried in California."

"Why California?" Ozzy asked. "I don't remember them having a connection to this state."

"Digger said that your mother seemed confused. She paid double what the grave and burial usually cost and left the moment your father was lowered down. I don't think your mother is well."

"Another sick burn," Clark chirped.

Sigi clamped back down on the beak.

"Ozzy, I don't think your mother is well," Rin repeated apologetically.

"How can you *know* that?" the boy said forcefully. "We don't even know for sure that she's alive. It was three years ago that my dad was buried—she could be dead too."

Ozzy sat down on the granite bench and Sigi joined him.

"You're not wrong," Rin said respectfully. "I know that for years after your parents were taken from you, Charles and Ray forced them to work on the serum. When they continued to fail, they were used as test subjects, injecting the serums into themselves to see if they worked. They never got it right, and over time they became ill from the effects and were then disposed of by Ray. By that point they were no longer themselves. Their brains were addled, and their ambitions and desires had poisoned them from wanting anything other than the control of other minds. The Cloaked House wasn't the only safe house they had set up. They went there to get away from Ray the first time. But they also had a lab in Colorado, and a submarine off the coast of Oregon. I think at that point they were hoping to recreate the formula so that they could best Ray. But they had forgotten too many things. Their minds no longer remembered the Cloaked House or the tapes with the formula. Or . . ." Rin paused. "Or you, Ozzy."

Sigi put her arm around the boy she had first met years ago on the beach. He was so much taller and wiser— and much more wounded. She leaned against him and squeezed her fingers around his arm while waving away a bug with her other hand.

"I realize it does nothing to help," Rin said softly, "but I want you to know that when I first told you that the answers we might find won't always be warm, I was not thinking they'd be this cold."

Ozzy raised his head and stuck out his chin. His dark hair blew softly into his eyes as he looked out at the dying light. His grey eyes matched the color of the granite bench and made his insides look rigid and rock-like.

"How do you know all of this?" he asked Rin.

"I found their lab in Colorado," he answered. "There were countless papers and books. What they didn't tell me, your mother did."

"You've met my mother?" the boy said with a face full of shock.

The wizard nodded.

Ozzy was speechless.

"I can't believe it," Sigi said in disbelief. "You found her? You were hired to locate her, and you did?"

Another wizardly nod.

"Why didn't you bring her back?" Ozzy asked.

"I tried." For the first time since Ozzy had known Rin, he saw tears in the wizard's eyes. "She's not well. She disappeared before I could get her to come with me."

Clark hopped onto Ozzy's right shoulder and patted his forehead with his right wing. The bird, the wizard, and the girl all knew that it was a moment to not speak. After a few minutes, the bird forgot that.

"I can't remember a lot about your parents," Clark said as he jumped off Ozzy's shoulder and onto the top of the headstone. "I know your mother was kind to your father. And I know that your father could get so caught up in his work that he'd have to shelve me away to think clearly. But I know that they must have been amazing to have a person like you. And even if he's dead . . ." Clark pointed down to the grave with his left wing. "And she's lost it, that doesn't take away from the fact that at one point you were loved and that is more than most objects or humans ever have."

Clark flew onto Ozzy's lap.

The bird's words seemed to lighten the mood in a small way.

"This is it?" Ozzy finally asked. "You've done what you were hired to do, Rin. You found my parents. And like Clark said, one's dead, and the other's lost and doesn't remember me."

Rin and Sigi and Clark stared at the trainee as he tried to process everything. Ozzy glanced up at Rin.

"Thanks, Rin," the boy said sincerely.

Sigi watched her dad, her own eyes filled with worry.

"It's okay," Ozzy continued. "You told me that the answers might be more painful than not knowing. But you were wrong." The boy sat up straight. "I would rather know everything as it is than be left in the dark. I know my parents loved me when they were taken. I know they were changed by the greed and power the serum caused. And I know I want to be like them in good ways, but I don't have to continue with any of the evil they put into the world."

Ozzy looked around at the cemetery as the night grew another shade darker.

"Can I at least get a ride back to Otter Rock?" he asked.

"What do you mean?" Sigi said.

"You two have done enough."

"Two?" Clark complained.

"You three," Ozzy corrected himself. "But I was planning to take you with me."

"Hold on," Rin said. "This isn't over. I'm not going to close the case and go off to Quarfelt to relax. We're going to finish this by taking Ray down and saving the world."

"No," Ozzy said, "it's too dangerous. I need to just go away."

"You don't run away from problems," the wizard counseled. "You run toward solutions."

"Well, my solution is to run," Ozzy insisted. "Let me go and you'll never have to deal with this again."

"Do you not understand how family works?" Rin asked. "Do you think Sigi and Clark and Patti and I are just here for you to bump into while you try to figure life out? No. Wrong. You are more important to me than the family I was assigned in Quarfelt."

"They assign you families?" Clark complained.

"Yes," Rin said, "and I did not do well."

"You don't need to do this," Ozzy said. "If I'm gone, the formula is lost forever."

"And so are you," Sigi pointed out. "We're not letting you go. And if you sneak off, Clark will find us and rat you out."

"That's true," Clark said. "I'm not good at minding my own business."

"And remember . . ." The dying light was behind Rin's back, making the wizard's silhouette tall and commanding. It also had the effect of making his voice sound more intimidating than usual. "You are a wizard-in-training. I must see you through. And you'll need every ounce of magic you can muster. It won't hurt to have someone with experience along for the ride."

"And that's you?" Ozzy asked.

"You know I hate to brag," Rin said humbly.

Clark was confused. "Nobody knows that."

"I don't want to hurt anyone else," the boy said, looking at Sigi. "I don't want anything else to burn down, or be torn apart, or to die because of me. I don't want to control anyone's will. It tears me apart."

"How about you give me until the end of the week?" Rin said. "If you're not happy with the results you can have your money back."

"What money? I have never paid you."

"That's true. Maybe you should give me some so that I can give it back if needed."

"That makes no sense," Ozzy insisted.

"Reality rarely does," the wizard spoke. "Sure, things fall when they are dropped, and get wet when they're rained on, but hearts break in thousands of ways. Futures change with the wave of a hand. And minds never seem to settle in until it's too late and life is waning in full."

The four of them stared at the tombstone as the bugs continued to buzz and bite.

"That's what makes life so fantastic," Rin continued. "Most don't know what tomorrow will bring, but there is always the guarantee of change."

"How do we stop Ray?" Ozzy asked.

"We stop him with a bird, a trainee, a full-fledged wizard, and his remarkable daughter."

"Seems like a powerful team," Clark squawked. "Especially the bird part."

"What about my mother?"

"I found her once," Rin said. "I will do my best to find her again. Now, let's make like a wizard and leave."

"It's 'make like a tree and leaf,'" Sigi corrected.

"That makes no sense. Trees never leave. But wizards are constantly moving. Unless you're talking about Spencer. He mistakenly turned himself into a mouthless mountain range. How can you turn yourself back if you can't speak the spell?"

The bugs were growing thicker.

"Nature needs to knock it off," Rin said, slapping at a mosquito on his left ear.

Having had their fill of the great outdoors, graveyards, and grief, they all made like a wizard and left.

CHAPTER FORTY

CHANGE

Ray sat in his office fuming. If it were physically possible, his ears would have been smoldering from the intense anger he felt inside. The call from Ty had not been what he was expecting, because the call had come from another source, who reported that Ty, the pilot of the helicopter, and another man had been taken into custody by the local police. An anonymous call had been placed, and when the police showed up at WetLand, they found the three individuals tied tightly to the bottom of a rusty roller coaster.

Ray wished the wizard hadn't broken his hourglass. Because had it still been on his desk, he would have personally picked it up and heaved it through a window.

Charles had failed.

Jon had failed.

Ty had failed.

Ray was running out of contacts he could trust with

such an important task. The trouble with what he was trying to accomplish was that he couldn't let just anyone find out what he was after. If others knew the power Ozzy possessed, the competition to get it would be out of control.

An idea came into his carefully coiffed head. There *was* someone else he could use. Someone who would make sure the job was completed as needed.

Ray pressed a button on his desk.

A mere moment later, Susan entered the office doors.

"Yes, Mr. Dench?"

"Sit," he said. "I have some instructions that need to be followed."

Susan sat on one of the leather chairs and took out her notepad. It was an antiquated way for someone to take notes, but once Susan scribbled anything on the paper it was always followed and executed to a T.

"Your instructions?" she said neatly.

Ray let her know what needed to be done.

The instructions were shocking, but ever the professional, Susan kept a straight face and jotted down every word.

CHAPTER FORTY-ONE

WHEN THE RAVEN CROWS THRICE

The van was an upgrade from the little white ex-hybrid. Ozzy was able to stretch out on the padded bench in the back and Sigi could lower her seat all the way down. At the end of the bench near Ozzy's feet, Clark made a nest from the wrappers of the snacks they'd eaten. It was comfortable and crinkly. Rin drove them north as he listened to a radio program about aliens. Every few minutes he would comment about what was being said.

"Some people are so gullible."

"That doesn't sound true."

"If there were aliens, you'd see millions of pictures of them on Instagram."

When they reached the turnoff for Otter Rock, Rin kept rolling.

An hour outside of Portland, the wizard pulled the van over onto a dirt road hidden by tall trees and thick brush.

With the vehicle parked, he leaned back in his own chair and got comfortable.

"We'll stop here for a few minutes," Rin explained. "Wizards don't need sleep, but we enjoy closing our eyes."

He closed his eyes and instantly began snoring.

Three hours later they were all still sleeping, and Clark was bored.

The bird decided to wake everyone up by attempting to imitate a rooster. His efforts produced an unpleasant noise that any actual rooster would be ashamed of.

"For the sake of all things audible," Rin complained. "What is that sound?"

Clark did it again.

Sigi blinked and glanced around the van. "Is something dying?"

"No," Clark said with attitude, "I'm just doing what those fat birds do on farms."

"Roosters?" Sigi asked.

"I don't know whose farm they do it on."

Clark tried once more.

"Stop it!" Sigi begged.

"It's an awful sound," Clark agreed. "How do they shut those other birds up when they do it? Rocks?"

Ozzy sat up on the bench. "You don't throw rocks at birds!"

"Darts?"

"Would you like it if someone threw a dart at you?" Sigi asked.

"If I could keep it."

Ozzy looked at the clock on the dashboard of the van.

"I think you slept for more than a few minutes."

Rin adjusted his seat and straightened his hat and robe as best as he could.

"I was having such a good time with my eyes closed I decided to keep at it."

"Where are we?" Sigi smacked her lips and looked at herself in the mirror on the visor. "I miss my toothbrush."

"We're about an hour or so from where we need to be." Rin shivered as he said the words.

"Are you cold?" Ozzy asked. The van was stuffy and hot, and the wizard's shivering seemed out of place.

"No," Rin said. "We should get going."

The wizard shivered again.

"Are you sick?" Clark asked. "Your hair looks unhealthy."

"I'm trying a new conditioner," Rin replied. "But I'm not sick. I'm just aware that we are going to do what has to be done."

"What has to be done?" Sigi asked. "Is it one of your list items? Because we still don't know where we're going."

"We're going to a spot just outside of Portland."

"To see your sister?" Ozzy asked. "Because if we are, I'd like to get something to eat before we get there."

"No," Rin replied.

"What spot?" Sigi asked.

Rin looked around the van as if someone else might be listening.

"I need to tell you something," he said seriously.

Clark squawked. "Before you tell anyone anything, could someone crack a window? I want to stretch my wings," Clark explained. "Also, I don't want to hear what the wiz is going to say. No offense, Riny."

"Some taken," the wizard said, nodding politely.

Sigi opened her door and Clark shot out into the forest. The fresh air coming in smelled of pine and grass and helped suppress the scent of morning breath.

Rin cleared his throat. "In the past . . ." He paused to sniff. "Well, it is important for everyone . . . for people to have answers." The wizard adjusted his hat so that the brim came down over his left eye. "We are going to a place with answers."

"Good," said Sigi.

"But these answers come with a cost."

"Like money?" Ozzy asked.

"If only. Then I could just pay and move on."

"You mean Ozzy could pay."

"You're right, I do mean that," Rin agreed. "But that's not the case now. These answers could very well be the death of me."

"Then don't do it," Ozzy said. "I told you, I don't want anyone to get hurt."

Rin looked at the boy and smiled. "It's too late for

that," he said compassionately. "I still have a knot on the back of my head from where that ogre hit me."

"I mean hurt worse," Ozzy clarified.

"No," the wizard spoke, "we will get what we need. We will tempt fate and be triumphant."

"You can see that?" Sigi asked. "You can see that we'll be okay?"

Rin shook his head. "I can only see that it will be worth it."

Clark flew back into the van through the open door.

"Wow," he said happily. "I can really move without all that gunk on me. What'd I miss?"

"My dad wants to tempt fate," Sigi said.

"Who's that?" the bird asked, trying to sound interested.

"It's not a who," Ozzy said. "It's a thing."

"Who's it?" the bird said, sounding sincerely interested.

Rin fielded the question. "Fate is the very thing we have had on our side since the beginning."

"Is it the thing that almost got me killed on that mountain?" Ozzy asked. "Or is it the thing that burned down the Cloaked House? Or is it the thing that blew up the boat?"

"It's all of those things," Rin said happily. "But now, we must head into the ugly side of it."

"Must we?" the bird asked. "Really?"

Rin started the van and drove north toward the next item on his list.

CHAPTER FORTY-TWO

PALE SHELTER

Because everyone was feeling nervous both as individuals and as a group, Rin made a point to stop for breakfast in Portland first. They had a meal at a place called Biscuits I Love You. The food was as magical as breakfast food can be. The biscuits were football-sized and tasted like a soft bit of handspun heaven. The smell of all things fried and creamy filled the air. And the eggs and bacon they ordered were cooked to the kind of perfection that only a wizard could produce.

"I bet the chef is one of us," Rin said as he pushed a bite of gravy-covered biscuit into his mouth.

"If he is, he's certainly ranked higher than me," Ozzy replied.

"I wish we could see his trousers," the wizard added.

"Please don't try," Sigi insisted.

Rin took a picture of his meal to post on Instagram.

After a breakfast that none of them would soon forget,

they climbed back into the van. Ozzy gave Clark a bit of greasy hash browns he had smuggled out. The bird couldn't taste, but he liked the feeling of grease on his beak.

"Loosens me up," Clark said as he mashed the fried potatoes around.

"Ready?" Rin asked them all.

Ozzy and Sigi nodded.

They pulled away from the café and drove down a city street lined with brightly painted buildings.

"I like Portland," Ozzy said as they drove.

Rin didn't comment.

After taking a wide street for a few miles, the wizard headed up a small street with thick brick walls along both sides. Behind the walls the tops of green trees stuffed with yellow and red flowers poked up. Unlike the road to Rin's home, this thin street worked the opposite way—each few feet it got quainter and prettier and even more lush.

"If I could paint, I'd paint a picture of this street," Ozzy said almost reverently.

"Remember," Rin warned him, "it's just as easy to choke on pretty food as it is to choke on ugly bits."

"That's a ridiculous statement," Sigi said. "Just what are you trying to say?"

"I'm saying things that look beautiful and charming can often hide things that don't have . . . I don't know what I'm saying."

Ozzy and Sigi had never seen Rin acting like he was.

"This place has answers?" Ozzy asked.

"But at what cost?" Rin replied.

The wizard pulled the van up to the front of a large iron gate. The gate was the only gap in a long brick wall that looked as if it went on forever. Rin rolled down his window and reached out. He pressed a few buttons on a keypad and the gate began to open.

"How do you know the code?" Ozzy asked.

"Wizards have access to information that not everyone else does."

"You said *I'm* a wizard. And I don't have the code."

"I don't know everything."

Rin was on edge.

Inside the gate, the cobblestone path wound around beautifully manicured gardens and ended in front of a house twice the size of Rin's, but not half as interesting. It was white and stiff; if a home could be starched and ironed, it would resemble the one they saw in front of them. Dark black shingles lined the roof with perfect spacing and symmetry. There were countless windows, and a tall front door that was the opposite of welcoming. Magnificent old trees surrounded the place, but they all were too scared to touch—not a single branch brushed up against the home.

"Wow," Clark said. "I didn't know a house could look stuck-up."

Rin stopped the van near the front walkway and turned off the vehicle.

"Ready?" he asked with uncertainty.

"To go inside a beautiful house?" Sigi asked.

"No," Rin said, "to meet my mother."

Ozzy looked at Sigi. Sigi looked at him. Clark looked out the window and commented on the size of the garage.

"It'd be fun to see that one burn down."

"Who knows what the day will bring," Ozzy said sadly.

The wizard stepped out and bravely walked toward the home he had once lived in many years ago.

CHAPTER FORTY-THREE

MONSTERS

Ozzy wasn't sure what they were walking into. He had met Rin's sister, Ann, and she was both impressive and kind. He knew Rin's ex-wife, Patti, and she was impressive and kind. He also knew Rin's daughter, Sigi, and she was impressive, brilliant, funny, quick, strong, kind, and a whole list of other interesting things. He had also met Rin's father in New Mexico. And even though the old man had been a bit rough, he had helped them get away from Charles. Ozzy had never met Rin's brother, Woody, but anyone who builds an amusement park in their own backyard can't be too bad.

So as they stood on the porch, in front of the tall unwelcoming door, Ozzy didn't know what to expect.

"Get into Ozzy's pocket," Rin instructed Clark.

"Why?" the bird asked. "You want me to jump out and surprise her like I did to your sister?"

"No," Rin said emphatically. "She hates animals."

"The world can be so ugly," Clark said before flying down and crawling into the front pocket of Ozzy's plaid pants.

Rin rang the bell and a high-faluting chime went off inside of the house.

"Have I ever met her?" Sigi asked. "I mean, she is my grandma."

"When you were very young," Rin said. "She's never wanted to be a part of my life or yours. And she didn't like your mother."

The door opened and a woman in her late forties with red-framed glasses and a white jumpsuit looked at them with a wary eye.

"Yes?" the woman said as she tried to visually digest what Rin was wearing.

"Is Candy in?" the wizard asked.

"Who may I say is calling?"

"I'm not calling," Rin argued. "I'm standing right here. The name's Rin. She'll know who I am."

"Do you mind waiting in the sitting room while I see if she's available?" the woman asked nicely.

"I mind a lot of things," Rin replied, "but sitting's not one of them."

They all stepped into the house and took a seat in a room near the front door. The space was immaculately decorated and clean. Colorful art hung from white walls and above white modern furniture.

"I like when rooms are called what they are," Clark

said, sticking his head out of Ozzy's pocket. "Sitting rooms make sense. Bedrooms make sense. But why aren't kitchens called food rooms?"

"You can call them that if you want," Ozzy said quietly.

"I heard some mention of candy?" the bird said.

"That's my mother's name."

"Is she sweet?" Clark asked.

"No."

"Is she a wizard like you?" Ozzy questioned.

"No. Her genealogy leans more toward the witch side."

"Whatever she is, her home is so clean it's suffocating," Sigi whispered. "I feel like we should take off our shoes and burn the rest of our clothes. Then take a bath in bleach and get dressed back up in sterile plastic bags."

The woman in red glasses returned.

"She will see you," the woman reported. "Follow me."

They walked down what appeared to be the main hall and then back to what could only be described as a bragging room. The space was the size of a small gymnasium with plush white carpet covering every inch of the floor. The walls were papered with white textured wallpaper and at least twelve feet tall. The furniture was opulent and excessive and uncomfortable looking. In the middle of the room, sitting on the biggest chair Ozzy had ever seen, was Rin's mother, Candy. She was wearing a light blue shirt and white pants. Her hair was the color of the walls and longer in the front than the back. She motioned for Rin to move closer toward her.

"Hurry, hurry," she said. "I don't want to waste time with you taking little steps."

The three of them scrambled closer.

"Sit on that couch," she said, pointing to a long white leather couch festooned with leather-covered buttons.

The three of them sat.

"It's been too long," Candy said. "You should have visited sooner. Look at your clothes. Is that how you're dressing in public?"

Rin bristled. "You know that I am."

"And that hat? I didn't raise you to be the kind of person who keeps his hat on indoors."

"I didn't care for a number of ways you raised me."

"Is that a jab?" Candy asked. "I always want to describe you as clever. I suppose it's well that I don't."

From inside Ozzy's pocket, Clark guffawed.

"Have you seen your father?" she asked.

Rin nodded. "We visited him a while back."

"I suppose he's still poor and principled?"

"He's doing remarkably well," the wizard lied. "He owns half of Albuquerque."

"What's that worth? A fraction of Portland? Water is life," Candy insisted. "And we have the water. It's quite a blessing. I see your sister, Ann, from time to time."

"Me too."

"I know." Candy sighed as if the entire world was picking on her. "She always fills me in on your disorder."

"It's not a disorder."

"Really?" Candy obviously disagreed. "A grown man walking around and telling people he's a wizard isn't a disorder? I suppose I shouldn't be surprised. We're all supposed to accept any label anyone wants to be called. Maybe I'll be a chair someday."

Ozzy looked at Rin in confusion. The woman sitting in front of them was as horrible as any monster he had ever met in a book or in life.

"Can you turn *me* into a chair?" Candy asked. "Is that something a wizard can do? You know, I always feel so badly that you don't stop by more often. But then when you do, I wonder why I ever felt that way. I've offered to get you help. I'll pay for the whole thing. We'll get the deluxe package with the padded walls, the straitjacket, the works."

Candy laughed at her own joke as if it were funny.

"Maybe they can clean you up a bit," she went on. "A grown man with a beard? What's next, a face tattoo? How can you have employment when you have hair growing out of your face? It's a health issue."

Clark began to squirm, and Ozzy put his hand on his pocket to keep the bird calm.

"Do you want me to die disappointed?" Candy asked Rin. "Is that what you want? I'm just trying to help. You've made bad decision after bad decision. A teaching degree, your marriage. At least you figured a way out of *that*."

"Stop," Rin insisted.

"She wasn't right for you or the family."

Rin stood up.

"Calm down," Candy said. "People today are so thin-skinned. You give them a little of the truth and they fly into a convulsion."

"Patti wasn't bad for our family," Rin argued.

Candy smiled so smugly all three of them wanted to throw up.

"Of course she was," Candy insisted. "You know what I thought of her. And I say *thought*, because I no longer think of her. I mean, imagine Henry Owens swooping in and buying up all that beachfront property in Otter Rock. We weren't the only family who had been waiting for that opportunity."

"Stop," Rin said again. "We've been through this enough. None of those 'other families,' including ours, had the foresight to ask to be notified when the owner decided to sell. Patti's father did."

Candy made a rude noise. "He never, and she never— and *you* never—did understand how money and privilege work. You don't just do what he did and not have consequences. I still don't see how it was that you ended up marrying his daughter."

Rin made an exasperated face. "You know who this is," he said, motioning toward Sigi.

"I know who it is," Candy said coldly. "She looks much like her mother—and her grandfather."

"Don't start," Rin said angrily.

"Wait," Sigi said. "Is she talking about me being black?"

"Please," Candy said haughtily, "*I* don't have a racist

bone in my body. Adults are talking, child. Adults who know their place."

Rin sat back down and put his hand on Sigi's knee to prevent her from jumping up and attacking her grandmother.

"Who's the boy?" Candy asked, switching subjects as casually as someone switches forks. "I don't remember you having another child. Although he appears to be more from our side of the family. That's something."

Ozzy looked at Rin and asked loudly, "Why are we here?"

"Yes," Candy said, "the boy makes a good point. Why *are* you here? Are you finally going to get what you've never retrieved? Or did you come to show off the leftovers of your failed marriage?"

Sigi jumped up, shaking. "You're a monster."

Candy looked unperturbed. "I am a mother," she said calmly. "Sit down."

Sigi remained standing.

"Either way," Candy said. "I am a mother and as a mother I will always put the well-being of my children first. You can't blame me for wanting to help Brian make the right choices in life."

"His name's *Rin*," Sigi said angrily.

Despite all the hostility in the room, the wizard smiled slightly at Sigi's defense of his wizardly name.

"You need to learn some manners," Candy said. "You don't shout at grownups. But I suppose the upbringing that a wizard father and *your* mother provided doesn't amount to much."

"I didn't know there were such hideous things in Portland," Sigi said. "I'm just embarrassed that our lives have any connection at all."

Candy laughed. "Embarrassed by the one thing you could be proud of."

"What are you doing?" Ozzy demanded.

"Excuse me?" Candy said.

"Why are you acting like this?" The boy was so baffled by the horrible behavior he couldn't tell if it was real or an act.

"I'm not acting," she insisted. "Sit down."

"No," Ozzy said, continuing to stand next to Sigi. "I'm not sure why Rin brought us here. You're terrible. You're the kind of person that needs to pass on so that greener things can grow."

Candy stood and brushed at the sleeves of her shirt. She appeared to be done with the conversation, but for some reason she didn't leave.

"My mother was taken from me when I was seven," Ozzy continued. "I've wished every day that she would come back. But you've shown me that just because something's called Mom that doesn't mean it has the attributes that come along with the label. Patti is one of the most impressive people I know. And Sigi is something your horrible life missed out on. I don't care how rich you are, or how clean you can get things. This house is grotesque and nothing but a monument to a human being who doesn't know how to actually be one."

Candy looked as if she wanted to speak but kept still.

Ozzy turned to Rin. "Why did you come here?"

"She has something of mine," Rin answered. "It's in the safe behind that painting."

The wizard pointed to a small painting on the back wall. It was a picture of a bowl of fruit with a vase of flowers behind it. The image was framed in gold and worth more than most people's homes.

"Get it," Ozzy said.

Rin walked over to the painting and pulled it off the wall. Behind it was the safe that had always been there. Candy just stood there, watching it all happen and not making a move or a sound.

"Do you know the combination?" Sigi asked, still angry about everything that was happening.

The wizard nodded.

Rin pulled open the safe and reached in. He shuffled through a few papers and coins until he found what he was looking for.

The woman with the red glasses came into the room. She took one look at Rin by the open safe and grew frantic.

"What are you doing?" she demanded.

"I'm getting my stuff," Rin answered. "My mother has held onto it for long enough."

"Your mother?" Glasses asked. Her voice made it

sound like she had never thought someone like Candy could be a mother. "Is that true?" she asked Candy.

The wizard mom nodded and smiled awkwardly.

"Well," Rin said happily, "we're done. I'll leave the safe open. My mother said she thinks you deserve a bonus."

Candy stood there looking stiff and immovable—only her head bobbed up and down as she approved the bonus.

"By the way," Rin said. "I'm not shaving the beard."

"And I'm never coming back," Ozzy insisted.

"You may not think you are, but among a whole lot of other horrible things, you're a racist, Grandma," Sigi added.

The three of them left the bragging room. As they stepped out, a small black object shot out of Ozzy's pocket and raced toward Candy. Clark smacked the back of her knees, making her legs buckle and forcing her to fall backward into her seat.

"Sit down," Clark tweeted.

He then zipped out of the room and joined the others.

As they sped away from the horrible home and the far-less-charming-than-it-had-once-seemed street, they all kept quiet while trying to make sense of what had happened in their own heads. Clark was the only one to speak.

"Candy," he said with disgust. "She's as mislabeled as a kitchen."

Rin took out his list and checked off another item.

"Don't check and drive," Sigi said nicely.

The wizard smiled. "What would I do without you?"

CHAPTER FORTY-FOUR

HOTEL

Emotionally drained from their visit to Candy's house, Rin, Sigi, Ozzy, and Clark decided to get a hotel room in Portland for the night. They weren't sure what to do next and they wanted to take a night to figure things out. Rin sprang for the Marriott hotel in downtown. He got two adjoining rooms with a connecting door. It cost more, but it meant that all four of them had their own bed.

"*Finally,*" Clark said as he began to peck and tug at the blankets on his bed. "This is how it should be."

It was three in the afternoon and not another word had been mentioned about what had happened at Candy's house. The situation felt just ugly enough that everyone was afraid to bring it back out into the open. After Ozzy and Sigi had gone down to check out the pool and Rin had ironed his robe while Clark built his nest, they decided to make themselves feel better about things by ordering a bunch of overpriced room service.

The hotel restaurant didn't serve breakfast all day, which prompted Rin to leave a negative review on Yelp and forced them all to have to order food items more suited for the non-magical person.

When the food arrived, they all sat in Ozzy and Clark's room, eating while watching a show on mute about maverick chefs.

"Doesn't all this cost a lot?" Ozzy asked Rin, submerging the end of his French dip sandwich into a cup of au jus. "The rooms? The food?"

"I was thinking the same thing," Sigi said. "But I was too hungry to bring it up." She finished a cup of clam chowder and picked up her club sandwich. "We don't usually stay in such nice digs."

Rin took a picture of his fettuccine Alfredo and posted it to Instagram.

"I wish I were photographing an omelet."

Sigi patted her father on the back.

Clark, who had been busy finishing up his blanket nest, completed the project and decided to jump into the conversation by saying, "Your mom seems like a horrible person, Riny. Normally, I'd add 'no offense,' but this time I mean to offend."

"I agree with Clark," Ozzy said, relieved that the sticky situation was being brought up.

"Me too," Sigi added. "I'm happy you never sent me to spend the summer with her."

"I would never have allowed that," Rin said. "She has

a hard time accepting anything she doesn't understand. And she fears anything that doesn't fit her idea of valuable."

"Although," Clark said, "when I die, I want to be buried in that metal box she has on the wall. What did you take out of it?"

"It's not important," Rin said. "What matters is . . ."

Sigi interrupted her dad. "I think it *is* a big deal. Didn't we go there to get what was in the safe? Wasn't that what you checked off your to-get-done list?"

Rin nodded. "It was necessary, but . . . this order of fettuccine is wizard-sized." Rin's hope was to change the conversation with his tone and topic.

They all stared at his huge plate of cheese- and cream-covered noodles.

"We're not talking about your noodles, Dad."

Rin slurped one of the noodles they weren't discussing and glanced at Sigi.

"I'm really sorry you had to see that."

"The noodle?" Clark asked.

"No," the wizard said. "I'm sorry about Candy. You all should have waited in the car."

"You're wrong," his daughter said sincerely. "I wish she was different, but I'm glad I saw her. It would be hard to describe someone as terrible as her. She has to be part of the reason you and Mom got divorced?"

Rin nodded. "That and the fact that your mother didn't want to be married to someone so magical."

All three of them took giant bites of the food they had before them and spent a few moments chewing. Clark watched enviously.

"I wish I could eat," he lamented. "You all look funny doing it, but from the noises you make it must be worth it."

Ozzy handed Clark a small cup of ketchup the restaurant had included for the purpose of dipping fries in.

"Here."

The bird pressed his beak in and out of the red stuff, happy to be included. He smeared some of it on his metal underbelly and smiled at the results.

"I'm red-breasted."

Clark eyed the small cup of mustard near Sigi's plate.

"Are you using that?"

She handed it over to him and he began to streak lines of yellow mustard on his wings.

"What you took from the safe isn't important?" Ozzy asked Rin, still wanting to know.

"What I took is something that belonged to me."

"And the safe still had the same combination?"

"I'm not sure," Rin said. "She never told me the combination."

"Then how did you know it?" Sigi asked.

"Lucky guess."

"If what you took out of the safe isn't important," Ozzy said, "then why did we have to go there?"

"It needed to be done," Rin answered. "I can't run from what I must face."

"Because of your knees?" Clark asked, still applying ketchup and mustard to his wings and body.

"No," the wizard said kindly. "And I should say that I was hoping for a different response." He glanced at his daughter. "I thought that once she saw the kind of person you are, she would have softened."

"It didn't work," Sigi said.

"Was your mom *ever* nice? I mean, was she kind when you were young?" Ozzy asked, the subject of mothers being close to his heart and mind.

"Not particularly," Rin answered. "I grew up in parts of Otter Rock and Portland. I think we moved a lot because other people also had a hard time getting along with her. I remember when I was nine and she told me I had good form while riding my bike. That was nice. Of course, she followed it up by telling me not to look so much like a child when I smiled."

"How'd she get so rich?" Sigi asked.

"She comes from very old money," Rin answered. "Her great-grandfather made a fortune in the stock market and that money has continued to grow into embarrassingly large amounts."

"How embarrassing?" Clark asked, dipping his left talon in mustard.

"Obscenely embarrassing," Rin answered. "She acts the way she does because she's ignorant to anyone else's condition. She feels invincible because of her wealth."

Sigi set the last bit of her sandwich down. Her dark

eyes flickered with the reflection of the muted TV. "I used to ask about your side of the family all the time," Sigi said. "But it's not a subject Mom ever liked to talk about. So I stopped asking. It's weird that Mom's never told me how horrible Candy is. Actually, I don't think she's ever brought her up."

"That's wise," Rin said. "Patti is remarkably fair. But when I married her, my mother acted like the world had come to an end and as if I had destroyed the family. The truth is, she had destroyed the family years before."

"When did I last see her?" Sigi asked.

"I think you were one and Patti was done."

Clark raised a ketchup-covered right wing.

"Yes?" Rin said.

"Did you mean to rhyme?"

"I did." Rin took a bite of his fettuccini and continued with a mouth full of noodles. *"My moom wouldn't knowledge ing I ever don."* He swallowed. "My marriage was the beginning of my family falling apart. That's about the time my dad left."

"Families are complicated," Clark tweeted.

"I used to blame them both for being such horrible parents." Rin slurped down another noodle. "But then I grew up, became a teacher, got married, had a daughter, and became a wizard. So, it all turned out in the end."

"You're not angry?" Ozzy asked.

"About what?"

"Dad," Sigi argued, not buying the idea that he was

okay with being raised by the terrible woman she had just met, "don't be thick. It's okay to be angry."

Rin looked at both Sigi and Ozzy—he would have included Clark in his glance, but the bird was so covered in condiments that he was uncomfortable to look at.

"I don't know if you know this," the wizard said, "but sometimes people laugh at me." The sauce that Rin had in his beard made it hard for Ozzy and Sigi not to laugh now. "They laughed when I wanted to be a teacher. They laughed when I told them I was marrying Patti. They laughed when we got divorced and things fell apart. And . . . ," he paused for dramatic effect, ". . . now some of them laugh because they don't believe I'm a wizard."

Ozzy and Sigi tried their best to look surprised by the information.

"I think they're mainly laughing at your pants," Clark said.

Rin ignored him and Clark looked bothered by the lack of reaction.

"Quarfelt is real," the wizard said quietly. "I know how unbelievable that might seem to others, but having even one person believe in you makes the challenge surmountable. You don't know what you did when you picked up that phone and dialed my number," Rin told Ozzy. "You altered the course of my life and gave me the kind of purpose every wizard needs."

"That still doesn't explain the pants," Clark tried again.

Nobody said anything.

"Dad," Sigi said, "I'm really sorry I didn't believe in you before."

Rin smiled. "Befores are forgotten when the now is so nice."

Ozzy looked around for a refrigerator magnet or a poster with the saying Rin had just said printed on it.

There weren't any.

"Hard to forget the before when the now pants are so awful," Clark tweeted loudly, tired of nobody paying attention to him.

Rin looked at the bird. "Sometimes being quiet is the most impressive thing a person, or a bird, can do."

Clark tipped his ketchup-topped head. "It's hard to be quiet when your pants are so loud." The bird looked around, wondering why Ozzy and Sigi weren't laughing.

"Pearls before pigeons," he complained.

Frustrated, Clark began to smear tough-looking circles of mustard around his eyes. Unfortunately, the tips of his wings were not made for precision painting and the thick mustard blinded him.

"I can't see!" he scream-tweeted.

Confused, the bird jumped up from his nest, flapping his wings madly. He flew up and against the window. With a hard thud, Clark bounced off the glass and fell onto the floor. He thrashed around Ozzy and Sigi's feet, sending drops of ketchup and mustard everywhere.

"Hold on!" Ozzy yelled while putting his food down. "You're making it worse!"

The wizard-in-training tried to grab the wailing bird, but Clark was almost completely covered in smeared ketchup and mustard. He slipped through Ozzy's hands and shot toward Rin. Clark hit the wizard-sized plate of fettuccine hard. Wet creamy noodles flew up into the air and stuck to the ceiling and walls. A dozen strands clung to Clark as he tried frantically to fly.

"What are you doing?" Sigi hollered. "Stop moving!"

Clark's ear holes were filled with ketchup and alfredo sauce. He twisted through the air and crashed down on the fat end of the ironing board that Rin had used to iron his robe. Ozzy jumped to grab him, but slipped on a mound of floor noodles. The boy slammed forward and onto the pointed end of the ironing board. His force and mass sent the bird rocketing toward the door.

Thwapt!

Clark's beak stuck into the door like a dart. The bird struggled to get loose, but it was no use. He gave up and hung limply from the back of the door, dripping various goop down onto the floor.

Ozzy looked around at the red-and-yellow speckled room. Noodles hung from the ceiling and walls and laid in random lines on the beds and carpet. With the TV and bird muted, the room was silent.

"See," Rin said cheerfully. "Sometimes being quiet is—"

A loud knock on the door disturbed the newfound peace.

"Were we expecting more food?" Ozzy asked.

"No," Rin replied.

"If it's one of the staff, they're not going to like what we've done to the place," Sigi said.

"Don't worry," Rin said. "It's not one of the staff. If I had to guess, I'd say it's the beginning of the end."

"What?" Ozzy and Sigi asked in unison.

"Of course, by my calculations, it's about a day early."

The wizard stood up, straightened his hat, and walked to the door.

CHAPTER FORTY-FIVE

YOU WALKED INTO THE ROOM

The wizard stood up, grabbed a small towel from out of the bathroom and quickly wiped bits of goo from his hands and face. He straightened his hat and walked to the door.

There was a second knock, a bit more forceful this time.

"Coming," Rin said, almost cheerfully.

The second knock caused Clark to vibrate. The bird was still stuck in the back of the door, hanging two inches below the peephole. Rin took the towel he had used and hung it over Clark. The white material covered the twitching metal bird completely. Without taking the time to see who had knocked, the wizard reached out and opened the door. Standing in the hall, wearing the kind of expression a vengeful shark might show a pesky shrimp, was Ty.

Rin tried to look past him to see if there was anyone else, but Ty's bulk blocked his view and made it difficult to see anything beyond the large man's shoulders and neck. Despite the sorry view, the wizard didn't seem surprised.

Ozzy jumped to his feet and tried to lock into Ty's will, but just like at Rin's house, his ability didn't work on the man.

"I thought you were in jail," Rin said, like a friendly neighbor interested in Ty's life.

"You'd be surprised what money can get you out of," Ty said.

"Well, I'd invite you in, but the room's a mess."

"Where's the bird?" Ty asked, stepping into the room.

"He's indisposed at the moment," Rin answered. "But if you want to leave your name and a message, I'd—"

Without warning Ty pulled a weapon from under his blue jacket and shot something into the wizard's neck.

"How many licksch," Rin slurred as he fell to the ground in a pile of crushed green velvet trousers and yellow terrycloth robe.

"What are—" Sigi was going to protest her father's treatment, but she too was stopped by another ogre in a blue suit who slipped into the room through the adjoining door and injected her with something that knocked her out.

Unlike the other two, Ozzy didn't even get the chance to try to talk. He was ambushed by a third ogre who shot a dart into the side of his neck without Ozzy ever seeing him.

The boy fell with a thump to the ketchup-, mustard-, and fettuccine-covered floor right next to Sigi.

Two more men entered the room. Ozzy, Sigi, and Rin

were all picked up and whisked away like a trio of old rugs. Then Ty quickly searched the space for any sign of Clark. He checked the drawers, the bathroom, and inside the ice buckets. He checked under the blankets and behind the nightstands. Seeing no sign of the bird, Ty signaled for his men to follow him. The lurch of blue ogres slipped out of the room and down the hall.

Ty smiled, feeling as if things were finally running smoothly.

His smile might have been lessened had he known what his search had failed to discover.

CHAPTER FORTY-SIX

THE HURTING

Sheriff Wills sat on a chair in Patti's front room. Patti was sitting next to the dirty couch facing him. He glanced her way and smiled sincerely. The sheriff felt sorry for her. Patti had married a wizard by mistake, and now she and her daughter and her house were paying the price for it.

"You still haven't heard from them?" Wills asked.

"I haven't," she said. "I'm not trying to keep anything from you. I want my daughter back and I want Rin to get the help he needs."

"He didn't say anything about where he was heading?"

"No. He just caused a traffic jam, took Sigi, and ran off."

Patti's short brown hair wasn't as neat as it usually was. Her eyes weren't as bright, and her smile was missing in the same fashion as her daughter, her ex-husband, and Ozzy.

"I didn't think things would get so out of hand," Patti insisted.

"If you had to guess," the sheriff asked, "where do you think Rin took them?"

"It's Brian," Patti said angrily. "I'm not going to feed his delusion anymore."

"Okay, where do you think Brian took them?"

"To a magic shop?" she said sarcastically and out of her mind with a lack of sleep and an abundance of worry. "To a bathrobe factory?"

Sheriff Wills pretended to write something down in his notebook to give Patti the time she needed to breathe.

"We'll find them," he finally said calmly.

Patti looked at the sheriff. Her dark eyelids closed and opened quickly. The expression on her face was one of defeat mixed with a new understanding.

"This must be one of the strangest cases you've worked on," she said, sounding as if the thought had only just occurred to her.

Wills smiled. "Yeah. I really don't know what to make of it."

"I'm sorry if I've pushed in the past," Patti said. "I honestly don't know the right course of action a mother should take in a situation like this. I only want them all to be safe."

"They're lucky to have you looking out for them."

"It's not done Sigi much good."

"Who's to say?" Wills said. "You might have done exactly what you should have."

Patti smiled weakly.

"I'll tell you this—I have to believe that despite Rin's condition, he's not going to harm them." Sheriff Wills stopped to consider his own words. "Not intentionally, at least."

"Do they know how the fire started?" Patti asked. "Did Rin start it? He burnt down Ozzy's home, you know"

The sheriff nodded.

"I'd love to blame him for your garage as well, but my officers never saw anyone other than Ozzy. And the fire marshal still hasn't found the cause."

"What about Jon?"

"He's still missing," Wills said. "But I wouldn't worry about him too much. I have a feeling he's cleared out for good."

Patti stared at the sheriff until he felt self-conscious.

"What?"

"Remember, years ago, when Brian first started telling people he was a wizard?"

Wills nodded.

"Wasn't it you who told me not to worry because it was just a phase?"

Wills nodded again.

"It's been a long phase," Patti said, her voice filled with exhaustion.

"I don't get everything right," Sheriff Wills admitted. "But I'm going to do my best to bring this phase to a safe ending."

Patti stood up.

"Are you hungry?" she asked. "I can make you something before you leave."

"If it's not a lot of trouble."

"No trouble," she said. "And I'm starving. What do you like? And don't say breakfast."

"It's my least favorite meal."

Patti fixed her and the sheriff a sandwich. She ate hers there and he ate his in the car as he drove back to the station to make more calls, attempting to connect a few more dots.

CHAPTER FORTY-SEVEN

WHAT HAS HAPPENED?

Ozzy thought he could hear the soft sound of the ocean. The noise was comforting but wrong. It was like hearing a Christmas song in July. The ocean in his head turned into a far less pleasant ringing in his ears.

Ozzy opened his grey eyes and instantly knew what the problem was. He wasn't lying on the sand watching the waves come in. He was tied to a chair in a fancy room with low lighting. On his right, he could see Sigi tied up, not moving, her head hanging down in front of her. To his left, he saw Rin, also tied to a chair, white rope wrapped around his arms and torso in a way that gave very little room for circulation and even less room for breaking free. Unlike Sigi, Rin was awake. He wasn't wearing his hat and his long hair and beard looked more mountain-man than magical.

"My head is ringing," Ozzy mumbled. "Where are we?"

"Reality," Rin answered.

"Yeah," Ozzy said. "This looks like my reality."

The room was a circle with no windows. It had a high ceiling and the wall was covered with a burlap material. The carpet was beige and a large round table was in the middle of the room. The table had nine wooden chairs with high backs. The chairs that Rin, Sigi, and Ozzy were tied to matched the set.

"You can't always tell," Rin said. "Round rooms are more of a Quarfelt thing. Wizards hate corners."

Ozzy struggled with the rope around his body.

"I can't move."

"Yeah, someone knows their knots."

Sigi started to stir.

"Where are we?"

"In a round room," Ozzy answered.

"Are we still in Oregon?" she asked.

Ozzy hadn't thought about it. The idea that they could have been transported somewhere far away had never crossed his mind.

"I'm not sure," the boy admitted.

"Uncertainty is intoxicating," Rin said.

"Not to me," Sigi told him.

"Is this like a dining room for the knights of the round table?" Ozzy asked.

"They did business at a round table," Rin informed the boy. "You know, quest updates and pillage reports. But they ate at rectangular ones just like the next guy."

A space in the wall opened, revealing a hidden door. Ty stepped through the opening and approached the captives.

"Where's the bird?" he asked bluntly.

"It's nice to see you love animals," Rin said. "You must have a kind heart after all."

"I hate animals," Ty insisted. "But that bird is something Mr. Dench is interested in."

"Ornithology can be very enjoyable."

Ty didn't smile.

"Where are we?" Sigi asked bravely.

"Does it matter?" Ty said. "Wherever you are, you're out of luck. Now, I need to talk to the boy."

"We'd plug our ears," Rin said. "But our hands are tied."

Ty grabbed the bottom of the chair Ozzy was tied to and picked it and the boy up as if they were nothing more than a duffel bag filled with wind and air.

"Wait," Rin said. "Where are you taking him?"

Ty didn't answer. He just carried Ozzy and his chair out of the room and let the hidden door slide quietly closed behind him. The wizard's daughter was beside herself.

"This is bad! Why would they take just him?"

Rin's eyes were closed.

"Are you going to do something?" Sigi pleaded. "He's in trouble."

"We're all in some sort of trouble," the wizard said wisely. "Be it a tiny ding, or the sting of death, we all have reason to worry."

"What? Change into something!"

Rin looked confused. "I didn't bring other clothes."

"No, no, change into *something*. Like you did in the ocean. You have to help Ozzy."

Rin stared at his daughter.

"Ozzy can take care of himself," he said proudly. "I've taught him everything he needs to know. Yes, it looks as if the student has become the—the student has become the—"

"Teacher!" Sigi said exasperated. "You should know that word. It's what you used to be before you decided to put our lives in danger!"

Rin didn't reply. His eyes were shut, and his head tipped slightly to the left. Hearing the word *teacher* had done something to him.

"What are you doing?" Sigi demanded. "Come on!"

The wizard didn't move. His hair didn't blow, his eyes didn't blink, and his expression didn't change. After a full minute he opened his eyes and showed his daughter a look of panic she had not seen him have before.

"Ozzy's in trouble," Rin said seriously.

"What? How do you know that?"

"Some things are too obvious to ignore."

Rin closed his eyes again as his daughter continued to shout and shake in fear.

CHAPTER FORTY-EIGHT

HOOKED ON A FEELING

Bennett had only worked at the downtown Portland Marriott for three weeks. He had recently moved from Missoula, Montana, where he had worked cleaning rooms for Holiday Inn Express. So far, the job in Portland had been similar—you clean up after other people, act courteous when anyone passes you in the hall, and occasionally get a tip.

Room 321 had been a different story. It was the first room of the day, and it was also the worst one he'd ever encountered. The guests had left without finishing their food and after knotting up blankets in a complicated ring on one of the beds. They had also spent some time redecorating the place with ketchup, mustard, and noodles. The dried pasta on the ceiling was the hardest to get off. It took hours to get the room looking like it was supposed to.

"People are the worst," Bennett said, still needing to

vacuum and put out the new bedding. "All that and not even a tip."

He scrubbed a rogue bit of alfredo sauce off the base-board, and as he stood up, he noticed a small towel hanging on the back of the door. He pulled the towel off the hook and gasped.

"That is the ugliest hook I've ever seen."

Bennett adjusted his glasses and studied the piece of hardware. The hook was large, bird shaped, and smeared with dried condiments. The beak of the bird was strongly adhered to the door and the body hung straight down. There was a small strip of silver on the odd hook.

Bennett stuck his head out into the hall.

"Mary!" he yelled.

His co-worker had been co-working on a room across the hall. She stopped what she was doing to check out what Bennett had found.

"Weird," she said, adding little to the discussion.

"Is it supposed to be there?" Bennett asked. "Is this like, the bird room?"

"We don't have a bird room."

Mary turned her headphones back on and returned to the room across the hall to continue her work.

"What's your story?" Bennett asked the hook.

He grabbed the bird as tightly as he could and pulled. Pushing up as he pulled out, he began to feel a little give. With a hard tug, the hook popped loose and flew across the room. It landed on a green leather chair next to the window.

Bennett stepped over and picked it up. He studied the beak and hefted the thing in his hands.

"Whatever you are, you're unusual," he whispered. "Ugly, but unusual."

Clark's eyes and beak flashed open, prompting Bennett to scream and toss the bird onto the bed.

"*Ugly* and *unusual*?" Clark said with disgust.

"What the—?" Bennett backed up toward the door.

"I'd say something about you and your curly hair and eye windows, but I have too much class."

The condiment-covered bird stood up on the bed and flapped his wings.

"Who am I kidding?"

Clark said a few unkind things and then flew past Bennett and into the hall. The bird zipped up and down the hallway looking for a way out. All the room doors and elevator doors were closed.

Bennett was now in the hall shouting things to Mary. As Clark raced back toward him, the curly haired boy ran for the stairs. Throwing open the door, Bennett ran down the stairs, taking them four at a time. Unfortunately for him, Clark had been able to slip into the stairwell before the door had closed. He followed Bennett down, nipping at the back of his wavy hair, and giving him a few more of his opinions.

"Nest head," Clark squawked. "You run like a human!"

On the first floor, Bennett charged out of the stairwell with Clark right behind him. The bird instantly gave up on the boy and shot through the lobby and out the open front doors.

Clark was free, but he had no idea where his group had gone.

"Damp," he chirped.

The bird searched the parking lot for any sign of Ozzy or Sigi or Rin. But there was nothing but parked cars and black asphalt. And even though he couldn't smell, the number of trees in the area made him certain that the air smelled like pine.

Circling the parking lot twice, he flew through some active sprinklers to wash off and then flitted down and stood on top of a trash receptacle near the front door. Through the glass he could see Bennett in the lobby trying to explain to his boss what had happened.

"Unusual and ugly," the bird said with a sniff. "Some people have no taste." Clark spread his wings and saw bits of dried ketchup and muck still clinging to him. "Maybe he has a point."

Clark looked out across the parking lot.

"Now," he said. "If I were a wizard and a daughter and an orphan, where would I go?"

The bird adjusted his dirty tail feathers, spread his messy wings, and flew north.

CHAPTER FORTY-NINE

SURPRISE, SURPRISE, SURPRISE

Ozzy sat alone in a small dark space not much bigger than the hidden basement room he had fallen into at the Cloaked House. Ty had dropped him off and left him sitting alone. He was still strapped to the chair and wondering what was coming next. His hands had been untied from the chair and then bound back together at the wrists. They were resting in his lap, but he was able to lift them and stretch just a bit. A metal chair with a low back and high seat was sitting empty four feet in front of him.

Lifting his head, he twisted to see more of the room. There was nothing there, just blank space with a bright light hanging up above him.

Ozzy stared at the light.

A door opened to his left and someone entered the room. Ozzy tried to see who it was, but the light he had been gazing at was now making it hard for his eyes to focus.

"Hello, Ozzy," the voice said.

The wizard-in-training was struck dumb.

"It's so nice to finally see you again. Your hair's gotten longer. I know a good barber back in New York. I'll set you up next time you're there."

Ozzy's eyes adjusted as Ray Dench took a seat on the chair in front of him. The red-headed man was wearing a brown dress shirt with a brown tie. He had on slacks pressed to perfection, if your idea of perfection was well-pressed slacks. Ray's hair had not gotten longer; it was neatly trimmed, and his skin looked shiny, as if he had been recently shellacked.

The junior wizard tried to hook into Ray's brain, but he couldn't.

"How'd you get us here?" Ozzy asked.

"It wasn't a problem," Ray said.

"Did we take a plane?"

Ray laughed. "Where do you think you are?"

"New York?"

"You are only a few blocks from the hotel we just snatched you from."

"I thought you couldn't leave New York."

"I am capable of anything!" Ray barked. He then quickly cooled. "I don't like getting out of my routine, but I will make the sacrifice on rare occasions," Ray said. "And this is one of those occasions."

The way Ray spoke made it sound like his being there was a prize Ozzy had won.

"Do you know what you possess?" Ray continued.

Ozzy didn't answer.

"You know, I'm not sure you truly understand just what is going on."

"I know enough to not trust you," Ozzy said.

"Good," Ray replied, "it's wise to be skeptical. But if you think I'm the enemy, you have it all wrong. I knew your parents. I know what they hoped to do. I was the one who helped them achieve their dream."

"Their dream of you kidnapping them and having me left for dead?"

"That's an unfortunate bit of history," Ray said with a sniff. "But when all of this is said and done, you will see how even that played a part in *us* changing the world."

Ozzy bristled at the way Ray said *us*.

"You've tried to kill us more than once," the boy reminded him.

Ray's eyebrows arched in surprise. "Is that how you see it? I apologize. I only want to finish what your parents began. My desire has been to bring you to me, not to kill anyone. The serum you have coursing through your veins is the key to great peace. Great peace. People keep making mistake after mistake, and our planet and way of life are paying the price for it. This isn't about me wanting to control everyone—this is about me wanting to give everyone the lives they want."

Ozzy stared confidently at Ray. "You can say it however you want, but I know you're wrong. And I will never help you."

"Oh," Ray said waving casually with his left hand, "I don't need you to help me. I don't know where you got that idea. I can take what I want from you without much effort. But I'm a dreamer, and it would be so much better if you went willingly. You know what this serum can do. You were the great experiment that we didn't know about." Ray sighed like a father who had just lost a child. "Had we known they had pumped you so full of the serum, we would have taken *you* from the woods, not your parents. But they fled New York and . . . well, you know the story from there."

Ozzy was quiet.

"Now, I know the path to this point has been filled with hardship and sorrow, but the future can be just the opposite. I'm sorry, truly sorry, for any pain I have caused. I loved your parents. But I promise you that with your cooperation I can make the future something spectacular."

"What about my friends?"

Ray smiled. "The wizard? The girl? Oh, they're of no importance to me. Your cooperation will give them the possibility of living a long and peaceful life."

"A life where they don't make their own choices," Ozzy said.

"That's not true," Ray insisted. "There will still be plenty of choices for them to make. We'll just guide them and the rest of humanity with the hard ones."

"You can't win," the boy said bravely. "You don't know what Rin is capable of."

Ray tried not to laugh, and the attempt made his already hard-to-look-at face harder to look at.

"I do know what *Rin* is capable of," Ray said, pronouncing the wizard's name like a bad taste. "And I know what he's not capable of."

Ray shifted in his seat and pulled something out from behind his back. It was a small yellow pamphlet, a single piece of shiny paper folded into three sections.

"Do you honestly believe that man is a wizard?" Ray asked Ozzy in a fake but fatherly tone.

Ozzy kept quiet.

"I didn't want to do this, but I think it's time that we all start acting like grownups."

"I'm a junior in high school," Ozzy protested. "I'm not a grownup."

"You know what I mean."

"I do?" Ozzy asked. "Are grownups the kind of people who destroy lives like you do? Because if that's the case, I hope I never grow up."

"Cute," Ray said condescendingly. "No, grownups are the kind of people who have to make big decisions. Decisions that are hard sometimes. Grownups are also the kind of people with problems. Some problems are fixed by a dentist or an accountant. Some problems require more help than that."

Ray handed Ozzy the pamphlet. He held onto it with his bound hands.

The wizard-in-training reluctantly glanced at the

front. The folded yellow pamphlet was an advertisement for the Healing Winds Mental Institution in Olympia, Washington. The picture on the front was of a tall brick building surrounded by trees. There was a line beneath the picture that read:

Life can be beautiful again.

It was difficult, but Ozzy unfolded the pamphlet and read the words inside. His bound hands shook as he held it. A feeling of something ominous and growing began filling his body from his bare feet up. Healing Winds had been established more than a hundred years before. It was a place for those who could no longer handle life. It wasn't a resort that famous people went to when they needed a rest. It wasn't an addiction center for those whose lives were ruined by addiction. It was a mental hospital for those who had lost it.

"What is this?" Ozzy asked quietly.

"I think you know," Ray said just as softly. "It's where your friend once lived. It is a place for people who are unstable. You see, Ozzy, the man you think is a wizard is nothing but a confused and unstable individual. He should be locked up, not worshiped."

"I don't believe it," Ozzy said. "This proves nothing."

"You might want to look at the pictures closer."

Ozzy studied the few pictures on the brochure. There was one showing the beautiful grounds where the patients could walk around. There was one showing the rooms they would be kept in. There was a photo showing a doctor talking to a group of patients.

Ozzy stared at the photo.

"You see it, don't you?" Ray said.

Most of the patients in the photo were strangers to Ozzy, but there was one in the back of the picture that stood out. He had only a mustache and no beard, and he was missing his hat and robe, but it was clearly a much younger Rin.

Ozzy's insides burst—he felt like he had while watching his parents being taken away. The wizard he knew was no wizard at all.

"I don't get it," Ozzy said, his breathing beginning to grow labored.

"I have the records," Ray said, his voice getting stronger. "It wasn't easy. But I found all of Brian Mortley's information and medical history at Healing Winds. He checked in for the first time many years ago because he was sick. He spent a year there before he was able to leave. They call his condition bipolar, but there are a few doctors there who didn't agree. Some listed him as psychotic. He has checked back in several times over the years. His last visit was about nine months ago. He stayed for three weeks."

Ozzy looked like he might throw up.

"He is not a wizard," Ray said. "He is a fraud and potentially dangerous."

The boy said nothing.

"I'm sorry it had to be me to tell you," Ray said. "But

that lunatic has almost derailed one of the most important discoveries in human history. The discipline serum can solve the very problems your friend is suffering from."

Ozzy's head rested on his chest as he struggled not to cry. Breathing hurt, thanks to the tight ropes binding him to the chair. He wanted to bust out and run unhindered to the ocean. His mind buzzed with the things Patti had told him, the words Sheriff Wills had said, the reality that didn't include wizards, and the pamphlet he now held in his hands. He thought back to the magnet Rin had quoted:

Believe nothing unless it agrees with your own reason and your own common sense.

Ozzy had questioned the possibility of Rin being real many times. He knew he didn't fit in reality; he knew he was unusual; he knew he defied all common sense.

"I've given you a lot to think about," Ray said. "Just remember, I want to help. Don't make this harder than it needs to be."

The boy said nothing—things were already much harder than they should ever have been.

The door opened and a man in a stylish green suit walked in, pushing a small metal cart.

"It's time to give up your secrets," Ray said happily. "This is the beginning of a new world."

The man in the nice suit lifted a syringe off the cart and walked closer to Ozzy.

The boy said nothing.

CHAPTER FIFTY

SPEAKING ONE'S MIND

Rin and Sigi sat impatiently and uncomfortably on the chairs they were tied to. Ozzy had been picked up and taken out long ago. Since then not a single ogre had returned to check on them.

"If I ever hold anyone captive," Rin said with disgust, "I'm going to make sure they still get something to eat and drink."

"I hope Ozzy's okay," was Sigi's reply.

"Do you think they fed him?"

"I mean, I hope he's not hurt."

"Right."

Sigi looked at her dad. His hat was on the ground and he was tied up tightly. Folds of his robe pushed through the strands of rope and made him look as if his body were made up of a stack of yellow fabric.

"Dad. Can I ask you something?"

"Of course."

"You're a wizard, right?"

Rin laughed like it was a joke. "Oh, you're serious. Yes, I'm a wizard. I thought we'd gotten past that point."

"Me too," Sigi said. "I mean, I understand that you're not a wizard in the traditional sense, like Dumbledore or Gandalf."

"Sure," Rin agreed. "Those two are made up."

Sigi blew a piece of curly hair from her eyes. "Okay, what I mean is you don't go around shooting spells out of your wand and cursing people."

"I apologize again for my language while we were driving. Sometimes people perceive my offensive driving as a personal offense. When, in reality—"

"Dad," Sigi said, bringing him back to the conversation at hand, "not that kind of cursing. You don't stand in front of a cauldron or ride a broom."

"You shouldn't stereotype wizards," Rin said sternly. "I thought I taught you better than that. I know several wizards who refuse to use cauldrons due to the trouble of having to wash them out. Do you know how hard it is to get rid of the ring of residue mugwort leaves behind?"

Sigi was as flustered with her father as she was with being tied up.

"Forget about cauldrons," she said. "My point is that you're a wizard."

Rin smiled. "I'm glad this conversation had a happy ending."

"It didn't," Sigi insisted. "It's not over yet. My point is

you're a wizard, so why don't you wizard our way out of this?"

Rin looked around the room, acting as if he hadn't noticed they were in any kind of a bind.

"We're tied up?" Sigi reminded him. "Clark's still stuck in the back of a hotel door, and Ozzy is missing! Can't you act like a wizard?"

"Check," Rin said.

"What could you possibly be checking off?"

The wizard smiled.

"Really? You have nothing to say?"

"Sometimes the wisest person in the room is the one who does nothing."

"Ahh," Sigi hollered. "I wish you *were* Dumbledore."

"He's not real."

"Well, I'm having a hard time thinking you are either."

Rin smiled. "I like when you doubt," he said kindly. "It's typically the precursor to magical things."

Sigi said a few unmagical things to her father as she continued to work at the ropes binding her.

CHAPTER FIFTY-ONE

A CHANCE FOR REPENTANCE

Ty drove quickly down the street toward the Marriott. He cursed himself as he traveled. His hands gripped the wheel tightly as he swerved around a car going too slow for his personal taste. Ty was angry at himself, but happy about what he now knew. The room where Rin and Sigi were tied up was not only round, it was wired. Microphones had been hidden in the room so Ty and his men could listen in to what their prisoners were saying. They hadn't gotten much information; in fact, the conversation was hard to listen to due to some of the things the wizard said. But it had been a line that Sigi had thrown out that had changed everything.

"Clark's still stuck in the back of a hotel door."

Ty cursed himself again. Had he done a more thorough job of checking the hotel room, the bird Ray wanted so desperately would already be in their possession. Now, as he raced through the streets, he was filled with anxiety.

The metal nuisance could have gotten loose or maybe been taken away.

It wasn't easy working for Ray. The job was even harder when you didn't properly finish the tasks that you had been assigned. Ty was supposed to have captured Ozzy at WetLand. He had failed. Ray had gotten him out on bail so that he had another shot at making things right. He couldn't let the bird get away.

Traffic in front of him came to a stop at a red light.

Ty would have swerved around the cars and driven through, but the crosswalk was filled with half a dozen old men riding recumbent bicycles. Their low-to-the-ground bikes all had flags sticking up on the back to let people know they were there. The old men were shouting at vehicles and ringing bells on their handlebars to alert the cars of their existence.

Not wanting to be slowed down by accidentally plowing over them, Ty waited with the rest of the cars for the light to turn green. Once it did, he wasted no time speeding the last few blocks to the hotel.

CHAPTER FIFTY-TWO

JUMPING INTO THE MIND
OF A WIZARD

Clark was mystified. For his entire existence, he had believed that he was capable of almost anything—if anything didn't require opposable thumbs or patience. But now with the ones he loved in danger, he could see no way to find them. Not having the ability to eat made it clear that he lacked guts. So when he tried to go with his gut instinct it didn't pan out.

"Where would a wizard go?" he asked as he flew above Portland.

Knowing that Rin liked to burn things, the bird scanned the entire city for some sign of fire. Sadly, there was none.

"Sigi," Clark chirped.

Knowing the girl liked math and cat videos he flew through the streets looking for a group of nerds standing around a phone or TV. There were plenty of nerds in

Portland, but nobody he saw was talking about math or watching cat videos.

Clark thought of Ozzy.

Knowing the boy liked Sigi, he flew through the city looking for her by looking for nerds who were watching cat videos. His search quickly became an unfruitful loop of dead ends.

With gut failure, Clark decided to try intuition.

The bird flew through a couple McDonald's drive-thrus knowing they served all-day breakfast. Nothing. He thought he was onto something when he spotted a cart near a park selling dreamcatchers and colorful witch hats. But that hunch ended with an upset cart owner with an upset cart, and Clark no closer to finding his friends.

The dirty bird landed on top of a streetlight and took a moment to think things over. His non-gut instinct had failed him, and his intuition had been even spottier.

"If I were a human who always said dumb things, where would I be taken?" Two ravens settled on the street-light next to him. "I hate to be an unkindness. So, shoo." Clark waved his wings and the birds took off. "Ozzy likes Sprite. Is that something?"

The sentient bird was thinking about giving up and going back to the upset dreamcatcher cart to stare at some of the handmade jewelry again when he heard bells. He glanced down and saw an unkindness of old men riding squished bikes. The flags on the back of their bikes were appealing as they flapped in the wind. Clark considered landing on the helmet of one of the men and getting a free ride through downtown, but his considerations were dashed as he looked through the windshield of a sleek looking vehicle stopped near the light.

It was Ty.

The thought struck Clark that it might be wise to follow the car and see where Ty went. Another thought that struck Clark was that it might be fun to follow the old men and see where they went.

"A bird's time is never his own," Clark complained.

The nearby traffic light turned green and the cars began to move forward. Clark opened his wings and followed the ogre in the aerodynamic car.

CHAPTER FIFTY-THREE

A STROKE OF LUCK

Ty went directly to the front desk of the hotel and requested to speak with the manager. A bubbly little man came out from the back. The name tag on his dark blue shirt said Waldo. Ty apologized for the mess he and his friends had left in the room and offered to pay for any damages.

"That would be appreciated," Waldo said.

Ty pulled out his wallet and handed the manager a credit card.

"It was all an accident," Ty explained. "I hope it isn't too much trouble to clean."

"It was a bit of a chore."

Ty looked upset. "It's already been cleaned?"

"Yes." Waldo handed the credit card back. "I believe it's finished."

Trying not to appear bothered, Ty smiled at the bubbly man.

"Oh," he said snapping his fingers, "I just remembered. I left my glasses in the room. Do you mind if I take a quick look?"

"It's been cleaned," Waldo said. "I'll see if anyone reported them."

The manager lifted a walkie talkie and communicated with someone in housekeeping. There was a brief exchange of words and he signed off.

"They didn't find any."

"Can I speak to the person who cleaned the room?"

"He's gone home," Waldo said. "He wasn't feeling well."

"I know the glasses are in there," Ty said seriously. "Let me just take a quick look."

Waldo appeared a few bubbles shy of his normal effervescent self.

"I can let you take a quick look."

Ty followed Waldo up to the third floor. Waldo let Ty into the room and the ogre checked behind the door. There was nothing there but a peephole with a small dent beneath it.

"Not good," Ty said.

Waldo let him check the door on the adjoining room, but it was missing a beak-sized hole.

"You said the boy who cleaned all of this went home?"

"He wasn't feeling well," Waldo said. "It's the weirdest thing. A bird chased him down the stairs."

"A bird?"

OBERT SKYE

"That's what he said. It flew right out the doors of the lobby."

Ty wanted to strangle the bubbly man, but instead he pushed him aside and ran down the hall toward the stairs.

"What about your glasses?" Waldo yelled.

Ty was already in the stairwell and descending at a rate much quicker than four steps at a time. He burst out of the stairs and ran through the lobby. Once outside, he jumped into his car and sped away.

He raced down the street saying the kind of words one expects an angry ogre to say.

Behind him, twenty feet in the air, a spot of speckled black followed.

Ty drove wildly, slowing only when he arrived at the gate to the Infinity building. The gate opened for him and he drove in.

He was not in good spirits.

Ty parked his car and walked quickly toward the building. The automatic glass door at the front slid open and he stepped inside. Behind him a flying dart shot through the air, tracking the man like a missile. Just as the door closed . . .

The door didn't close.

Instead, there was a horrible squawking noise. Ty turned around to see a metal bird caught in the door. Clark was four feet off the ground and pinched between the two glass doors. He was also dotted with bits of red and yellow and struggling to get free.

Ty leapt at the fowl creature and grabbed him with his big hands. He held the bird tightly, thrilled by his stroke of good luck, and staring at the elusive angel of death.

"Take a picture," Clark chirped. "It'll last longer."

"I can't believe it," Ty said.

"You seem like someone who has a hard time believing," Clark said. "Now, where's Ozzy?"

Ty gripped the bird in his hands and went to find Ray. He had something positive to report.

CHAPTER FIFTY-FOUR

THE PRISONER IS NOW ESCAPING

Sigi struggled with the ropes around her, rocking the chair she was in as she fought with the thick twine. Her arms were tied to her sides and the fight for freedom caused her curly hair to stick to her forehead and create almost as much irritation as the ropes.

"We've got to get out of here," she insisted.

Rin sat calmly in his chair, gazing at his daughter.

"What do you think of Ozzy?" he asked.

"Please," Sigi begged. "I think he's in trouble. Just like us."

"There's that," Rin agreed, "but has it been difficult having him live at the house with you and Patti?"

"Difficult? We're tied to chairs after being tranquilized and brought here by a madman. So yes, it's been a little difficult."

"I think you're handling it well."

"Would you—!"

Sigi was planning to say a few unkind things to her father, but her mood was altered by the sight of Rin's ropes dropping from around him and falling to the floor.

Rin instantly put his finger up to his lips to silence his daughter.

"Boy, I sure do hate being tied up," he said loudly as he slipped out of the rest of his ropes and stood up from the chair. He motioned for Sigi to join the pretend conversation.

"Oh, . . ." she said, catching on, ". . . me too."

Rin came around the back of Sigi's chair and untied her.

"I guess we're stuck here for good."

"Right," Sigi said as the ropes around her fell to the floor.

As quietly as she could, she stood up next to her dad. The sensation of being untied was painful but exhilarating. The two of them quietly stretched and flexed as they carried on with their fake conversation.

"If only we hadn't been captured," Rin said, stepping carefully toward the door.

"But we were," Sigi said sadly.

Rin found the small hidden handle on the round wall. He looked at his daughter as he stood next to her.

"Ready?" he mouthed.

Sigi nodded and Rin gave the handle a gentle pull.

He pushed open the hidden door and found a hallway with two tall ferns sitting in two tall pots. Between the ferns there was a long hallway that led to a white door with a gold handle.

"What—?" Sigi started to whisper before her dad signaled to still stay quiet.

The two of them walked down the hall and stood near the white door. The doorknob rattled and both Rin and Sigi stepped to the side and stood with their backs against the wall.

The door opened and an ogre in a blue suit walked out. He was moving so quickly that he didn't notice the two people at the sides of the door. In his right hand he was holding a strange-looking gun. Rin stuck out his foot and yanked it backwards. He caught the man on the right shin and the motion sent the ogre hurling forward toward the ground. The falling giant hit his head squarely on the edge of a potted fern. A loud fleshy clunk filled the hallway and the man's gun flew out of his hand and skidded across the floor.

Blue suit lay face down and motionless.

"He's not dead, is he?" Sigi asked.

Rin reached down and picked up the gun. Without hesitating, he shot the motionless man in the back of his left leg.

Sigi jumped, expecting there to be noise, but it was a tranquilizer gun that shot small darts.

"Is that what we were hit with?" Sigi said.

Her father wasn't there to answer the question. Rin

had already dashed into the room that the man had come out of. Sigi joined him.

Inside the room there was a table covered with electronic surveillance equipment. Next to the table were two chairs. There was no sign of anyone else.

"Where's Ozzy?" asked Sigi.

"Somewhere," Rin answered as he searched through all the equipment on the table. "This room was just for listening to us."

"How'd you get your ropes untied?"

"Wizards have complete power over ropes," Rin said. "Here it is."

Rin picked his phone up off the table and pressed the screen.

"You're not posting something, are you?" Sigi said angrily.

Rin looked at her. "No." He tapped at his phone a few more times. "There. I just needed to send a couple of texts."

"To who?"

"You wouldn't believe me if I told you. Now let's find that boy you're sweet on before that man in the hall regains consciousness."

"That's not a line most dads say to their daughters."

"I'm not most dads, and you're definitely not most daughters."

Inside the surveillance room there was another door that led them down a different hallway.

"How do we know where Ozzy is?"

"We don't."

Rin began opening doors, but they were all just dark empty rooms.

"This place has no windows," Sigi said.

"I think they're hoping it keeps out the birds."

"I hope Clark's okay."

"Have you ever known him not to be?"

"Countless times, thanks to you."

Rin opened a door near the end of the hall, and sitting in the middle of the room was Ozzy. He was still tied to a chair and his head was hanging down to his chest. The light above lit him up but did nothing to make things brighter. Next to Ozzy was a man in a green suit. He was sitting by a cart that had tubes running from it to Ozzy.

The man stood up and opened his mouth to holler. He was too slow. Rin shot a dart into his leg and the man and his green suit collapsed on the chair.

Rin and Sigi ran to Ozzy.

Moving quickly, Rin removed the needle from Ozzy's right arm. The wizard grabbed the tubing and a small glass case containing four vials of blood. He shoved everything into the pocket of his robe as Sigi worked at the ropes that were tying up Ozzy.

"Ozzy," she whispered fiercely. "Ozzy! Wake up."

The boy didn't move.

"Help me," Sigi said to her father.

Rin stepped over and undid one of the knots. Sigi

tugged at another and the rope loosened and slid down around Ozzy's lap.

"He's still not moving," Sigi said frantically.

"They've taken a lot of blood," Rin told her.

Sigi lifted Ozzy's head up and his dark hair hung in front of his eyes like frayed leather.

"Ozzy," she whispered again. "Ozzy."

"We don't have time to waste," Rin told his daughter.

"Come on," Sigi begged while trying to lift him up out of the chair.

"Leave me alone," Ozzy said mournfully, his eyes still closed.

"What?" Sigi asked. "Why?"

"I know the truth."

"Okay, fine," Rin sighed. "So, I'm not really a size thirty-two; I'm a thirty-six."

"Stop, Dad. What do you know the truth about, Ozzy?"

"Healing Winds," the boy whispered.

"What do you mean?" Sigi said, sounding confused. "Healing winds?"

Rin pulled out his list and checked off another item.

Ozzy looked at him. The boy's grey eyes were ringed with red the color of the plaid stripes on his pants. He appeared lost and afraid and checked-out.

"Come on," Rin said kindly. "We need to move."

"If you want me to go," Ozzy said in a whisper, "you'll have to use magic."

Rin shrugged. "There's nothing more magical than the human body."

The wizard reached down and yanked Ozzy up out of his seat and threw him over his right shoulder. The loose rope fell to the ground, but the boy didn't protest. Rin protested a little by groaning under Ozzy's weight.

"Let's go," Rin said to his daughter.

At the end of the hallway, they turned and saw a set of automatic glass doors in the distance. The natural light looked like a miracle and gave them something to run toward.

Moments before reaching the doors, two shadows approached the building and the automatic doors slid open.

Ty and Ray stepped in.

Rin stopped and stood twenty feet away from the two men. He still had Ozzy over his shoulder and the weight of the boy was beginning to take a toll.

"What are you doing here?" Sigi yelled, standing by her dad and staring at the two men, who were backlit by the light coming in from the doors.

"What?" Ray asked. "No hello?"

Sigi gave him a different mix of those two words.

Ray ignored her. "I see you found Ozzy. Sorry, but we can't let you take him."

Sigi looked at her dad as he stood there trying to keep Ozzy on his shoulders. The wizard was shaking like an enchanted leaf. She glanced down and saw the end of the gun sticking out of his right robe pocket.

"Well, then," Rin said grunting. He shifted Ozzy, trying to get a better hold on him. "I guess we're at an impasse. Because we are a package deal and we're not leaving without him. You have his blood back in the room. That should be enough."

Sigi knew her dad was lying; she'd seen him take the glass case and tubing.

"We made the mistake years ago of not collecting the boy," Ray said with no trace of good humor or grace. "I will not have any loose ends again."

The situation felt hopeless, so Sigi did the only thing she could think of.

With a quick jerk, she reached down and pulled the gun from her father's pocket. Then before anyone could react, she pointed it toward Ray and pulled the trigger. The dart hit his right shoulder. The red-headed man's knees folded, and he crumpled like a dirty towel that had been dropped down a chute.

Sigi turned the gun toward Ty and pressed the trigger. Nothing happened.

She pressed again, but the weapon was out of darts.

Ty laughed.

"I'm going to enjoy this," the large ogre said cruelly.

Ty began to move closer and Sigi threw the gun like an axe. It hit the man squarely in the forehead. Ty swayed for a moment before his eyes crossed and he fell backwards. His falling body activated the automatic doors.

Rin looked at his daughter and smiled proudly.

"You know that in normal situations you shouldn't shoot people with darts, right?"

Sigi nodded.

"I'm glad this wasn't a normal situation," the wizard said.

"Me too."

Rin hauled Ozzy out the open doors and across the parking lot toward a bus stop. They reached the stop just as a bus pulled up and opened its doors.

They climbed on.

"That was good timing," Sigi said as they sat down on the back row and propped Ozzy between them.

"Wizards and buses have a special bond."

"Well, maybe you and this bus and that rope back there should run off together."

Rin pulled a length of rope out of his pocket.

"You never leave good rope behind," he lectured. "So, I guess in a way I am."

Sigi leaned back and closed her eyes, too tired to even ask where they were going, and too smart to know she wouldn't get a straight answer anyway.

The moment felt like a brief respite from the storm, a well-earned break. But they would have all felt different if they had known that at that moment, locked in a box, locked in the trunk of a certain car, a certain bird was very much in danger.

CHAPTER FIFTY-FIVE

DON'T PRETEND YOU CAN JUSTIFY THE END

Ozzy woke up in a bed so soft he felt as if he had died and gone to marshmallow heaven. The sheets he was under were smooth, like a silk only a poet could describe. The room felt familiar and, as he rolled over, he saw a square window that helped him identify what spot on the globe he currently occupied.

Ozzy was at Ann's house.

Ann was Rin's sister and Ozzy had stayed in her home once before. She was a kind person with more polish than one would expect a sibling of Rin's to have.

Ozzy looked out the square window at the stars. As before, the view made him miss the superior view he used to have from his attic room in the Cloaked House.

The boy tried to piece together what had happened. The last thing he could remember was talking to Ray and hearing the truth about Rin. He also remembered the picture of Rin in the pamphlet.

Recalling the conversation made Ozzy feel sick again. He sat up in bed and looked at the bandage on his right arm. He had no recollection of what had happened there.

"Clark?" Ozzy whispered. "Clark?"

The bird didn't reply.

Ozzy thought about getting out of bed and trying to find Sigi or Ann, but the bed was soft, and it seemed easier to stay put.

There was a timid knock on the bedroom door.

"Yes?" Ozzy called out in a volume that suited the timidity.

The door opened slowly, and Rin came in.

Almost involuntarily, Ozzy scooted his whole body back on the bed and as far from the door and the false wizard as possible.

"Can I come in?" Rin asked kindly.

Taking the silence as an invitation, Rin walked in and sat down on a small plastic desk chair across the room. He didn't turn on the light or close the door. He just sat and let the stillness of the room erase some of the awkwardness of Ozzy's reaction. The boy didn't look at Rin; he kept his gaze directed at the stars outside of the square window.

"Are you hungry?" Rin finally asked.

Ozzy was starving, but he didn't say so.

"Ann fixed you a plate of food. It's downstairs in the fridge."

"I'm not hungry," Ozzy said, wanting nothing to do with the kind of food Ann made.

"I thought that might be the case."

Rin stood up and set a box of zebra cakes down on the end of the bed and returned to his chair. Ozzy took the box, opened it up, and began eating. The familiar, sugary taste seemed to soften his nerves just a bit.

"Why are we here?" Ozzy asked between two big bites.

"This felt like the right place to come," Rin said. "Hotels can be dangerous."

"Sigi's okay?"

"She's asleep in the next room."

"And where's Clark?"

Rin took a deep breath and sighed. "I went back to look for him. He wasn't there. The only thing there is a small hole in the back of the door where his beak was stuck. But talking with a girl at the check-in desk, apparently there was a bird loose in the hotel today. It chased a kid down three flights of stairs and flew out the front door."

Rin couldn't see it, but Ozzy smiled.

"He's probably looking for you now, unless he's waiting for the sun to charge him. I don't know if he remembers this house, or if he'll just head back to Otter Rock. What I do know is that he's resilient and probably falling in love with a spoon somewhere."

Ozzy polished off another pack of zebra cakes and Rin handed him a bottle of Sprite he had smuggled into the house. Ozzy took a long drink. Then, with sugar coursing through his veins, he found the courage to say what he wanted to say.

"You weren't in Quarfelt," he said sadly. "You were in a hospital."

"A story can have more than one twist," Rin replied.

"Ray said you were sick. He said he has records that show you going in and out of Healing Winds for help for years. Does Sigi know?"

"No."

"Patti told me you were sick," Ozzy said. "I didn't believe her. I thought you were a wizard."

"And what if I'm not?" Rin asked, his face more shadow than definition.

"Then there's no point to this. My parents were good, then horrible, now my dad's dead and my mother might be as well. Ray is evil and wants to ruin the world and we helped. I should have stayed in the Cloaked House. I should have never gone looking for answers. I should have never made that call."

"Ouch," Rin said softly.

"Sorry." Ozzy breathed out. "That's how I feel."

"No," Rin corrected, "my shoulder's just sore from carrying you."

The boy opened another pack of cakes. After swallowing a couple more bites he said,

"This is all a mistake."

The stars outside of the window stopped blinking.

"I could argue about what Ray told you," Rin said. "I could say he was lying and that I never went to Healing Winds."

"It'd be a dumb argument," Ozzy said. "I saw the picture."

"You saw the pamphlet?" Rin asked with embarrassment. "I can't believe I ever had just a mustache."

"*That's* what you have to say? You have nothing to say about the fact that you lied to me—you just want to complain about a mustache?"

Rin stood up and walked to the window. He looked down at the neighborhood park below and saw no movement or motion in the dark.

"Becoming a wizard isn't easy," he said in a voice so low Ozzy could barely hear it. Rin turned. "Everyone needs help, Ozzy. I'm not embarrassed to say that in the past I accepted some. The intensity of magic is hard to manage. Just like the pursuit of one's dreams can be deadly. I needed help in the past. But that doesn't change what I am. In fact, it has only made me stronger. There is a saying in Quarfelt, 'What doesn't kill you makes you tired.' Well, I was tired. I was hurt from experiences I couldn't avoid. I was also trying to accept Quarfelt in my own mind."

"You still say it's real?"

"Whether I say it or not, it is."

"Then do something," Ozzy said frustrated. "If you're a wizard, do something. Make this room light up. No, turn my pants green. No, bring my family to me."

"What would that prove?"

"It would give me hope that you can do what you've promised."

"It would give you nothing but memories and markers that indicate how weak your will was. What would you do with green trousers? Show them to others and insist they believe because of them?" Rin sighed sadly. "I thought I taught you better than that."

"You've taught me nothing!"

The weight of the room grew heavier. The darkness made the space feel like the bottom of the ocean, with millions of pounds of pressure pushing in threatening to crush the life out of everyone in the room.

"I'm sorry, Ozzy," Rin said. "Perhaps I should have led with the fact that I've spent time in a mental hospital. But believe it or not, I'm sane enough to know that doesn't look well listed in a classified ad. 'Struggling human for hire.' You wonder why I'm not pulling flowers from my sleeves or making the bad guys disappear? Well, those kinds of tricks are not magic. They're a glitch. They're a distraction that steals your attention. The true sadness of reality is that it has forgotten that magic is everywhere. We bury it with worry and tedium, because deep inside we all know it takes strength to wield a wand. It takes energy and belief to step out of the fog of reality and recognize the wonder in almost everything. You are resisting what is inevitable. And when you finally figure this all out, things will be both heavier, and more fantastic."

"Figure what out?" Ozzy asked angrily.

"I can't tell you."

The room was still.

Outside, the black sky began to fill up with thin ghostly clouds. When Ozzy finally spoke again, his voice was as soft as a feather, but it had the impact of a large stone.

"What you're really saying is that you won't do any magic?"

Rin took off his hat and ran his long fingers through his long hair.

"I'm saying I already have."

Ozzy laughed scornfully.

"You may not know it, Ozzy. But I am glad Ray told you the truth. It needed to happen. It was on my list. You deserve to have all the answers. You've had more to think about in your life than most people your age. Still, I need you to trust me for one more day."

"I can't."

"*Can't* is different than *won't*."

"I won't."

"Nobody can force you, Ozzy. But the conclusion of our quest is at hand. And I need you to believe in me one last time."

"Believe nothing," Ozzy said. "No matter where you read it, or who has said it."

"Nicely put." Rin stood up slowly. "Refrigerator magnets can be powerful."

Ozzy shook as he sat on the bed. "Well, I don't believe what you've said."

"Okay," Rin adjusted the belt on his robe. "I get it."

The once-wizard walked out of the bedroom and closed the door behind him.

Ozzy looked at the dark, vacant room and couldn't decide if he should cry or scream. Before he could make up his mind, something tapped against the outside of the square window.

The boy turned and saw stars draped with gossamer clouds.

CHAPTER FIFTY-SIX

CALLS OUT IN THE NIGHT

zzy moved closer to the window, hoping to see the bird he desperately missed. Instead, there was another tap as something small hit the glass and bounced off. The boy reached down and undid the latch. Grabbing the windowsill, he pulled it up and open. A cool breeze dropped through the opening like a blanket that chose not to be comforting.

Ozzy stuck his head out the window and gazed down at the haunting night.

"Clark?"

"Stop looking up all the time," a voice from down below said. "Sometimes what you're searching for is more in reach than you think."

Ozzy looked down. It was hard to see clearly, but there, standing on the sidewalk in the middle of the front yard, was an old man. Strike that—a very old man. Burn that—a very, very, old man, the kind of man who looked like he had been born before electricity, the invention of the wheel, or the discovery of fire.

"You—Grandpa?" Ozzy said, not knowing exactly what to call the man.

"I don't care for that term, but yes, yes, it's me," the old man said. "Now come down here."

The boy rubbed his eyes in disbelief. The last time he had seen his grandfather (the term sounded weird even in his own head) the old man had let Ozzy know that he didn't want anything to do with the boy's life.

"Come down," the old man said.

Without thinking, Ozzy climbed out of the window and onto the roof. He scooted to the edge and then, using the rain gutter, shimmied and dropped down into the front yard. He turned to see his grandfather staring at him. The old man was holding a book in his right hand.

"I wondered if you'd use the stairs and come out the front door like a civilized human," he said. "I knew you wouldn't."

"You did?"

"Yes, yes." The old man was flustered. "There's a table at the park."

Ozzy's grandfather walked down the front path, crossed the deserted street, and entered the neighborhood park. The boy followed ten steps behind him, wondering where he was being led.

"I don't understand why you're here."

"Please let me sit down first."

They came to a picnic table sitting empty under a small metal shelter. The park was empty mostly because it was midnight. The old man sat down and let out a dusty sigh. The expression on his face made it clear that he wasn't pleased about being there. Ozzy sat directly across from him.

Their arrival caused a light to flick on beneath the shelter.

Ozzy opened his mouth to speak but his grandfather stopped him by showing him the wrinkled palm of his left hand.

"I realize that on paper I might be your . . . well, your mother's father, but I don't want to be called anything like *Grandpa*. My name is Omen, and if you need to address me, use that."

Omen then set the book he was holding on top of the table. Under the light, Ozzy could see that the cover was purple leather and there was gold lettering on the front that read:

Oz

It wasn't surprising to see Omen with a book. The man was a bibliophile who lived and breathed them—well, *lived* was a bit generous. The surprise was in the fact that his grandfather was there at all.

"I don't understand why you're here."

"Any other day I would have said the same thing," the old man grumbled. "I hate being away from my books.

Or outside. But yesterday at three o'clock, when I went to answer my door and receive my latest titles, this was the only one that arrived. To say I was surprised is an understatement."

Omen pushed the book toward the boy.

Feeling like it was a trap, Ozzy didn't touch it.

"Go on," his grandfather insisted, "open it up."

Ozzy opened the front cover carefully. The end pages were orange and felt like a stiff satin. He turned the page and looked at the title.

The Trials of Oz
By Labyrinth

"What is this?" Ozzy asked, his messy bed hair making him appear extra surprised. "Is it a joke?"

"Do you think I'm funny?" Omen asked.

"No, not at all."

"Read the first page."

Ozzy turned to the beginning and began. Each word he read filled him with awe and fear. It was an account of his birth and his first years in New York. The information wasn't new—it was all things that Rin and he had discovered in the last while, but it was in a book and written as a story.

The boy looked up.

"I don't understand. Rin wrote this?"

"That's what it says," Omen said. "At least according to the bio on the last page."

Ozzy turned to the About the Author page at the back of the book.

Labyrinth was born in a hospital that has since been torn down and made into a supermarket and a Starbucks. He has a brother, Woody (deceased), a sister, Ann (alive), and a daughter named Sigmund (alive and quite brilliant). He is best known for being a wizard.

Looking up from the page, Ozzy said, "Sigi's name is really Sigmund?"

"Makes sense. That family seems to have a lot of issues."

Ozzy began to flip through the book. He spotted pages and paragraphs that described everything he and Rin and Sigi and Clark had been through. The mountain in New Mexico, the trouble in the ocean.

"There was a submarine out there?"

"At one point," Omen said. "It was once a lab in international waters. But that was a long time ago. That submarine no longer exists."

"So, it was Rin that destroyed the *Spell Boat?*"

"Read," Omen chastised. "Don't look at me for answers when there is a book in your hands."

Ozzy read the pages about Rin meeting and talking with Ozzy's mom.

She was a lovely woman, with eyes like those of her son and posture that would put a post to shame. What she wasn't was kind. Her mind seemed to be in a constant state of drift. She was forgetful and confused and stubborn. When I asked her what she could remember from the past she answered coldly, "All I remember is my work."

The words pressed on Ozzy's chest like a thick slab of granite. No mention of her son. Just the all-consuming work that had torn his family apart. He tried to catch his breath and then quickly flipped the pages. His fingers fell on one of the last chapters.

Omen put his old hand on the book and pulled it back.

"That's enough," Omen said.

Ozzy blinked slowly. "You told me to read."

"Old men are fickle."

"At what point does the story end?" Ozzy asked.

"It ends tomorrow," his grandfather said. He flipped to a page near the back and showed the boy. "But you should focus on tonight."

Omen pointed to page 350.

As Ozzy read the words, something inside of him began to grow. It was a feeling of energy so raw and swelling that he felt as if his skin couldn't hold it in. He read the word-for-word conversation he had just had with Rin in the room with the square window. He read about the pebbles his grandfather had thrown at the window and how his grandfather had said:

"Stop looking up all the time. Sometimes what you're searching for is more in reach than you think."

Ozzy looked at Omen.

"For the record," Omen said, "I never would have said that if I hadn't read it in there first."

There was the account of Ozzy climbing down the roof to meet with his grandfather.

"How . . . ? How is this possible?"

"I think your friend might be a wizard," Omen said. Only a book would have motivated me to travel here and tell you this. I enjoyed the read. It is sorcery and magic in the most outstanding way."

"Maybe he printed it a while ago and just guessed at what you were going to do?"

Omen eyed Ozzy. "You don't believe that."

Ozzy didn't.

"I don't know what to believe." A sudden realization dropped down from the thin clouds and landed on the boy. "Wait—you said the story ends tomorrow."

His grandfather nodded.

"So you know the ending?"

Another nod.

Ozzy reached out for the book, but his grandfather pulled it away.

"It would do you no good to know."

"I think it would."

"What you think you want is often the thing most dangerous to acquire."

"Does the book say you would say that?"

"Yes," the old man said. "Otherwise I never would have. Now, I'm old, it's the middle of the night, and I miss my other books. Tell that wizard he's brilliant. I can think of no other way anyone would have gotten me out here to meet with you had I not read it in a book. He is truly a genius."

"Is that another thing the book says you'd say?"

"Yes," Omen admitted sadly.

Ozzy's grandfather stood up, his bones and joints snapping like bubble wrap as he stood.

"You're just going to leave?"

Omen nodded.

"Do you play a part in what happens tomorrow?" asked Ozzy.

"Only if my influence now helps you discover what you should already know."

"What do I know?"

"I hope you find out."

Omen turned to leave.

"Wait," Ozzy pleaded. "You could stay the night here. I'm certain Ann would let you."

Omen looked at his grandson. "That's not the way the story goes."

Ozzy stood up and as he turned from the table, his foot caught on the edge of the cement pad. He stumbled onto the grass face-first. His grandfather did nothing to assist him getting up.

Once on his feet again, the boy dusted himself off. There were long grass stains on the legs of his pants.

"Look," Omen said.

Ozzy saw that his grandfather was pointing back toward the house. When he looked, he saw that the home was still dark. Only the open square window was lit up.

"What am I looking at?"

"I have no idea," Omen said. "But in the book, I tell you to look."

The old man walked away from the covered table and disappeared into the night. His image vanished quickly, but the sound of his snap, crackle, and pop took longer to drift away. Ozzy stood alone wondering why his grandfather had told him to look at the house. There was only the one glowing window.

Ozzy laughed in amazement.

He looked down at his green-stained legs, back up at the glowing window, and then into the darkness where his grandfather had gone.

"He lit up the room," he whispered in disbelief. "My pants are green, and I was led to family."

"Daaammp."

It wasn't in his personality to swear, but there was magic—or trickery—afoot and he didn't know how to react. His body continued to expand and contract with a feeling of unstable possibilities. His mind could make no sense of the book Omen had shown him, or of what was happening, but the trainee was now willing to give the wizard one more day.

Unable to climb back up onto the roof to get into his room, Ozzy tried the front door.

It was unlocked.

As he stepped into the dark house, he heard a voice.

"Do you know what time it is?" Rin asked.

Ozzy turned around and saw the wizard lying on the couch. He had a blue quilt on him and was propped up on his elbows.

"I don't."

"Neither do I," Rin admitted.

Ozzy nodded, but it was doubtful if Rin could see. He stepped quietly past the couch and toward the stairs.

"Are we good?" the wizard whispered.

Ozzy stopped stepping. "We are."

"Good." Rin pulled the blanket up to his chin. "You should get some sleep. Tomorrow's a big day."

"Good night, Rin."

"Good night, Ozzy."

The boy's heart and mind were buzzing comfortably as he ascended the stairs.

CHAPTER FIFTY-SEVEN

PROPER FOOD CHOICES

Ozzy got very little sleep—he lay awake until four and was awakened shortly after six by Sigi. She shook him in a way that made it clear there would be no more rest in the immediate future.

"Get up," Sigi said urgently. "Ray has Clark."

Ozzy sat up instantly. "What?"

"Ray sent my dad a picture of Clark. He was tied up and caged."

"No." Ozzy jumped out of bed. He looked around the room frantically and picked up a blue T-shirt from the floor. "What do we do?" he asked as he put the shirt on. "Where's Rin?"

"Well, . . ." Sigi said nervously. "He went to pick up breakfast."

"Are you kidding?"

"Apparently he worked something out with Ray," Sigi

quickly explained. "We're going to make an exchange for Clark later today."

"What are we exchanging?"

"I'm not sure. But my dad thought we might as well eat breakfast while we wait. Also, Ann was about to make food. He wanted to get something before she insisted on feeding us."

Ozzy walked to the square window and looked out at the sky.

"Is Clark hurt?"

"I don't think so. He actually looked really good in the photo Ray sent. I know that sounds weird, but it was a well-photographed picture."

The boy stared at the girl, and the girl stared back.

"It's stupid, I know," Sigi admitted. "I don't know what to think. I'm as worried as you are."

Ozzy looked out the window and down at the park.

"Are you okay?" Sigi asked. "You were in rough shape when we brought you here."

"I won't be okay until we have Clark," Ozzy said honestly.

"Me neither."

Sigi put her arm around Ozzy and gazed at the park with him.

"I saw my grandpa last night."

"In a dream?"

"No. He was down there, in the front yard. We went to the park."

"That sounds . . . fun?"

"It wasn't fun. It was strange. His name is Omen."

"That's foreboding."

"He came to convince me that your dad was really a wizard."

"I thought you already believed that."

"I didn't yesterday."

"Really? But you're the one who used to think that Harry Potter and other books were real."

"I grew up with no one to tell me differently."

"What else did your grandpa say?"

Ozzy wasn't ready to tell her everything, so he went with, "He told me your name was really Sigmund. I thought you said it was Sigourney?"

"My mom never liked Sigmund. She changed it to Sigourney."

"Well, I need to know what you prefer so I can get it tattooed on my arm correctly."

"Sigi," she said. "And don't."

"Breakfast!" Rin's sister hollered up from downstairs. "Come down when you're ready."

Ozzy broke out in a cold sweat.

"I thought Rin was getting breakfast," he said.

"Maybe he didn't tell Ann."

The two of them split up and took an inordinately long time getting ready, in hopes of Rin returning before they went down.

When the two of them finally came downstairs, Rin

was back and arguing with his sister about him bringing in outside food.

"Do you know what's *in* that?" Ann asked as the wizard held up a wrapped sausage McMuffin.

"Yes," he said. "Magic."

Ann was wearing a pink bathrobe longer than the yellow one her brother was sporting. Her black hair was pulled back with orange barrettes and she had on fuzzy red Elmo slippers.

"I don't allow sugar in any form in this house, Brian!"

"It's Rin, and we have a rather big day ahead of us," the wizard argued back. "We need to eat well."

"I made yum-yum yolks," Ann snapped. "They're vegan eggs with vegan mayonnaise and a touch of dry, saffron-infused tofu."

"Just a touch?" Rin said with disgust. "How about you save it for later."

"You'll be back later?"

"No, I meant save it for you later."

Ann left the kitchen in a huff. Ozzy and Sigi dug into the McDonald's bags as Rin filled them in.

"Ray has Clark."

He showed Ozzy the photo Ray had sent.

"That *is* a good picture," Ozzy said as he chewed.

"How'd Ray even get ahold of you?" Sigi asked.

"I called him," Rin admitted. "It really is just lucky that they had Clark."

"Lucky?" Ozzy asked.

"Well, magical." The wizard winked at Ozzy.

For the record, Rin was not a great winker. It was a friendly gesture that he liked to use, but it always made him look like he was in the middle of a sneeze.

"Okay," Ozzy said. "Magical. Why?"

"Because now Ray feels as if he has something to trade. We are going to meet them at twelve-fifteen and give them the vials of Ozzy's blood in exchange for Clark."

"If we give them the vials, they win," Sigi pointed out.

"No," her father insisted. "I won't let that happen. But Clark is the main concern now."

"He'd appreciate that," Ozzy said.

Ann came back into the room to chastise her brother further. "I just think it's so disrespectful to come into my house and bring that." She pointed at the McDonald's bag. "What's next? Full-sugar soda? Candy?"

"That reminds me," her brother said. "We saw Mom."

"Really?" Ann asked, suddenly more curious than angry. "You haven't been *there* in a long time."

"I wanted to show her my daughter."

Ann gasped and glanced at Sigi. "I'm so sorry," she said. "I can imagine how that went."

"It wasn't pretty," Rin added.

Ann put her arm around Sigi as she sat at the kitchen bar and ate a stack of pancakes.

"Are you okay?" Ann asked. "Aside from the poor food choices you're consuming?"

"Yes," Sigi said confidently. "I'm fine, but I don't think Candy will be leaving me anything in her will."

"Don't worry about that," Ann said. "She'll never die. Besides, your father has enough money to set you up when he kicks the bucket, which will be sooner than later thanks to all the sugar he eats. Of course, he can only get the money if he takes . . ."

"That's it," Rin said interrupting. "Look at the time?" He glanced around for a clock but couldn't see one. "We've got to get going!"

"But—"

"Buts are for interrupting," the wizard insisted as he pushed his chair in. "Come on, you two. Bring the food you haven't eaten."

"I'll pack up what I made for you as well."

"There isn't time for that," Rin said. "We've got a bird to save."

The wizard, the trainee, and Sigi thanked Ann for the hospitality and then split the scene before she could wrap up a single thing.

"What was she talking about?" Ozzy asked as they drove away from Ann's house. "What did you need to get from your mom?"

"Is it that thing you took from the safe?" asked Sigi.

"It's not important," Rin said. "What's important is that we get to where we're going on full stomachs. Hand me a breakfast burrito. I suddenly feel international."

"Where are we going?"

"Are you two ready to be famous?"

"Depends," Sigi said. "Famous like movie stars, or famous like two kids who are driven off a cliff by a wizard?"

"Famous like movie stars."

"I can live with that," said Sigi.

"I'd prefer not to be a star."

"One of you is going to get their wish."

"If we're making wishes," Ozzy said. "I'd like to wish for Clark to be back."

"Classic mistake," Rin said kindly. "You should have wished for more wishes."

The international wizard took a bite of his burrito.

"Are you really not going to tell us where we're going?" Sigi asked. "Where are we making the exchange?"

"Let's have it be a surprise."

Ozzy and Sigi didn't say anything, knowing they had no say in the matter anyway.

CHAPTER FIFTY-EIGHT

URGENCY AND FEAR

Sheriff Wills flew down the freeway, Patti sitting in the passenger seat. He had the lights of his patrol car flashing, but the siren was off.

"Are we going to make it there on time?" Patti asked.

"I'm sure hoping so."

"Why Portland?" she asked.

"I have no idea where any of this is heading," Wills said. "I just want to get Sigi and Ozzy safely away from Brian."

"Thank you," Patti said sincerely.

Sheriff Wills and Patti had a single purpose. Over the last couple of days, they had spent a lot of time together trying to figure out where Rin had taken Sigi and Ozzy. They were at their wits' end with all that Rin had done. They were worried about the danger Ray represented, but they were equally uneasy about what Sigi's own father was capable of.

"He won't hurt them," Wills said, trying to sound comforting.

"I know," Patti agreed. "I don't think he'd purposely do anything to harm them, but I do think he's more than capable of putting them in a situation where they will get hurt."

"The place is going to be packed with cops," Wills said. "They'll find him."

The sheriff looked at the GPS on the patrol car's dashboard. He pressed on the gas and sped even faster to the Oregon Convention Center.

CHAPTER FIFTY-NINE

DRESSING THE PART

Jon was new to Instagram; he followed only one person—a wizard named Rin. He had watched Rin post pictures of breakfast food and zebra cakes, but nothing that let him know where he and Ozzy and Sigi had gone after they had left WetLand. But this morning that had changed. Rin had posted a picture of himself standing in front of the Keep Portland Weird mural and holding a breakfast burrito in his hand. The single hashtag below the picture said,

#PortlandComiConTodayAtTwelveFifteen

It was a very clear clue.

The moment Jon saw the post he knew where he needed to be. He had holed up in a vacant vacation home near Corvallis, but it was time to leave. He slipped out of the cabin and jogged calmly down to a nearby street. He found a car to hotwire and then drove north to Portland. It was an hour-and-a-half drive to the Rose City, but Jon had just enough time to make one stop along the way. If things went right, he would arrive at the convention center dressed properly and on time.

Of course, nothing had gone right for Jon in quite some time.

But with his belief in the possibility of magic, the average man was hopeful today would be the day that his luck would turn around.

CHAPTER SIXTY

COULD A PERSON BE SO MEAN?

Ray put on an avocado-green dress shirt and closed the sleeves with cufflinks that had cost as much as a good used car. He threw a white tie around his neck and tied an impressive-looking full Windsor knot. He stared at himself in the large closet mirror and smiled. It was the kind of smile that normally gave children bad dreams and caused people to close their curtains as he walked by their windows. But today the smile was all for himself.

Today he would finally get what he wanted.

It had not been easy for him to leave New York and come to Oregon. Thanks to the right medication and proper motivation, he was doing just fine. He had surprised himself with how easy it was. It had caused him so little stress that he was having to rethink the way he would live once he achieved world domination.

Ray stepped out of the closet and into the large bedroom he was staying in. The house he had rented for the visit was opulent, extravagant, and massive. If he had to be away from New York, he would at least stay somewhere comfortable.

Just outside of the bedroom was a formal dining area with a long table centered under a massive crystal chandelier. Standing near the table was Ty. He had on his official blue suit and was waiting stoically for his next order. Sitting on the table near Ty was a black wire cage. The top of the cage was rounded with a steel loop in the middle for hanging. Inside the cage was a small metal bird tied up with black wire, lying on its side.

Clark saw Ray come in and instantly began to aggressively chirp and tweet.

"Is that what you're wearing?" Clark scoffed. "I know where we're going, and you're going to stand out like a cruel thumb."

"Quiet," Ray insisted.

"You like to cage things that should fly? And silence things that should sing?"

"I like to control things that are too stupid to know how to act."

"Well, good luck with that," Clark said. "Even if you get that serum, it won't work on me. I have no brain."

"That's obvious."

Clark tilted his head to the left while looking out of the cage.

"You seem really short for a villain," he said. "You should make this lump of a human," Clark nodded in Ty's direction, "carry around a box for you to stand on."

Both Ray and Ty appeared to be unfazed by what a brainless metal bird was calling them.

"You know what, Clark?" Ray said. "Once I figure out how you were created, I'm going to make an army of clones. Then I'm going to run you through a shredder."

"Do you kick your mom with those lips?" Clark squawked.

"It's *kiss*," Ray said impatiently. "Do you *kiss* your mom?"

"I don't think so," Clark argued. "Who kisses their mom? Of course, I don't have one. Which makes me a bor-phan."

"I assume that means bird-orphan."

"Looking at you, I bet you assume a lot," the bird chirped. "I wouldn't even be here if you didn't have your glass doors do the dirty work."

"Clamp his beak," Ray ordered.

"With extreme pleasure."

Ty opened the cage and grabbed Clark. Holding the bird's body and head, he pinched the beak closed and twisted a small piece of wire around it to create a muzzle of sorts. Clark tried to tweet, but no sound came out.

"Cover the silver strip too," Ray added. "I want him silent and still."

Ty took a strip of black tape and put it on top of the silver strip.

"Now," Ray said, "that's better."

"Much better," Ty agreed.

"I didn't ask for your opinion," said Ray, harshly reminding his lead ogre where he stood.

Ty apologized.

"We should go," Ray instructed. "I want to get a good look at the convention center before that wizard and his friends show up. Bring the bird."

Ty picked up the cage and followed Ray out of the house and to the large black SUV waiting in the drive.

CHAPTER SIXTY-ONE

COMICON

The Oregon Convention Center was teeming with fantastical life. Everywhere you looked, there were booths selling small figurines and costumes and posters. There was an entire floor for anime and another for gaming. The multinational media conglomerates were there too, all hoping to cash in on the geek culture they used to scorn. Those companies had massive booths filled with products like energy drinks, toys, and candy.

Ozzy walked around in awe.

He had never seen anything like what he was now seeing, and he had seen some amazing things in the last half year of his life. Everywhere he looked there were superheroes and aliens and movie characters walking around like they owned the place.

"Who's that?" he asked Sigi.

"A truly fat Thor," she answered.

The best part about the Portland ComiCon was that

Rin fit right in. He walked through the crowd of people like a magical Moses, parting the sea of geeks and nerds like a pro.

"This seems like a strange place to meet up with Ray," Sigi hollered as someone dressed as R2-C4, half-robot half-explosive, bumped into her.

"It's a public place," Rin shouted back to her. "Ray's a powerful person who hates crowds. This will throw him off his game and give us a sea of witnesses. Plus, Jeff Goldblum's going to be here tomorrow. Now let's hurry."

They reached a large ballroom that had a healthy stream of people heading into it. Near the ballroom door was a small screen, listing what events were happening in that room.

Rin stopped to read the screen.

Ozzy and Sigi looked past him to do the same.

12:15 *The Perennial Five:* Cast and Crew

"What's *The Perennial Five?*" Ozzy asked.

"You'll see," Rin said as he pushed into the stream of people still moving into the room.

The large ballroom was packed. Lines and lines of folding chairs were filling up with people of all races, creeds, religions, sexes, colors, wings, horns, spandex, and makeup.

"What are we doing?" Ozzy shouted. "Aren't we here to get Clark?"

The wizard nodded.

Ozzy and Sigi followed close behind Rin as he shoved

his way toward the front of the big room. Up ahead they could both see a long row of tables covered with black fabric on top of a platform and next to a podium. Sitting behind the tables were four remarkably interesting people: two women, one thin man, and one man so large he took up two seats.

Rin kept walking closer to the front and Ozzy and Sigi kept following. The wizard led them to the front row, and then to their great surprise, he didn't stop. Rin walked around a short barricade and jogged up three steps leading onto the platform.

"What are you doing?" Ozzy hissed.

"Taking our places."

Behind the long line of covered tables were nine chairs. In front of each chair there was a microphone and a bottle of water. Five of the chairs were occupied by the four interesting cosplayers. Rin took a seat at a spot that had his name on it. It was then that Ozzy noticed there was a place next to Rin that had Sigi's name, and a place next to her that had his.

"What is happening?" Sigi said as she looked out at the thousands of people filing into the ballroom and sitting to face the stage.

Ozzy sat down in his chair without answering. He picked up the name card on the table and read the small print under his name.

OZZY TOFFY
Artifice Wump

"Artifice Wump?"

"Mine's not any better," Sigi said, showing him her card.

SIGI OWENS
Merry Dangle

Rin was talking with a heavy man named Bill who was taking up the two seats next to him. Sigi tugged on her father's sleeve.

"What is all of this?" she said with a smile, pretending to be calm so that the growing crowd in front of them wouldn't realize how confused she was. "Merry Dangle?"

"Congratulations," Rin said as he turned to her. "She has the meatiest part in the movie."

"What movie?" Sigi hissed happily.

"The one we're pretending to be in."

Ozzy leaned in closer to Sigi and looked Rin in the eyes.

"Can't you do *anything* normal?" he asked, trying hard to not look frazzled.

"Normal has no set definition."

"Who are those people?" Sigi pointed to the other five table guests.

"They're backup," Rin said.

"For what?" Sigi asked. "A sad prom?"

Rin smiled. "Look around."

Ozzy and Sigi both took a moment to look out at the crowd. The room was loud and chaotic as more and more people continued to pour in.

"Are we fighting *all* these people?" Ozzy questioned, wondering if he had the strength to take over the will of everyone there.

"Look closer," Rin suggested.

A second sweeping glance helped the two teenagers to see what Rin was talking about. Standing against the back wall were at least twelve large ogres in blue suits.

"Ten rows up," Rin said. "On the left."

Trying to appear casual as they glanced, they saw Ray, sitting ten rows back and on their far left. In front of him was another ogre. Behind him was another. And sitting next to him another.

"This feels like the mother of all bad ideas," Ozzy said.

"What?" Rin asked with genuine surprise. "You two are playing the cool teenagers in an important movie. You'll be a part of the PFU."

"Really?" Sigi complained.

"Perennial Five Universe," Rin said proudly.

"I thought perennials were flowers."

"Some are. Here." Rin handed Sigi a printed program. It was flipped open to the current date and time. "This should explain things."

Ozzy and Sigi read the short paragraph Rin was pointing to.

12:15 Ballroom B. *The Perennial Five*: Cast and Crew
Come experience a rare opportunity. This is your chance to know more about the most anticipated movie of the year—*Perennial Five: The Comeuppance.*

Meet the cast and crew of what is sure to be a movie for the ages. Find out about the PFU and all upcoming information. Bring your questions and enthusiasm. This panel promises to be one of the most popular and engaging ones. #wherewondertakescontrol #nottobemissed #PFU

Ozzy and Sigi finished reading the paragraph and looked up at Rin.

"I wrote that," he bragged.

"This movie doesn't exist," Sigi whispered intensely.

Ozzy shook his head. "Are we going to have to answer questions?"

"About a movie that doesn't exist?" Sigi reiterated.

"Yes," Rin said excitedly. "But don't worry—your answers can be anything."

The wizard's reply was not comforting.

"There's so many people," Sigi said as she glanced out at the noisy crowd.

The wizard's daughter was right. The room was at capacity. People were standing in the aisles and edges. Beyond the open doors at the back of the room, more people were outside of the room looking in. Ray had his eyes on them and wasn't blinking.

"All this for a movie that's not real?" Ozzy questioned.

"If you think about it, no movies are," Rin replied.

A pudgy man with hair where it shouldn't be and no hair where it should be walked up onto the stage and stood behind a podium at the end of the table. He gazed down the row of guests and nodded politely. Rin and the rest of the Five nodded back.

"Here we go," the wizard whispered excitedly.

The vast crowd before them began to quiet down in anticipation of Wrong-Hair saying something. The man checked his watch.

"I see it's time," he said into the microphone on the podium. "If you could all take your places and silence your cellphones?"

Though the crowd was made up entirely of people who claimed to be rogues and independents, they all did exactly as they were told.

"Thank you," Wrong-Hair said. "My name is Martin Foote, and I will be the moderator for this session. I believe we are all in for a treat. In my opinion you have picked the right spot to sit. Because I feel we are at the cusp of something extraordinary. Sitting before you are the stars of the upcoming movie *Perennial Five: The Comeuppance.*"

The crowd clapped and cheered as if they had any idea of what the movie was or who Rin and his cohorts were.

"We'll begin by hearing an introduction from each of our guests." Martin looked down the row of people sitting behind the long table. "Would each of you please tell us who you are and who you play in the movie. We'll start with you, Flora the Older."

Flora stood and adjusted her black beret. She started to talk and then realized that the mic was on the table. She sat back down and moved her mouth close to the mic. "I am a witch," she announced. "Classically trained. And I play a very important and crucial part in the movie. But not wanting to spoil anything, I will say no more."

The crowd clapped as Martin thanked Flora and introduced Gemi.

"I play Gemi the Younger and I too am a witch. Self-trained. I'm good with curses, and I play a role every bit as important as Flora's."

More clapping and Jayson was introduced.

"I am an alchemist," he said in a deep voice.

The crowd wasn't impressed.

"I'm really important as well," Jayson insisted in a much higher voice.

It was Bill's turn.

The big man shifted in his two seats and pulled both microphones up to his putty-like face. He winked with his one eye and swiveled his head so that everyone could clearly see his eye patch.

"I be Bill," he said. "A wizard and a scourge. My role is as big as my backside."

The audience loved that. So did Bill.

When it was Rin's turn, the wizard had surprisingly few things to say.

"My name is Rin, and I am the ending."

The crowd loved the veiled and mysterious answer.

Rin nodded in a way that he probably thought looked gracious.

"And finally," Martin said. "We have the young stars

of the film, Sigi Owens and Ozzy Toffy, who play the roles of Artifice and Merry."

"Hello," Sigi said into her mic.

"Hello as well," Ozzy added, hoping the attention would quickly move off them.

Sigi saw the need to add something more.

"The two of us loved being in this movie. It was sort of a dream role." She reached under the table and took Ozzy's hand. The gesture helped calm them both down. "I don't think I've ever done anything that meant this much to me. And I've had the time of my life starring with these people."

Rin winked at his daughter, and Bill handed him a tissue.

The audience clapped about what Sigi had said and cheered in celebration for the fake movie and all that was attached to it.

"Wait," Rin said into his microphone, "we're missing something."

The crowd held their breath.

"This movie would not have been possible without the world's greatest producer," the wizard said. "The man who believed in this when no one else did. The man who was willing to sacrifice everything so that the true vision of the PFU could make it to the screen. And that man is here today. Please welcome Ray Dench!"

Rin pointed to Ray, who sat dumbfounded ten rows back and to their left.

CHAPTER SIXTY-TWO

GRIP OF TENSION

The audience in Ballroom B had no idea who Ray Dench was, but they clapped as if they'd like to.

"Please," Rin said with glee as he looked out at Ray, "it is my highest honor to have him here. Let's give him the kind of hand you would give someone who granted all your wishes and made all your dreams come true. Come on up, Ray."

Ray Dench did not look like himself now. He looked like a lost dog being threatened by a cruel owner. His cold exterior blinked off for a second before he was able to gather his wits and regain his composure. He waved Rin's request off, refusing to get up as the crowd went wild.

"This is for you, Ray," Rin shouted. "Get up here!"

The nicely groomed man with the green shirt and red hair was livid. His face matched his hair and made it appear that his head was on fire.

"Come up!"

Ray was not used to other people besting him. His desire to be anywhere else was overtaken by his need to show Rin that he did not have the upper hand. His face cooled, and he stood like a statue that had grown tired of sitting. Then he walked up to the stage as the entire room cheered. He climbed the three steps and took the seat next to Ozzy.

He smiled at the boy.

The junior wizard could feel the hate coming off him. Ray leaned forward and talked into his microphone.

"Thank you," he said coolly. "I am not one for public appreciation."

Someone whistled and another person made some sort of beeping noise.

Ray casually glanced out at his army of ogres stationed throughout the crowd.

Ozzy saw what Ray was doing and wanted to run. He wanted to leave the stage, the room, the building, reality. He wanted to be anywhere Ray wasn't.

"Now that we have almost everyone," Rin said. "Let the questions begin."

There were microphones on stands in the aisles so that people could ask questions. Behind the microphones were lines of people waiting to be heard. Martin gave a few rules of question etiquette and then motioned for them to begin.

A woman dressed as some sort of evil Pippi Longstocking was the first.

"I haven't really seen anything about this movie," she

said excitedly, "but I would love to interview you for my blog."

"That's not a question," Gemi said.

"If you want an interview, find me on Instagram," Rin added. "I'm at well-managed-magic."

Martin took a moment to remind the audience once more what was and wasn't a question.

The next question came from a man/tree/pancake.

"Hi, I'm Rooty-Grooty-Fresh-and-Fruity," he said, describing his outfit.

The crowd sort of liked it.

"Anyway, I was wondering if *Perennial Five* is set in our reality, or if it takes place in an alternate one?"

"I like the pancake part of your outfit," Rin responded. "It shows signs of strong magic. As for your question, I'll let Ray answer that."

Ray sniffed calmly. Then trying hard not to appear rattled, he leaned into his mic and said, "It takes place in a reality where all magic is dead."

The audience oohed and ahhed.

"It's dark," Ray added, "but I guarantee that the ending will blow your minds."

It was a strong line, delivered by a cruel man, and the crowd was into it. It took Martin a full minute to calm everyone down. With order restored, a man dressed as SpongeBob No-Pants stepped up to the mike.

"Um, . . . I have a podcast," he seemed to brag, clearly

not knowing what kind of things people should brag about, "and I'm wondering what the plot of this movie is?"

"It's an exciting one," Bill answered, bragging about something he didn't know. "There's all the elements you want, and none of the ones ye don't want."

For some reason, people continued to clap and cheer.

In the back of the room, Ozzy saw someone in a green uniform. He did a double take and saw that the man in the uniform was standing next to someone in a white blouse. Though they were far away, their expressions were easy to read—neither the sheriff or Patti looked happy. Sheriff Wills leaned over and whispered into the ear of a nearby Portland police officer. That officer waved at another officer a few feet away from him.

Ozzy squeezed Sigi's hand and she squeezed back to let him know that she'd seen them too.

Ray was tired of only acting half-creepy, so he reached over and put his hand on Ozzy's knee. Then leaning in a few inches, he whispered,

"You should have accepted my offer when you had the chance."

Ozzy smiled nervously while a woman who said she was Marley Quinn stepped up to the mic to ask a question.

Ray had more to say to Ozzy. "You and your friends will not make it out of this alive." He smiled as he whispered into his ear.

The boy tried to brush Ray's hand off his knee, but it only made him squeeze tighter.

Martin informed the half-dog, half–Harley Quinn that the story idea she was going on about sounded interesting, but it wasn't a question. The woman sat down, and a man dressed as a Spiderman from a dingy and low-rent part of the Spiderverse took the mic and said,

"This question is for Labyrinth."

Rin doffed his hat politely.

The man at the mic was nervous. He took a deep breath and asked.

"Are wizards real?"

Ozzy looked at Sigi. There was something about the off-brand Spiderman's voice that was familiar. With Ray's hand on his left knee, and Sigi holding his right hand, Ozzy felt planted in his seat—unmovable and frozen. Sigi's dark eyes made it clear that she too recognized the voice as belonging to Jon. Rin didn't seem to recognize it. He answered Off-Brand Spiderman's question as if it had been asked in earnest.

"Of course wizards are real," Rin said kindly.

"Then you're a real wizard?" Off-Brand asked.

Rin stared intently at the masked questioner. "I believe you know the answer to that," he said seriously.

Ozzy took a sip of water and found it hard to swallow. The room was growing smaller and pushing in on him. He could feel something building to a dangerous point—like an overheated radiator about to give.

Off-Brand was supposed to sit down and let the next person ask a question, but he remained standing and continued to shake. The audience could feel a shift of weird energy in the room. Things had been lighthearted and funny, but now they were heavy and intriguing.

"You know," Rin continued, his eyes on the spider, "Bill gave a fine answer about the plot earlier."

Bill smiled proudly.

"But," Rin went on, "I feel I should share something with all of you that no one else has yet seen. An exclusive."

The audience went silent and slid to the edge of their seats.

Rin reached into the pocket of his robe and pulled out the glass case with the four vials of Ozzy's blood in it. He set the case on the table in front of him. The audience gasped as if he had just shown them a real infinity stone.

It had not seemed possible, but Ray sat up even straighter. He eyed the vials, knowing that they were more valuable than any infinity stone could ever hope to be.

"These are an important part of this story," Rin said dramatically, "but their purpose can't be understood without the most remarkable part of the movie." The wizard turned to look at Ray. "Mr. Dench, will you bring in the bird?"

Stuck between Rin and Ray, Ozzy and Sigi could feel daggers being thrown back and forth.

"What are you saying?" Ray asked.

"Let's show them the bird," Rin said, "the most interesting part of the movie. You do have it, don't you?"

Ray looked at the glass case in front of Rin. "Of course."

He waved to Ty in the back and the man stepped out a side door.

"This is exciting," Rin cheered. "Due to Ray's generosity, this room gets a sneak peek at my favorite character."

The audience was so pumped up that the possibility of some of them passing out seemed like a real concern. Off-Brand Spiderman continued to stand at the mic, shaking.

Ty was back, and in his right hand he was carrying what looked like a covered bird cage. Cellphones exploded with flashes of light as the ogre delivered the object to Ray. Ty climbed the three stairs and set it on the end of the table near Ray.

Ray glanced at the vials. Rin, Ozzy, and Sigi only had eyes for the cage.

"Do you mind if I do the unveiling?" Rin asked. "Here, you can hold these."

The wizard pushed the glass case in front of Sigi toward Ray. Ray reluctantly pushed the covered cage past Ozzy toward Rin. The dangerous exchange was taking place in front of thousands of people who had no clue what was really happening.

Ray grabbed the glass case and Rin pulled the cage directly in front of him. The Perennial Five all leaned in closer to see what the wizard was about to do. Ray put the glass case in his lap.

"*The Perennial Five* is a movie," Rin said, "but this item makes it a masterpiece."

The crowd went wild.

Rin pulled off the cover. Lying on the bottom of the cage was a lifeless black metal bird tied up with wire.

The crowd and the rest of the Five were confused.

"It don't look like a masterpiece," Bill said.

Ozzy began to stand up to reach for the cage, but he could feel that Ray was now pressing the end of a gun up against his hip in a way that no one else could see. The boy sat back down.

Rin and Sigi opened the cage and Sigi pulled Clark out. She ripped the tape off his back as the wizard undid the wires that were holding his body and beak. They set the bird on the table, but he didn't move.

Rin rolled Clark over a couple of times, but he wouldn't perk up.

For the first time there were a couple disappointed groans from the audience.

"Don't worry," Rin said. "He'll come around."

Ray knew that when Clark came to life, his odds of escaping dropped dramatically. He was done with all of this. He was done being tricked by someone who belonged locked up. He was done wasting his time. He nodded to Ty, who was still standing on the platform. Ty walked over the podium and handed Martin a note.

The crowd was very interested in what was happening.

Martin looked flustered. "I need to read this?" he whispered to Ty.

Ty nodded.

Martin tugged on his collar. "So sorry to have to

announce this, but this session will need to end early. We ask that everyone please exit the room in an orderly fashion."

The crowd was confused.

"Please gather your things and leave," Martin added.

Some of the audience stood up and began to exit, but most of them began to complain loudly.

"It's an emergency," Ty added, leaning into the mic.

That was enough to make everyone move faster. The police at the back of the room were trying to figure out what was going on, and what their role should be.

Ray used the chaos of the standing crowd as an opportunity to jump up from his seat and reach for the bird. Ty stepped away from the pulpit hoping to help. The Perennial Five were not having it. They all jumped to their feet and began to push Ty back.

The various ogres in the audience were pushing through people to get to the stage. Three of them were already there trying to escort Ray safely away.

"Get the bird!" Ray insisted as he was being whisked off the stage.

The hand of a boxy ogre reached up over the front of the table and grabbed Clark. In an instant the bird was swept away into the sea of people.

"Clark!" Ozzy yelled.

Ozzy was grabbed by Ty, who was attempting to drag him away. Sigi picked up the metal bird cage and swung it into Ty's face. He fell into the tables, knocking the whole line of them forward and off the stage.

The room was in complete pandemonium. Cops were trying to get control of something they didn't understand, while people dressed as things they wished to be were being pushed around by ogres.

"We need to get you two out of here!" Rin shouted.

"No," Ozzy said. "I have to find Clark."

"And Mom," Sigi added.

"She's here?" Rin glanced around excitedly.

"Yes," Sigi yelled. "She came in with Wills."

Rin smiled. "Well, why didn't you say so?"

The wizard turned and clapped his hands together. Instantly everyone not wearing blue dropped to the floor.

Ozzy and Sigi stared at the wizard.

"Marvel later," he said casually. "Find Clark."

With only the ogres standing, Ozzy spotted the boxy one who was still holding Clark.

People had begun to get back up.

"I got this," Bill said.

The big wizard jumped off the stage like a nimble ninja, and when he came down, the floor shook, sending everyone to the ground again.

Ozzy leaped from the stage, running in the direction he had last seen Clark. Sigi kept pace with him.

"Did you see what my dad did?" she yelled.

"How could I have missed it?"

Police officers were yelling at Ozzy and Sigi to stay

still, but Gemi was too quick. She cursed them with painful feet, and they all began to howl and writhe in agony.

"They went out those doors!" Ozzy yelled.

Outside of Ballroom B, the scene was equally chaotic. Everyone had heard the commotion and now superheroes were running scared. There were so many people that it was hard to see anything well.

"Don't worry," Jayson said, "I'm an alchemist!"

Both Ozzy and Sigi were surprised to see Jayson running beside them. He muttered a few words and clicked his fingers. The move was more pretentious than interesting.

Soda from food carts and food stands shot out of their dispensers and up into the air above everyone. At the same time, candy from a giant booth promoting a giant candy brand unwrapped itself and shot up into the cascading soda. The affect was a sweet cloud of wet mist descending over everything.

"How does this help?" Ozzy yelled.

"I'm an alchemist!" Jayson cried triumphantly. "Look."

The cloud of sweet mist was causing everything besides Ray and his ogres to look blurry. The blue men stood out like bright lights.

"Unbelievable," Ozzy said, as he instantly spotted who they were after.

Ray and his men were on one of the large escalators moving people down and toward the first-floor exits. The moving stairs were crammed with more people than was conceivably safe. Ozzy could see the boxy ogre standing next to Ray as they descended.

"They're on the escalators!"

The crowd of people trying to get onto the moving stairs was blurry and so thick Ozzy and Sigi couldn't push through.

"Did someone say Flora?" Flora the Older said, appearing out of thin, sticky, wet air.

No one had, but Flora shouted a few words and the escalators began running in reverse, bringing people back up.

Ozzy saw Ray and his posse still trying to fight their way down in reverse, but the throng of people in front of Ray was too thick.

Someone grabbed Sigi from behind. She turned to find her mother.

"What is going on?" Patti yelled, as a short Incredible Hulk bumped into her.

"Magic," Sigi yelled back.

"They have Clark!" Ozzy pointed at the hordes of people being forced back up the escalator.

"Who does?" Sheriff Will said.

"That's Ray Dench," Ozzy shouted, "with the red hair surrounded by blue ogres."

The sheriff began to push and shove his way into the bottleneck of people wanting to go down who didn't realize people were being forced back up.

A small planet came careening through the crowd behind. People tried desperately to get out of Bill's way. The big wizard had a wand in his hand, and he was zapping anyone he didn't like the look of.

The sound of gunfire filled the air.

On the escalator, one of the ogres began shooting into the air. Anyone around him did their best to scream louder and get out of the way. The group of ogres surrounding Ray forced themselves down and off the escalator. There were too many people. Ozzy couldn't move and Ray was getting dangerously close to getting away.

Ozzy's chest grew tight with anxiety. He felt a tap on his shoulder and turned around to see Rin.

"They still have Clark," Ozzy yelled.

"I know," the wizard replied.

"Can't you do something?" Ozzy, Sigi, and Patti pleaded in harmony.

"Why not?" Rin said.

The wizard smiled and lifted his arms.

CHAPTER SIXTY-THREE

LIFTED UP

As Rin raised his hands, everyone in the building slowly lifted seven feet into the air—every merchant, every cop, ever ogre, every visitor, every cosplayer, everyone. The only group still on the ground were Rin and his associates.

Ozzy gazed up at all the kicking feet and screaming mouths of those who had suddenly taken flight. Their cries and shouts were so loud that Bill couldn't take it.

"*Excesistaltalkus!*"

The hovering populace above them went silent. There was still the sound of emergency alarms going off, and assorted machines humming, but Gemi quickly quieted those down, making the building eerily quiet.

Patti was beside herself. She stared at all the squirming people above her and sat down on an empty couch nearby.

Someone's boot dropped off their foot and hit Flora the Older in the head.

"That's enough of that," she said. *"Expentestikpina!"*

The sky of patrons all became still and stiff.

"Are they okay?" Ozzy asked.

"They're fine," Flora insisted.

With nobody in their way, Rin walked freely down the escalator that had become stairs and onto the first floor. The wizard stepped beneath a hovering Ray and his ogres. The Perennial Five and the rest of the group circled around.

Rin reached up and took hold of Ray's right leg. He pulled the man down like someone might yank a mower cord.

Ray hit hard against the floor.

"Who has Clark?" Rin asked.

Ozzy pointed up at the boxy ogre.

The wizard pulled him down. He came to a stop on top of Ray. Ozzy leaned down and took Clark out of the man's coat pocket. The stripe wasn't covered, but Clark was still lacking enough charge to be alive. Ozzy held the bird in his hands so that the silver strip faced up.

Rin waved his right hand and Boxy Ogre shot back up again. He waved his hand again in Ray's direction and loosened the red-haired man's tongue.

"How?" he asked, looking up. "How are you doing this?"

Rin sighed. "I get so tired of saying this. Magic."

Both Ray and Patti looked sick.

The Perennial Five moved closer to Ray as the red-headed man stood up.

"That's not true," Ray insisted. "You found the formula. This isn't magic—it's the result of the serum. My serum. Don't you see what we could do if we worked together?" Ray motioned to the cloud of humans above them.

"We didn't do that together," Rin pointed out.

"That formula belongs to me!" Ray was unraveling. "We don't need the boy. I have the vials. I can crack the code."

Rin glanced at his counterparts in the Perennial Five. "Do you think you could give us a moment alone?"

They all nodded.

"And can you make sure nobody comes in or out of the building?"

"That's easy magic," Bill said happily.

The other four Perennials split up and vacated the area. The fifth stayed right where he was. Once Flora, Gemi, Bill, and Jayson were gone, Ray spoke.

"Good," he said. "This is a private matter anyway."

It was a silly statement, seeing how thousands of people were above them standing in the air.

"Forget this talk of magic," Ray insisted. "With those vials we can control the will of the world."

Rin sighed, sounding bored by how predictable Ray was. The wizard glanced at Patti, Sigi, and Ozzy, who was still holding an undercharged Clark.

"What do you think?" Rin asked the boy. "Do you think it's magic?"

Ozzy studied the wizard. His mind emptied quickly, as if it were a bucket and the bottom had dropped out. Then just as rapidly it filled up again. Wave after wave of new thoughts washed up and over his brain. The puzzle he had been trying to put together was coughing up the last few pieces, and the picture it was revealing was one the boy had never thought of.

"Those vials won't help," Ozzy said.

The wizard smiled.

"My parents never found the right formula," Ozzy went on, a new understanding taking over his whole body. "They tested it on me, but it didn't work. It only changed my finger."

"What?" Sigi said. "What are you talking about?"

"There is no working discipline serum."

"What about the people they tested it on?" Sigi asked. "That lady who acted out on stage? That man who walked into the polar bears? Tindale something . . . no, Timsby?"

Rin shuddered at the remembrance of the awful name.

"Those were attempts," Ozzy said, "but they never got it right. That's why they couldn't recreate it all those years—they never really had it. They moved to Oregon to hide from Charles and Ray, but they must have still had hopes of finding it on their own."

"What about you?" Sigi said. "You've made people

fight and cops drive into the ocean. You've made squirrels do what you want."

Ozzy was silent. He stared at the floor for a few moments before saying,

"It was magic."

The answer was as much of a revelation to himself as it was to everyone else.

"Finally!" Rin said with relief. "You figured it out."

"Well, this is nice."

Everyone turned to see Ray holding a gun and pointing it toward them. They had been so focused on Ozzy's words that they had failed to keep their eyes on Ray.

The angry man waved his gun from side to side.

"I don't know how you are doing all of this," he told Rin. "But it's a trick and I'll figure it out."

In the distance, the sound of something crashing down shattered the quiet.

"What was that?" Ozzy asked.

"It takes a lot of energy to keep everyone up there," the wizard explained. "I guess one dropped."

The sound of something falling was just enough of a distraction to give Ray the time to grab Patti's arm and pull her in front of himself.

Patti said a few things that made it perfectly clear what she thought about Ray. Sheriff Wills tried to move in, but Ray pointed the gun at him.

"Let her go!" Sigi demanded.

"Everyone stay right where you are," Ray insisted. "I'm

going to slip out of here. But this is not the end. I can afford to continue this fight forever. But to make it fair, I'm going to need to even the odds."

What happened next happened so fast that it would take a wizard to understand it. Ray pointed the gun at Rin and pulled the trigger. But like a low-budget superhero movie, Off-Brand Spiderman leaped in from nowhere and took a bullet for the wizard. Rin reached out and caught Jon in his arms as Ray released Patti and turned to run away. Ozzy set Clark down as he attempted to help the wizard.

Rin pulled off Jon's mask and tried to assess how badly hurt he was.

Jon smiled up at Rin.

"You're going to be okay," the wizard promised.

"I just wanted to believe in something."

"It looks like you do."

Jon smiled again and closed his average eyes.

Rin looked at Ozzy. "You two need to stop Ray!" The wizard's tone was one that made it clear how important it was to do what he was saying, while also letting them know it could be done.

Ray had run back to the escalators and was now at the top near the second floor. Ozzy and Sigi gave chase. The trainee looked at the hovering people and decided to see what he could do. Words formed in his head and sprang from his mind like flowers.

"*Sagutuosldropus!*"

People above began to sag in the air and then slowly drop back down to the ground. A man painted red and yellow clipped Ray as he got off the escalator. A wet-blanket kind of person who had worn a polo shirt and chinos to a ComiCon dropped near Ray and caused him to stumble and fall. Ray rolled over twice and then got back on his feet.

Ozzy and Sigi were coming off the escalators.

Ray ran into the large convention hall. Like everywhere else in the building, most of the people were still hanging in the air. A few had dropped down and they were trying to figure out what was happening.

Ozzy saw a huge stand of vinyl figures and more words popped into Ozzy's head.

"*Tolifusdefunco!*"

Thousands of figurines came to life and sprang from their boxes and shelves directly onto Ray. He slid to the ground and was buried by toys.

Ozzy and Sigi stopped at the pile.

"I can't hold it!" Ozzy yelled.

The young wizard's strength wasn't strong enough to keep it up. The vinyl toys became lifeless and Ray crawled out from under them.

He got to his feet and ran toward a wall of doors. It was a decent idea, but the doors led into a closed-off part of the Convention Center. So as Ray pushed on the handle, nothing happened.

Ozzy and Sigi easily caught up to him.

The man turned and growled. The two teenagers stood still as Ray pointed his gun.

"You can't win," Ray shouted, wishing desperately that he had never left New York. "You can't defeat me!"

Ozzy and Sigi showed Ray their palms, hoping he wouldn't do anything rash. The boy could feel magic building inside of him, swelling like a foam. He looked at his finger as he held up his hand. The purple was there, but in his mind, he now understood everything. He glanced at Ray knowing that it would simply take the right word to end it all. But Ozzy held his tongue. There was a more fitting way to finish this.

"I don't know what's happening," Ray shouted as more and more people dropped back down to the floor.

"I do," the boy said. "You've underestimated a wizard, and his daughter, and most importantly, a bird."

At that moment, a bullet of black shot through the falling people and hit Ray directly in the chest. Clark's force and momentum sent the man flying backwards into the locked doors. The bird looped up and then came back down, jabbing Ray in the left shoulder. The extra hit wasn't necessary, seeing how Ray was already down, but Clark needed the closure.

The bird flitted onto Ozzy's shoulder and cocked his head.

"You okay?" Clark asked.

"Now that you're here," Ozzy answered.

Sigi patted the bird on his wing as more and more people fell back down to earth.

"What happened here?" Clark asked.

"It's a long story," Ozzy said.

"Then don't tell me," the bird insisted. "I'm already bored."

A panting and confused Sheriff Wills came up behind them. He had his gun drawn and was pointing it at Ray. He looked at Ozzy and Sigi and Clark.

"I have no idea what's going on," the sheriff admitted.

Sigi pointed to the red-headed heap. "That's Ray."

"Are you okay?" Wills asked Ozzy, staring at Clark.

"Never better," Ozzy answered.

Ozzy reached for Sigi's hand and together the two of them and one bird walked off and faded into a waterfall of humans and a swamp of vinyl figurines.

CHAPTER SIXTY-FOUR

ALL AROUND ME ARE FAMILIAR FACES

The car stereo played as Rin drove. Clark sat in the passenger seat, making a nest out of old road maps and flyers he had found in the glove compartment. Ozzy and Sigi sat together in the back watching the landscape slide by like wet paint as the music filled the vehicle.

"And all the deeds of yesterday, have really helped to pave the way."

The car they were traveling in was the same one they had taken to New Mexico. It was also the only vehicle to survive the garage fire. Because of that, it still smelled faintly of smoke. Ozzy had suggested they use magic to remove the odor, but Rin liked the smell, insisting it was a nice reminder of what they had overcome.

"You won't tell us where we're going?" Sigi asked.

"Not this time," Rin said solemnly.

"You never tell us where we're going," Clark pointed out.

"Consistency is an admirable trait."

It had been over a year since the Portland ComiCon and life was beginning to settle nicely. There may be no way to describe what happened at ComiCon—unless, of course, you believe. Then the explanation is simple—it was magic. And when all was said and done, Ray was finished, and they had won.

To the consternation of almost everyone, there was no security tape footage, cellphone videos, or pictures of any of it. It was as if all traces had been mysteriously erased. People swore they had been covered with blurry soda, lifted up, made mute, and dropped down, but there was no actual proof. Rin would have liked to have been caught on camera, but Bill didn't like to be filmed. The only bit of video that survived was a short clip of security tape that showed Ray shooting Jon. It had helped nicely in the case against Mr. Dench.

Jon had survived the gunshot. Like Ray, he was now in prison, but unlike Ray, he had a chance of getting out someday.

"It's beautiful here," Ozzy said as they drove.

"Yes," Rin agreed. "Washington is a lovely place."

Clark looked out the front window. "Not enough objects."

The garage at 1221 Ocean View Drive had been rebuilt. The new one was bigger and much nicer. Rin thought it was vulgar, but Patti liked the space. And now that things were as they should be, there were no longer any cop cars parked in front—except for when Sheriff Wills dropped by. Wills always seemed to have one more question to ask Patti, and Patti always seemed to have one more answer.

"Does Quarfelt have this many trees?" Clark asked.

"You've been there," Rin said. "You should know."

Clark jumped from his nest to the dashboard. "There's a lot of things I *should* know."

They'd been driving for a couple of hours now. Nobody was complaining, but there was an unusual feeling of importance in the car. Over the last year, Rin had taken Ozzy and Sigi and Clark to several interesting spots. They had traveled back to Emmitt Toffee's grave, this time with bug spray—and flowers. They had visited Omen twice, and both times the old man pretended to be unhappy about being bothered. They had stopped by Ann's during non-mealtimes. Rin had shown them fields he thought were important, and mountains he claimed were just fat valleys. He had also taken them to visit Flora the Older, and Gemi the Younger, and Bill. They were planning to see Jayson at some point, but that point had not yet come about.

Ozzy breathed in.

The smell of the car reminded him of his room over the old garage. When the new one had been built, Patti had made sure there was a nice room above it. But Ozzy had never called that room his. No, the young wizard had happily moved in with Rin at WetLand. His bedroom was now an attic with an oval window that faced the forest and displayed stars in the same fashion the Cloaked House had. He loved the spot. The only negative to moving was that he no longer got to wake up and fight over bagels with Sigi. It didn't matter, seeing how she spent most of her time at WetLand, helping her father and Ozzy clean up the place, and finding moments to be alone with the boy she loved.

Clark liked the move to WetLand as much as anyone. The house and property were filled with new things for him to stare at and admire. He was currently in a somewhat serious relationship with an oversized ladle hanging on the kitchen wall.

"You know," Clark tweeted from the dashboard, "if you wanted to show us trees, we could have stayed in Oregon."

"But these trees are different," Rin insisted. "They're here."

Ozzy stared out the window, seeing the difference in each plant and tree. Recognizing the importance of every leaf and branch. He glanced down at his finger. The purple marking was still there, but he no longer saw it as anything other than a reminder of what his parents had tried to do, and how they had failed. His power to control minds was still there, but he knew now that it was an act of magic, not the discipline serum. He was growing stronger every day in his abilities. It helped, of course, to live with someone as proficient in magic as Rin was.

"You seem serious," Sigi said to her father as he drove. "I mean, more serious than other times."

"Sorry," the wizard replied, reaching over to turn off the radio. "I think I must be nervous."

Clark tilted his small head. "You?"

"I found something important," he admitted. "I just hope showing you is wise."

The words Rin had said came out like an incantation; they drifted through the car and caused everyone's thoughts to grow quiet. The car drove on without a bird tweeting or a boy asking or a girl commenting.

There was only a thick silence.

Rin slowed down the vehicle and turned off the road. Ozzy's insides began to tumble.

The wizard pulled through a large open gate. In big metal letters on top of the gate it said:

HEALING WINDS

"Wait," Sigi said nervously. "Isn't this the . . . ? Are you checking yourself back in?"

The wizard's daughter had long ago been filled in on the help her dad had needed in the past.

"No," he replied. "I've never felt better."

"Then why are we here?" she asked.

"There's someone I think Ozzy should see."

"A doctor?" Clark chirped. "He does get all weird around Sigi."

"No," Rin said in a tone that told Clark to hold his beak.

Ozzy could feel it. He knew exactly what was happening. His mind showed him everything and notified his heart of the possibility of new pain.

"My mother's in here, isn't she?"

Rin pulled into a parking space in front of the large stone building. Ozzy recognized the place from the pamphlet Ray had once shown him.

The wizard shut off the car and turned to look at the boy who had changed his life. His eyes were red and worried.

"I found your mother again months ago," he whispered. "She's not well. The years of testing the serum on herself have made her someone other than who she once was."

Clark chirped dramatically.

Ozzy reached over and squeezed Sigi's hand.

"I want to see her," he said resolutely.

"She may not know who you are," Rin warned.

"I know who she is," Ozzy said. "You paid to bring her here?"

Rin nodded. The wizard never asked to borrow money anymore—unless he had forgotten his wallet. The account book he had taken from his mother's safe had changed all of that. Years ago, Candy had let him know it was there and that she would hand it over if he would beg for it. Well, since wizards are proud, in a non-offensive way, he refused.

The money was his, but he couldn't give her the satisfaction of seeing him grovel. Now, however, knowing that his future would require him to be around a bit more than in the past, he realized that for the sake of all things Sigi and Ozzy, it would be wise for him to retrieve what was his all along.

The four of them got out of the car and Clark tucked himself in the front pocket of Ozzy's new shorts—the same shorts that had arrived a month early by courier. They were knee-length, with random stars in random colors stitched on them.

Inside the facility, everything was old but clean. The halls were wide, and the floors were a green linoleum. Rin checked in at the front and they were led to a small bedroom on the second floor. The orderly let them in saying, "She's not a risk. You should be just fine. I'll be here if you need me."

Ozzy followed behind Sigi, who was following behind her dad. The orderly shut the door after they had entered.

The room was plain, with a barred window. There was a sterile bed and a small dresser attached to the wall. A big pink padded chair sat in the corner of the room.

In the chair there sat a woman.

She had dark hair pulled back into a bun. Her features were soft and familiar. Her eyes made it obvious that Omen was her father, and her ears made it clear that Ozzy was her son. She looked both beautiful and lost.

"Hello, Mia," Rin said, taking off his hat. "I brought you someone."

The wizard stepped aside, and Ozzy walked closer.

Mia Toffy looked up at her son.

"Hello," Ozzy said softly, his heart on the verge of stopping—or beating out of his chest.

Mia stared at him intently, turning things over in her mind.

"Do you remember me?" he asked.

"I'm not sure," she replied.

Ozzy turned to look at Sigi, who had tears in her eyes and an expression of wonder. When he turned back, his mother was standing.

Mia touched Ozzy's cheek as the boy trembled.

"Wait a moment," she said with a gasp, "you're Ozzy."

Mia Toffy put her arms around her son and began to sob.

The rest of the room joined in, Clark wailing the loudest.

Amidst the noise and emotion, Rin pulled out his to-get-done list. "Check," he said softly.

And just like that, the wizard had completed the job he had been hired to do.

DISCUSSION QUESTIONS

1. Clark gets a chance to be something a little different than he's used to, but it doesn't work out. Would changing something about your appearance affect how you act? Why or why not?

2. Ray Dench is obsessed with obtaining the serum so he can control others. Even if he had good intentions, would it be a good thing or not to be able to control the actions of other people?

3. Jon has spent most of his life working for other people. Does the change he makes seem like he's following his own path, or is he still stuck in someone else's orbit? Do you think that will be good for him or not?

4. Ozzy learns some things about Rin from Ray Dench that throw him for a loop. What are some of the ways we can react when people we trust disappoint us? Which ways do you think are best?

5. Rin's mother, Candy, is a pretty horrible person, and it seems like she either doesn't know she is, or she doesn't

care. What's the best way to deal with someone like that? If you found out later that Candy's actions were caused by a mental illness, how would that change your answer?

6. Sigi and her mother, Patti, have a pretty good relationship, but also some pretty intense discussions about how each of them see Rin. Can good friends have different, strong opinions and still be friends? How does that work?

7. Patti, Sigi, and Ozzy have all had serious doubts about whether or not Rin is a wizard or has magical powers. When that question was answered, how do you think each of them felt?

8. Ozzy has several of his most important questions—about his parents, about magic—answered. Have you had any important questions answered? How did the answers come? How did you feel when they came?

9. What do you think will end up happening with Ozzy, Clark, Sigi, Rin, and Patti? What about some of the other characters (Jon, Ann, Ray, Candy, Sheriff Wills)?